Praise

DA
BLADE

'This has everything you want from an epic fantasy adventure –
devious Gods, hideous monsters, a portal to another
dimension and a hero with an enchanted blade. Great stuff'
Charlie Higson, author of the Young Bond series

'Fans of Rick Riordan and John Flanagan have a whole
new world of dark magic, mysterious gods and brave
heroes waiting for them'
Sebastien de Castell, author of the Spellslinger series

'A razor-sharp, spellbinding read full of intrigue and magic.
This tale truly takes the crown as the young heir to the
likes of *A Game of Thrones and Throne of Glass*'
Chris Bradford, author of the Young Samurai series

'The world of Strom is rich with peril, political intrigue,
conspiracies and betrayals ... Why aren't you reading this already?'
Sarwat Chadda, author of the Ash Mistry Chronicles series

'An epic dark fantasy set in an arcane world where kings
are murdered, monsters roam and ordinary boys are
given extraordinary gifts'
Mark Walden, author of the H.I.V.E series

'A powerful, compelling story in a world that stays with you'
Angie Sage, author of the Septimus Heap series

DARK
ART

Books by Steve Feasey

Mutant City
Mutant Rising

Dark Blade
Dark Art

DARK ART

STEVE FEASEY

BLOOMSBURY
LONDON OXFORD NEW YORK NEW DELHI SYDNEY

BLOOMSBURY YA
Bloomsbury Publishing Plc
50 Bedford Square, London WC1B 3DP, UK

BLOOMSBURY, BLOOMSBURY YA and the Diana logo
are trademarks of Bloomsbury Publishing Plc

First published in Great Britain in 2020 by Bloomsbury Publishing Plc

Copyright © Steve Feasey, 2020

Steve Feasey has asserted his right under the Copyright, Designs and
Patents Act, 1988, to be identified as Author of this work

All rights reserved. No part of this publication may be reproduced or
transmitted in any form or by any means, electronic or mechanical,
including photocopying, recording, or any information storage or retrieval
system, without prior permission in writing from the publishers

A catalogue record for this book is available from the British Library

ISBN: PB: 978-1-4088-7341-0; eBook: 978-1-4088-7342-7

2 4 6 8 10 9 7 5 3 1

Typeset by RefineCatch Limited, Bungay, Suffolk
Printed and bound in Great Britain by CPI Group (UK) Ltd, Croydon CR0 4YY

To find out more about our authors and books visit www.bloomsbury.com
and sign up for our newsletters

For Hope and Kyran, as they start out on their voyages into the turbulent waters of adulthood. x

Prologue
Gematik's Citadel, Eastern Hasz

High Priestess Elafir stepped out of the water of the sunken bath and into the robe her slave was holding out for her.

'You must be hot,' she said to him with a concerned smile. Indeed, she thought the unfortunate creature must be close to collapse. Though his head was shaved, he was fully dressed in his court attire and sweating profusely in the hot air of the bathhouse. The scar on his neck, where the sign of her house had been branded into the skin, was a livid red colour.

She knew there would be no response to her comment. The individual she had acquired the slave from had ensured the man's silence long ago by removing his tongue. The slave was, however, able to communicate with her using his hands and the language of signs that she'd taught him. It was how he'd delivered the perplexing news he'd brought to her a moment ago.

She waved him away, watching as he shuffled off through the swirling air. All of the servants in her citadel were mutes that she'd hand-picked from a nearby slave market. It was better than the alternative, which was to have her attendants come from the emperor's court, all of whom could be spies or possibly even assassins. Hasz was a place of distrust and subterfuge at the best of times, and right now, with Emperor Mamur old and frail, and no natural heir to take over the realm, his would-be replacements were circling the royal court like the carrion vultures often seen soaring over the arid plains a short distance from her citadel. Elafir smiled at the image. She was no vulture, no scavenger. No, she was a magnificent desert lioness, waiting patiently for the man to fall and the birds to land. Then, and only then, would she come out and lay waste to everything in her path.

She turned towards the closed door that led towards her chambers, a small frown forming on her otherwise perfect features. With a sigh, she adjusted her gown and made her way out. She had a visitor.

Now dressed in the garb of her office – a grand, floor-length robe of a purple so dark it was almost black – Elafir took in the four people before her. The quartet were in the main entranceway to the citadel, the great wood-and-iron doors closed and barred behind them, showing no signs that they'd been opened. Torches sputtered on the walls, throwing shifting shadows that invited the eye to chase them. Standing nearest was her acolyte, Alwa, and behind her were two of her household guards. But it was the sight of the young man they flanked that took her by surprise. His pale skin and light eyes betrayed that he was not a Hasz'een. If she had to guess, the priestess would say he was from the East, possibly Strom or Vorneland, but there was something about him – perhaps the sharp cheekbones – that suggested he had other blood in him from lands south of those kingdoms. The stranger met her stare.

The high priestess kept her features neutral, unwilling to give away her surprise at being summoned like this or her annoyance at being dragged away from her bath.

She nodded for Alwa to speak.

'This *esh-el* says he has business with you,' the acolyte spat, using the derogatory term for a foreigner. Her expression was a nervous one and she fingered the material at the sleeve of her smock. 'He claims you would want to speak with him.'

'A slave? Has business with me?'

The acolyte shook her head and frowned. 'He is not a slave as far as I can make out. He has no owner's marks on his face or neck.'

The priestess looked across at the stranger with fresh eyes. Alwa was undoubtedly right about the young man's status: no slave would dare look back at her with the arrogance this newcomer displayed. And there was something else ... something she sensed at an altogether different level. There was majik in the young man.

She turned her attention to one of the guards, the man visibly jumping when she addressed him. 'Where did you apprehend our visitor?'

The guard glanced at the acolyte before answering. 'W-we did not. The foreigner was already in the citadel when Mistress Alwa called for us.' He nodded in the acolyte's direction, relieved to be shifting the attention back to her.

A small laugh escaped Elafir, though her eyes held no hint of humour. 'That is not possible. As you well know, these buildings and the lands that surround them are protected by majik – ancient and powerful defences designed to destroy anyone foolish enough to enter without permission. Acolyte Alwa, I suggest you tell me the truth about where and how you found this young man before I lose what grasp I have on my growing displeasure!'

Alwa wrung her hands. 'I came down to the lobby area when I heard someone calling out in a foreign tongue. This –' she shot a hateful look in the newcomer's direction – 'person was standing inside the main doors, exactly where he is now.

4

Just standing here, waiting. When I challenged him, he said to me in the tongue of the Eastern Kingdoms that he had business with my mistress, and that I should bring him to you. That is when I raised the alarm. The guards are telling the truth.'

'And as I have already told you, that is not possible!' Normally serene and unflappable, Elafir gave in to the anger that had been growing inside of her. The high priestess's outburst struck fear into the members of her household.

Alwa was clearly struggling for a response that would not further incense her mistress. Before she could find one, the Easterner broke in, speaking for the first time since the high priestess's arrival.

'The majik bound around and through this place is indeed strong. And so it should be. The creature contained inside this body –' he gestured down at himself – 'helped weave it with Gematik, your famous ancestor, after whom the citadel itself is named. Of course, creating majik defences gives the creator a unique insight into how to get around them. I mean you no harm or offence in entering your citadel in this manner. It just seemed the best way to show you that I am who and what I say I am.'

Elafir narrowed her eyes at the intruder. He appeared to be about the same age as Alwa, but held himself with an assured bearing that suggested he was either extremely

5

self-confident or very good at hiding his fear. 'The man who worked here with my ancestor died a long time ago.'

'His body did, yes. But Yirgan was clever enough to trap his spirit – his lich – in a phylactery, a specially constructed magical container, before he died. I brought the lich back into this world and gave it physical form again.' He raised his arms, palms out, at his sides and offered her a sullen smile.

The priestess looked the intruder up and down, as if the legitimacy of his story might be written somewhere about his person. Whatever she saw there seemed to satisfy her. 'Leave us,' she said, gesturing for the guards and the young woman to go.

The citadel's sentries scurried off, but Alwa paused for a moment. 'Mistress, we don't even know who this foreigner is, let alone his motives for coming here. Shouldn't we—' She stopped when her mistress raised a hand.

A smile briefly touched the corners of Elafir's mouth. She turned to the newcomer. 'Acolyte Alwa is correct. Whilst you have told us *how* you managed to be here, you neglected to introduce yourself.'

The young man bowed his apology. When he straightened again his eyes never left those of the high priestess. 'My name is Kelewulf. If you would be so gracious as to grant me an audience, I would be happy to explain what I am doing in your homeland.'

* * *

'I remember the tales told me of Yirgan,' Elafir said. They were in her private rooms now, the high priestess sitting in a grand, ornate chair with Kelewulf sitting across from her in the much more modest seat she'd offered him. She studied the stranger, trying to understand how the young man before her could be what he claimed to be. 'The "last great mage" is what they call him to this day – at least those who dare to mention him at all. It is said his powers were even greater than those of my ancestor Gematik.' She picked at an invisible speck on her gown. 'It would be no mean feat to control such a force of majik, regardless of the form it took.'

'Yet here I am. Having done just that.'

The priestess made a dismissive gesture with her hand as if his response were not entirely to her liking. 'Why Hasz?' she asked.

'I'm sorry?'

'Why have you come to Hasz?'

She watched him studying the huge lion-skin rug on the floor between them. The creature's dead head still roared and its eyes stared out at the world, albeit through balls of black glass. The person responsible for killing such a magnificent and powerful beast must have been scared for their own life, knowing how one mistake could bring about their own demise, and Elafir wondered if the young man opposite her was feeling the same way. She noted how carefully he appeared to be weighing his response to her question.

'The Emperor of Hasz is not a young man,' Kelewulf said at last. He shifted his glance to the high priestess, looking for a reaction that did not come. 'It is said that he is … frail, but that his hatred of the Six Kingdoms remains as strong as ever, despite the two nations having had little to do with each other for so long. I imagine he might welcome information on the lands to the East. Information from someone who was very close to the ruling Rivengeld family. Intimate information about how the new King of Strom thinks.' He shot her another searching look. 'I would also imagine Emperor Mamur might be interested to know that the Six Kingdoms are more vulnerable now than they have been in a very long time. A vulnerability that was created by me before I left those lands to come here.'

Elafir made sure the flame of curiosity that Kelewulf's words had ignited inside her did not show on her face. What Kelewulf could not know was that his proposal had come at a very opportune moment. Mamur was amassing his armies and navies for an attack on the Six Kingdoms – one last great war to avenge the Hasz'een people's only ever defeat and mark the emperor's long reign as one of greatness.

8

It was a move that was not without its opponents. Many of those in the imperial court argued against it, not wanting to put an end to the peace the Hasz'een had for so long enjoyed, a peace that had been hard won after hundreds of years of conflict.

But Elafir knew how wars, or the threat of them, had a way of shaking up the balance of power in a country, and the high priestess wanted to be part of that shake-up.

Perhaps she could use this young man to further strengthen her own position in the imperial court. There was no doubt in her mind that the timing of his arrival was perfect; as if the gods themselves had dropped him into her lap at just the right moment. She pondered this, knowing how it always paid to be wary of the machinations of the gods, who seemed unable to keep out mankind's affairs.

The young stranger had sat unmoving throughout Elafir's long period of thought. She appreciated this. Many people in his position would have become increasingly nervous and tried to fill the silence with needless babble.

'Why would you betray your own kind?' she asked eventually. 'You are, if I am not mistaken, a child of the Six Kingdoms. What are you? Half Stromish, half Neshian?'

Something flickered behind the young man's eyes. It was the first loss of composure he'd shown, however fleeting, and Elafir stored the information away in case it should prove useful at a later time.

'You're very close. My father was of Strom. Some say he *was* Strom. He—'

'Your father was Horst Rivengeld.'

'You know who I am?'

'I didn't. When you first gave me your name I did not make the connection. But just in that moment there, when you let your guard slip, I noticed the family likeness.' She stared at a point somewhere over his head, trying to remember more. 'Your mother was from the Southern Kingdoms. She was Bantusz, not Neshian. She was forced to marry your father after he defeated an uprising by her people.'

'That is correct.'

'So why betray those kingdoms and their people? If, as you seem to suspect, Mamur's hatred of those over the Norderung Sea is as strong as ever, the information you bring him could motivate the emperor to launch an attack on those shores. He would start with Strom, but you must know if Emperor Mamur is successful he will not stop there. That is not the Hasz'een way. We will continue to press through all the lands to the east.'

'The people of the Six Kingdoms mean nothing to me. They are weak and backward in their thinking. They have largely turned their back on majik and knowledge of the Art. Unlike the Hasz'een. No, your people's love of dark majik, their relentlessness in taking over all of the lands around them, show a strength that is lacking in the East.'

'*Hmmm.* Indeed.' Elafir shifted a little in her seat, steepling her hands in front of her and peering at him closely over the top of them. 'You have told me what you believe you have to offer us, but not what you want in return. I take it you *do* want something?' She noted how, despite his desperate attempt to remain looking calm and unruffled, *this* was the question he'd been waiting to be asked.

'Yirgan was a great mage, and his lich is very powerful. But much of his knowledge and understanding of the dark arts were lost when he left his physical body. Whilst what is left is still useful, particularly when it comes to summoning, it is not enough. I want to learn from you, High Priestess.'

A thought occurred to her. 'Yirgan ... his lich. It cannot be an easy alliance. I'm surprised the creature has not tried to take a stronger hold of you.'

The young necromancer smiled slyly back at her. 'It did. But I defeated it, and now the mage's spirit is entrapped as securely as when it was in the phylactery I found it hidden in.'

'Would you say Yirgan is your slave now?'

'I would, yes.'

'Yirgan was Hasz'een. Why should I welcome some-body who has subjugated one of my own people?'

11

'The Hasz'een have a long history of subjugating others. I would have thought my actions might be approved of in these lands.'

His response irked her. 'Hasz has changed much in the long years since the war with the Six Kingdoms. Many of us on this side of the sea believe the practice of slavery should be abolished.'

She liked the impact her words had on him and sensed that he had not been expecting such a response. Even so, he maintained his composure and when he spoke again it was in the same unperturbed tone.

'Perhaps "slave" is not the right word.' Kelewulf frowned a little. 'Yirgan and I entered into an agreement together. I willingly gave him a physical body so that he might *live* again. In return he was to help me and provide me with the knowledge I sought. He betrayed our contract and the trust I put in him. If he is now in a position of servitude as a result of what he tried to do, he only has himself to blame.'

When Elafir stood it was to signal she had heard enough; that she had made up her mind. She admired the unblinking way met her gaze.

'I would be pretending if I said I was not impressed with what you have already achieved, young necromancer. That you are alive at all, having broken into my palace in the way you did, is testament to your skill. What you seek,

12

however, and the price you must pay for it are things I alone cannot decide upon. You will remain in my citadel while I try to ascertain if the emperor has any interest in an audience with you. If he does, and the information you give him is deemed of value, he will decide if you may become an acolyte here and I will try to teach you the things you desire to know.'

Kelewulf got to his feet, and the high priestess nodded in approval when he signalled his gratitude with a deep bow in the manner of her own people.

She looked towards the door just as one of her attendants appeared. 'Hukret will show you to your rooms.'

'I am to have rooms? I thought maybe I would be held as a prisoner. In your dungeons, perhaps?'

'Dungeons? What makes you think I would have dungeons?'

He shrugged.

'I told you. Despite what your people believe, we are not savages in Hasz. You will be placed under guard, yes, but you will be quite comfortable here, Kelewulf Rivengeld. That is, unless the emperor considers you to be of no use to him.' She gestured for Hukret to come forward. 'If that proves to be the case, and for having the audacity to enter my home uninvited, I will quite happily oversee your slow torture and eventual death myself.'

* * *

Kelewulf looked about him at the rooms he'd been given, taking in the strange furnishings and the art on the walls. The Hasz'een taste was more lavish than that of the people of the East, who favoured practicality over style. The chair backs were inlaid with intricate geometric woodwork, the candles were covered with shades of coloured glass, and even the bedding was edged with ornate patterns and images created using different-coloured cotton threads.

Throwing himself down on the bed, he stared up at the ceiling as he replayed his encounter with the high priestess.

Outwardly at least, Elafir appeared to have accepted his story about why he'd made the journey to Hasz. He knew that, as a devotee of majik, she would understand his thirst for knowledge of the Art. It was this he'd banked on to make the reason for his defection over the Norderung Sea sound authentic.

It would not do to underestimate such a talented practitioner of the Art, however, and Kelewulf knew he would have to be extremely careful if his true purpose were not to be discovered. He could sense the depth of majik in Elafir, and in some small way he wished he really *was* here to learn from her and the other masters in the citadel. But that would take years of studying the Art in all its forms, and he was impatient. He wanted to be powerful *and* young, not waste his youth cooped up in a place of learning like this with his head stuck in ancient books and scrolls.

That wasn't his way. He had already saved himself a great many years of learning by letting Yirgan's lich inhabit his body, and he would save a lifetime more if he could only find the thing he truly sought here: Lorgukk's heart.

With *that* in his possession, he would show this world what true power was. He would wipe out the memory of the suffering and indignity he'd endured in his young life by making everyone else understand what it felt like to be helpless and afraid. *Their armies, with their swords and spears and shields, will be useless in the face of the dark god, and they will beg me for mercy!*

The sound of a murmured conversation between the two guards outside his door broke into his thoughts. Getting to his feet, he walked across to the window and looked out at the grounds surrounding what was, for now at least, his prison.

The heart was out there somewhere, he knew it.

But where would such a precious thing be kept? Not here in Elafir's palace, that much was certain. No, that would be too easy, and nothing about his journey here had been easy. From narrowly avoiding death on the pirate ship he'd managed to get passage on, then almost being captured by a band of roving slave traders, to the enormous mental effort it had taken to majik his way into this damned citadel, everything was conspiring to make his quest as difficult as could be. The most he could hope for was that somewhere in this seat of learning there were clues to the heart's whereabouts.

It would take all his cunning and guile to find the artefact, and even then, he had no idea how he was going to steal it from beneath the very noses of the bloodthirsty maniacs that were the Hasz'een people. Still, he had spoken to Elafir and he was, as yet, alive. When he'd set out on this undertaking, he'd seriously doubted even *that* much was possible.

Flodjen
Vorneland

1

Lann hardly spoke a word to Astrid as they made their way across the market square. He was too fearful of what lay ahead of them and what they had to do.

The fine weather of the day was gradually giving in to cold as the sun made its way towards the horizon, and all around them the residents of the small farming town were scurrying back to the warmth of their houses, laughing and chatting as they went. He envied them.

As they rounded a smokehouse, the heady smell of fish and burning wood chips filling their lungs, Lann saw a cart carrying five farmhands pull up outside The Broken Staff inn. Astrid's light touch on his sleeve told him she'd spotted them too. Pretending to notice something of interest on a merchant's stall, they stopped and watched out of the corners of their eyes as four men and a woman jumped down from the cart bed and said their farewells to the driver before heading towards the front door.

Lann and Astrid had been expecting the farmhands' arrival. They'd been finishing up checking on their horses in the town livery minutes earlier when the Dreadblade had warned Lann that a powerful demon – a jurdlek – was on its way. Astrid too had had a premonitory warning: the bangle she wore high up on her arm had been sending increasingly strong pins-and-needles sensations through her bicep the nearer the creature got to the town.

'Which one is possessed by the demon?' Astrid asked, peering across at the group openly, now that they had their backs to them.

'I'm not sure, but if I had to guess, I'd say it was him.' He nodded in the direction of the man at the rear of the party who was not joining in with the others' jokes and excitement.

Nir-akuu, the dark blade hanging at his side whispered. Instinctively, Lann reached down and placed his hand on the pommel of the weapon.

Almost as though the straggler had caught an echo of the dark blade's utterance, the man turned his head to the side. His eyes momentarily filled with an inky blackness, transforming them into something dead and empty that had no place in any human face. It was only the briefest glimpse, and anyone else might have doubted that they had seen it at all, but it was everything Lann needed to confirm his suspicions.

It was clear from her expression that Astrid had seen it too, and her hand momentarily came up to her bangle. 'We need to be extra careful this time,' she said. 'That thing has given us the slip twice now, and I'm not willing to give it the chance at a third. Not after what it did to that woman in the last village. We can't let that happen to another innocent person. We made a promise.'

Lann grimaced at the memory. The woman had been left a gibbering mess, her mind apparently wrecked beyond repair when the demon gave up possession of her. Despite the local doctor's ministrations, it was unclear if the woman would ever recover.

'We did. We won't fail again.' He offered her a reassuring smile, but she didn't return it.

Nir-akuu ...

'Right then. Off you go.' Astrid gestured off to the group's left, where a narrow walkway led to the rear of the inn. She and Lann had scouted the place earlier in the day, discovering how the passageway provided access to the kitchens. From there, a person could make their way through to the large hall where visitors and locals ate and drank together.

'I still don't know why we have to do it this way round. We should rethink—'

'We agreed,' she said, cutting him off. 'We would do the jobs that best suited our skills.' Cocking her head to one side, the shield maiden gave him a look that suggested any further discussion was pointless.

Even when she was being cross and dismissive, as she was now, Lann doubted he would ever get sick of looking at Astrid Rivengeld. He felt his face colour a little and wished he hadn't had this last thought. They were friends – partners – nothing else.

'That *is* what we agreed, isn't it?' she asked.

'Yes. But—'

'Right. So you go sneak round the back and I'll go start a fight.'

Puffing out his cheeks and shaking his head, Lann did as he was bid and set off.

Astrid watched Lann cross the dirt track that the wagon had come along. As she did so she took off her sword belt, then unslung the fine bone bow she wore across her back. Hating the feeling of being disarmed, she placed both items under a nearby bush, pulling the greenery about them until she was satisfied they were well concealed. The bow, in particular, was dear to her, and she hated the thought of losing it, given to her as it was by her father, shortly before he died. Checking Lann was in place at the mouth of the walkway, she gave him a brief nod and set off towards the main entrance to the inn.

Astrid paused inside the door, scanning the place. It was busy, but two of the farmhands had just managed to get served with five large horns filled with ale. She headed straight for them.

Clutching the horns carefully so as not to spill the liquid, the pair were halfway back to the rest of the group when Astrid bumped into the man hard enough to send him crashing into the woman, so that both ended up sprawled on the ground. Covered in beer and muck from the sawdust-strewn floor, the pair glared up at the finely dressed young woman.

'You should watch where you're going,' Astrid said, shaking her head. 'You almost spilt that on me.'

The woman struggled to her feet first, a look of fury on her face as she squared up to Astrid.

'*We* did?! You – you barged into *us*! Look at the state of my clothes. They're soaked!'

Astrid looked up and down at the woman's costume, her nose wrinkling as she did so. 'Well, by the appearance of them that's the first wash they've had in a *very* long time.'

A few of the locals who had stopped to watch this exchange laughed at Astrid's comeback.

The female farmhand's face, already a shade of red, turned almost purple with rage. Without another word she swung a fist that might have taken Astrid's head off her shoulders had the shield maiden not smoothly rocked back out of the way, the intended blow narrowly flashing past her chin. She treated the woman to another shake of the head. 'You should do something about that temper of yours too.'

With a roar of fury, the woman threw herself forward, her fingers forming into ugly hooks as she reached for her tormentor's face. Astrid, her own arms still down by her side, waited until the last possible moment before moving her body out of the way, leaving one leg outstretched so that her foot caught that of the onrushing woman, who sprawled to the floor in a heap for the second time.

'Why don't you just stay down there, eh?' Astrid said to her opponent in a tone designed to make her do precisely the opposite.

Lann crept inside the rear door of the dining hall. He noted with satisfaction how the customers inside The Broken Staff were engrossed in the fight, and how the female farmhand was refusing to give up attacking her cocky young opponent. The man possessed by the jurdlek was still keeping himself slightly detached from everyone else. Cruel eyes stared out from his face, greedily drinking in the fight, as if he hoped it would escalate further.

Taking a bottle out of his bag, Lann drenched a rag in the noxious liquid it contained, taking care not to breathe in any of the fumes. The concoction was something his aunt had taught him to make from easily obtainable ingredients: a potion she'd used to quickly render a patient unconscious prior to surgery.

Lann crept up behind the possessed man. All he had to do was clamp the rag over the farmhand's face and he would slump to the floor. Then it was merely a matter of carrying the man out of the bar and placing his unconscious body inside a circle of salt to start the process of driving the demon out and give the man his life back.

It was a simple plan; the one he and Astrid felt carried the least risk.

Out of the corner of his eye, he saw the female farmhand throw a wild, looping punch that sailed well wide of its mark.

As Lann drew ever nearer to his target, any doubts that the man had been inhabited by the jurdlek were dispelled when he heard the callous laughter coming from his mouth. It was an ugly, cruel noise, devoid of soul and nothing like the raucous laughter elsewhere in the room. Lann stretched out his hand and was about to clamp it over the man's face when …

NIR-AKUU!!!

The jurdlek spun about, black eyes staring out from a face that was hardly recognisable as human. The thing screamed at him – a raw and harsh animalistic sound that caused Lann to hesitate for the briefest of moments. It was all the opportunity the jurdlek needed. It threw itself out of Lann's reach, turning and knocking people out of its way as it made for the front door.

'Astrid!' Lann shouted as he set off after it. The shield maiden was directly in the jurdlek's path.

Astrid looked up. Pushing the female farmhand out of danger's way, she balled her hand into a fist and threw a punch towards the face of the oncoming demon.

She'd been looking to connect cleanly with the jaw and render the human host unconscious, but Lann could see that the demon was wise to their deception now. It knew that she was part of a plan to destroy it. The jurdlek easily countered Astrid's blow and, when its other arm swung up, Lann saw the metallic flash of a baling hook gripped in its hand.

Time seemed to stretch out for Lann. He couldn't remember doing so, but he'd drawn the sword from its scabbard; the thing was screaming a death cry as it urged him onwards. Suddenly the memory of his Aunt Fleya's last moments returned: how, only a few weeks ago, he'd been too slow to stop her death at the hands of a demon. And with these unbidden thoughts came the chilling certainty that he would once again be too late to save a person he cared deeply about.

The baling hook flashed up towards Astrid, who tried to twist about on her front foot to avoid it. A master of fighting techniques, she would have succeeded had it not been for the woman she'd picked a fake fight with seconds before. Not realising what was going on, the woman grabbed Astrid about the hips, stopping her from moving properly and forcing her to lift an arm to stop the weapon instead.

The hook of metal sank deep into the leather vambrace that Astrid wore on her forearm, causing blood to immediately pour out from beneath the armour. Despite the pain she was clearly in, her eyes widened in alarm as Lann closed the space between them and raised his sword to swing the thing straight at the head of the jurdlek.

Lann was filled with something like the berserker rage that had overtaken him after his aunt's death, when he'd stood before a portal arch hacking and stabbing at the malevolent creatures that dared to come through it and killing everything in a desire to slake his thirst for revenge.

Astrid must have remembered that time too, because she screamed out at him in a voice that sliced through his thoughts and memories: 'No, Lann! Don't kill him!'

There was a sickening thud as the flat of the blade, not the sharpened edge, made contact with the farmhand's head; the force of the impact was enough to make the man's legs fold up, crumpling him to the floor in a heap.

What followed would be retold many times over by the villagers present that fateful day. There was no need for the storytellers to embellish events; the narrative was extraordinary enough as it was. They would recall how the young man had brandished the dark blade, warning everyone to stand back and leave the unconscious man alone while in the same breath demanding someone bring him a keg of salt. They would tell of how he had listened to his companion, despite his obvious concern about the blood pouring from her wound, when she told him to 'stop worrying about me and finish what we have come to do'. They would recount how he had poured the salt out of the keg to form a large circle around the prone farmhand, and how no sooner had the circle been completed than the man started to buck, his body racked by violent spasms as he shouted and pleaded to his friends for help. But none would come to his aid. Not while the dark blade was brandished at them by the young stranger.

Finally, speaking in whispers, as if fearful to say the words aloud, they would recall the dark and terrible creature that had eventually emerged from the farmhand's body. The thing had little substance at first – it came out of his mouth and nose, wispy and smoke-like – but it had quickly coalesced into a looming thing of terror. It stared about itself, that sinister figure, and when it saw how it was trapped inside a prison of salt it'd howled in rage and fear until the young man jumped into the circle, screaming out strange words that sent shivers down the spines of everyone there, and skewered it on his sword.

That night Lann and Astrid managed to secure a room each at The Broken Staff, despite the innkeeper making it clear he wanted them to move on. Astrid's offer of a substantial number of silver coins for a single night's lodging had quickly changed his mind.

Lying on his bed, still in his clothes, Lann stared up into the shadows of the beamed ceiling, knowing sleep would not come easily, if at all. It wasn't just the day's events replaying over and over in his head, although that was bad enough. It was the voice of the sword that was propped up against his bed stand, its familiar refrain repeating in his head.

Nir-akuu. Monsters.

'Look, we got it, didn't we?' Lann spoke out to the empty room, his voice wrought with emotion. 'We got the jurdlek, so quit it, will you!'

Nir-akuu ...

With a groan he pulled the pillow over his face and clamped it down over his ears, knowing it was pointless. If the last six weeks had taught him one thing, it was that there was no way to block out the blade's voice inside his head when it was in pursuit of its enemies.

Six weeks. That was how long had passed since Kelewulf Rivengeld had opened a portal into the Void and allowed a great host of vile creatures through it. If there had been a worse day in Lann's life, he couldn't remember it.

Fleya had been killed that day.

He shook his head, trying to eradicate the images this memory conjured up inside him, his aunt being brutally murdered by a foul demon that had come through in the first wave of interlopers. An all too familiar feeling of hope-lessness and grief filled him – like a tight knot of physical pain in his heart – and the sob that escaped him filled the room. Lann had failed to stop the creature before it killed her. He'd been *so* close, but ultimately it was his fault she was dead. He recalled the look on her bloodied face in those last moments and how, as his aunt lost her last tenuous grip on life, he had lost his mind.

Dreadblade in hand, he'd charged towards the great archway-shaped portal Kelewulf had created and stood there in the midst of the things pouring through it, hacking and slashing and stabbing until he was a thing of red in a ghastly sea of limbs and bodies.

The majority of the terrible horde had died at the hand of the young man wielding the supernatural blade that day. But despite Lann's efforts, many had still managed to escape and flee.

The Dreadblade would not tolerate even a single one of them to stay in a world they had no right to be in, and Lann, as its wielder, was obligated to see its work done. Since then he and Astrid had travelled through the land on horseback, guided by the weapon, relentlessly hunting the foul creatures down one by one.

It had not been easy, and the time they'd spent pursuing the creatures had left the pair mentally and physically spent.

Except it hadn't been just six weeks, had it? The exhaustion and distress Lann was experiencing was the result of that night, months before, when, as a blind boy all alone in his aunt's cabin, he'd been visited by the god Rakur, who had offered him the sword and his sight. He should have known better than to trust the trickster god.

Nir-akuu.

'Shut up!' Lann shouted, sitting up and staring across at the thing. 'You almost got Astrid killed today!' He swallowed, and when he spoke again his voice was full of menace. 'Listen to me, blade, and listen well. I agreed to wield you, and I now fully understand the cost of doing so. But, so help me, if you ever put somebody I care about in danger like that again, I will seek out the deepest, darkest ocean and throw you down into its inky depths forever. So ... please ... I'm asking you. Shut. Up.'

He pulled the hood of his cloak over his head and buried his face back into the pillow. It seemed an age until he eventually drifted off into a fitful sleep.

Lann stood and stared about him. He was like an island in an emerald-green sea of grass that stretched as far as the eye. A breeze blew in from his left, teasing at his hair and stirring the blades of grass so they whispered excitedly beneath its gentle caress.

He was dreaming. Some small part of his brain knew this, just as he knew his physical body was still sleeping in The Broken Staff. This dream, however, was strange in its vividness and clarity. His nose was filled with the rich, thirsty scent of the grasslands. Lann couldn't remember smells featuring in his dreams before – even when he'd been blind.

A crow called out somewhere overhead, the sound filling his heart with joy and sadness in equal measure.

'Nephew.'

His aunt's voice made him slowly turn around to face her, fighting the sadness and tears that welled up inside him.

Fleya inclined her head. She was smiling at him in a way that did nothing to lessen his grief.

His emotions were so high that he was unable to speak straight away, so he nodded back at her and did his best to return her smile.

'What is this place?' he eventually asked.

As if noticing the landscape for the first time, she looked about her. 'The Plains of Oonal.'

He shook his head to indicate he had never heard the name before.

'The Plains are not in the Six Kingdoms,' Fleya explained. 'They are in a land far beyond those in which you and I live. The horse tribes of the Manguls inhabit this place – a proud nomadic people who spend most of their lives on the back of their beloved beasts. I thought it would be a good spot for us to talk. It is peaceful here. You can almost hear the gods whispering their plans for us all.'

He liked the way she still spoke of herself in the present tense, but he knew it was only her spirit, her essence, left for him to interact with now.

Lann was about to respond when a sudden noise close by made him reach across his waist for the blade that was not there. It was only a small animal dashing from its den into its grassy hunting grounds, but his reaction was not lost on Fleya.

'It must be a welcome respite that the Dreadblade does not follow you into your dreams.'

It was true. It felt good to escape the dark blade's demands in this dreamscape; to be free of that voice and the words it spoke in a long-dead language.

She smiled sadly at him as if reading his thoughts. 'I'm here because I am concerned about you,' she said.

'I'm not the one who's dead.' No sooner had the words left his mouth than he regretted them.

If they upset Fleya in any way she did not show it. 'But you *are* angry that I am. And what is worse, you blame yourself for my death.'

A swell of emotion broke inside him and this time he did not fight the tears that sprang to his eyes. He let them roll down his cheeks. 'We shouldn't have split up. I should have been there for you, just as you were there for me during the long spell when I was blind. Wh-what is the point of bearing a sword of the gods when I could not use it to save you!'

'And if you *had* been there for me, a small child would have been killed instead. Is that, I wonder, a fair trade? I am over one hundred and twenty years old, Lann. I've lived more than my fair share.'

Lann paused. He knew what she said was true, but the loss was still so raw. 'I'll have my revenge on him,' he said in a small voice.

'Kelewulf?'

'Of course. Who else?'

'Kelewulf is as much a victim in all this as you or I.'

'How can you say that? He knew what would happen when he created that portal …'

'Perhaps.'

Lann ignored her. 'And even though he couldn't keep it open for long, he knew the horrors that would emerge from it and what havoc and misery they would wreak.'

'The sword and its wielder serve a purpose. In killing the jurdlek today you were fulfilling that purpose. Just as your father did when he wielded it before you.'

'The Dreadblade drove my father mad.' Lann paused and gave a little shake of his head. He did his best not to think about his paternal heritage; his discovery that he was the son of a god did not sit easily with him. 'It is not easy to be its bearer, and at times it feels little more than a curse. But it will give me the chance of avenging you.'

'What do you intend to do to Kelewulf when you finally do catch up with him?'

'I'll kill him. Just as he killed you.'

Her sadness at his response was easy to see, but Lann thought he detected something else in her look too: disappointment. 'Revenge is an ugly thing, Lannigon. It eats away at a soul, turning the good that lives inside a person into something foul and unpleasant. It was vengeance that motivated Kelewulf to open the portal, and it continues to drive him now.'

'What does *he* seek to revenge?' Try as he might, Lann could not keep the anger from his voice.

'He blames the people of the Six Kingdoms for the death of his mother.'

'His father was at fault for her death.'

'And his father was *king* of the most powerful kingdom at the time she killed herself. As far as the young Kelewulf was concerned, his father *was* the Six Kingdoms.' Fleya paused, turning her head up to the sun and letting it bathe her face with its light and heat. 'I miss the feeling of the sun on my face most of all,' she said quietly. 'That, and the touch of the wind.' Turning back to him, she gave a sigh. 'It is good that you finally caught up with the jurdlek.'

'If only we could have destroyed it sooner. We almost had it three days ago, in the town of Mjalvir. But it escaped us. The person it had been hiding inside lost her senses. When we left she was a gibbering wreck.' He shook his head at the memory. 'I think death would have been preferable.'

'She'll recover. It will take me some time, but …' Lann raised an eyebrow at his aunt, who responded with a knowing smile. 'I have visited her in her sleep, much as I am visiting you now. I have been calming her soul so she might regain her mind and have her life back.'

Lann's heart filled with love and pride again. In life, Fleya had always used her powers to care for others. It seemed that even death could not thwart her affection for humankind.

She looked away into the distance behind him, as if something were trying to get her attention out there. 'You must not blame yourself for everything that happens along this long and winding path you tread, Lannigon. To do so will drive you into a dark place from which you will struggle to emerge. You and Kelewulf are on different paths, but those paths will cross again before long. How you respond to this encounter will determine how deeply you go into that darkness.' She had not taken her gaze away from the horizon behind Lann. Now she narrowed her eyes, frowning a little at whatever she saw there.

Twisting about, Lann followed her line of sight but was unable to make anything out amongst that vast green ocean.

'What is—?'

When he turned back, she was gone.

'It's deep,' Lann said, peering at the wound on Astrid's arm. It was the following morning and they were in his room at the top of the inn, preparing to leave Flodjen. Before they set out, however, he was determined to check her injury was healing properly. 'I'll put some more luundret oil on it and replace the bandage, but I think it'll still leave a bad scar.'

'Lots of my sisters in the shield-maiden ranks have marks on their faces and bodies. They come with being a fighter.'

'It was too close a call. I – I should have …'

Seeing his distress, Astrid reached out with her good arm and placed her hand in his. 'It wasn't your fault,' she said.

'How can you say that?' He stared across at the Dreadblade, a strange expression on his face. 'The blade. It screamed out at the wrong moment. It wanted the demon to know it was there, even if that spelled danger to you. I don't know why it would do that after everything we've been through together …'

'The blade is not a person, Lann.' She winced a little as he applied the balm to the stitched wound, but waved away his apologies. 'It cares for little except its wielder and fulfilling the purpose it was created for. You yourself have told me that.'

'Perhaps. Maybe I haven't listened carefully enough to the many warnings I've been given about it.' He stopped and stared across at the sword in its scabbard.

Astrid watched a shadow pass across her friend's face. It was clear from Lann's expression that the weapon was talking to him.

'Be quiet,' he whispered to it, confirming her suspicions.

She reached out and turned his face so that he was looking at her again. 'You and the sword have done good things. Do not forget that. Together you have saved lives. Yesterday was just … an accident.' She paused to let him finish his ministrations before she asked her next question. 'What will you do next?'

Astrid could see the effect that the last few weeks had had upon Lann and knew he, like her, was tired and exhausted. She also knew it was more than that for him – the strain of the demands the weapon made on him were starting to affect his mood and his health.

'Hasz. I'll go to Hasz.'

'Straight away?'

Lann nodded. 'That's what we agreed.'

She pursed her lips, considering how best to continue. 'I … need to go home to Stromgard.' She let her words sink in for a moment, the silence of the room broken only by the wind worrying at the shutters outside the window. 'And you should come with me. Something tells me I need to see my brother, and goodness knows we both need a rest, Lann.' She reached out to him again, taking a firm grip on his hand. 'Afterwards, I'll come to Hasz with you as I agreed. But I'm exhausted right now. Exhausted and injured and homesick to the point that I really need to hear some friendly voices.' She hoped her words would strike a chord inside him and that he might understand that he needed a break every bit as much as she did. 'We haven't stopped since we left Stromgard, you and I. Please. Kelewulf can wait. For a short time, at least.'

'He killed my aunt.'

'And he killed my father – your king,' she shot back. 'He tried to frame my brother for that murder and have him executed. Do you think I have forgotten those things? Do you think I want revenge any less than you do?'

Astrid searched Lann's eyes with her own. It was obvious he was disappointed and angry. What she couldn't know was that Lann was replaying the conversation he'd had with his aunt the night before; remembering her warnings about how he should not rush into seeking vengeance.

She was about to appeal to him again when she saw the fight suddenly seem to go out of him. His shoulders slumped forward, head lolling down between them. When he raised his head again there was a different look in his eye. He let out a big sigh and even managed a small smile back at her.

'This is what you really want?' he asked.

'I believe it is, yes.'

'All right then, Princess Rivengeld. I am, as always, at Your Highness's command. Let's go back to Stromgard.'

'I'll give you "Princess",' she hissed, fetching him a heavy punch on the arm.

The sound of his laughter was like music to her ears.

Emperor Mamur's Palace
Hasz
2

The Hasz'een throne room was a cavernous space the like of which Kelewulf had never seen before. Huge pillars of stone towered upwards to support a roof painted with scenes depicting the history of the Hasz'een people, and from the upper galleries light streamed in through windows inlaid with multicoloured glass that painted the dust motes swirling and dancing in the warm air with their hues. Gazing about him, Kelewulf could hardly imagine how such a monumental feat of construction was possible, until he remembered how the Hasz captured and subjugated all of the peoples they'd defeated in battle. The magnificent structure he was entering was no doubt built on the sweat and tears of countless slaves.

Flanked on either side by the two armed guards who'd brought him here from his chambers in the citadel, Kelewulf turned his attention away from the architecture and began walking towards the black marble dais ahead of him, on top of which was a great throne of the same material, the sable stone inlaid with intricate patterns of gold. On the throne sat Emperor Mamur.

The man looked ancient.

Thin and shrunken, Mamur had the appearance of a skeleton that had been draped in ill-fitting flesh. His body was almost lost among the grand, flowing robes of his office. The emperor's skull-like face stared out at Kelewulf – or at least, one side of it did; the left eye was an unseeing milky-white colour. The right, however, shone with an intelligence and authority that left Kelewulf in no doubt that this man was a ruler of people.

Mamur wore no crown, but on the forefinger of his right hand was the symbol of his office: a gold ring into which was set a great black pearl the size of a robin's egg. It was the Ring of Hasz, and it had been on that finger for a long time. Longer than any previous emperor's.

Despite the light coming in from the overhead windows, the arches and porticos to either side of Kelewulf were dark and shadowy, and it took him some time to realise that many of these were occupied by more heavily armed guards.

Up ahead, standing to Mamur's right and dressed in almost identical attire as his emperor was the man likeliest to sit on the black throne next: Grad'ur of Rishtok. Heavyset, with a face that looked as if it had never laughed, the man watched Kelewulf's approach with an expression of disdain. To the left of the emperor stood Elafir, in her familiar purple robes. The high priestess looked down at Kelewulf with an expression that was impossible to read. It made him wonder just what she might have told Mamur about him.

'I guess we're about to find out,' he mumbled under his breath.

As he reached the foot of the dais, Kelewulf was pulled to a halt by his escorts. Both men stepped closer to him and drew knives from their belts. They held the weapons close to his side.

Nobody said anything.

After the silence had gone on for an uncomfortable length of time, Kelewulf took it as a sign that he was to speak.

'Emperor Mamur, I am here to—'

A raised finger from Mamur and suddenly the dagger to Kelewulf's right was being pressed to his ribs hard enough that he had to struggle not to cry out. Even without the threat of the blade, the warning look Elafir shot him would have been enough to stop Kelewulf's words.

Grad'ur leaned forward and whispered something in the sovereign's ear. Whatever he said was answered with an almost imperceptible nod, and the finger was lowered.

Grad'ur, not Emperor Mamur, addressed Kelewulf. 'We are led to believe that whilst you appear to be but one person, you are in fact two, and that our erstwhile country-man, Yirgan, is a … cohort of yours.'

'He is.'

'You have given him new life?'

'Not life. He is dead. But before he died, he managed to hide his lich … his undead spirit … inside a phylactery. It is this part of him that I brought back into existence.'

'And why w—'

The finger went up again and this time it was Grad'ur who fell silent.

Emperor Mamur leaned forward. His upper lip peeled back a little to reveal a mouth full of teeth the colour of weathered stone. When he spoke, it was in a guttural whisper that was difficult to catch.

'My great-grandfather, Emperor Lundazh, banished the necromancer Yirgan from these lands. Did you know that?'

'I did not, Your Imperial Majesty.'

'That banishment was interminable and permanent.' There was a cold look in the man's eye when he spoke again. 'So in coming here with the necromancer's undead lich inside you, you have defied an imperial order.'

42

Grad'ur moved to speak with the old man, but was cut off again by the merest twitch of that ringed digit.

Kelewulf swallowed the lump that had risen in his throat. Of all the problems he'd foreseen occurring during this meeting, and there were many, this had not been part of his considerations. He had come here to ingratiate himself with the emperor using information about Stromgard and the Six Nations. Now the old man was accusing him of committing treason!

'I ... I had no intention of—'

'I would speak with Yirgan's undead spirit.'

'I'm sorry?'

'You already have admitted that it resides in you, yes?'

'It does. But ...' Kelewulf looked up at each of the people on the dais, but there was no help on any of their faces. 'Forgive me, Imperial Majesty, b-but what do you mean?'

'Here. Now. I will speak with the last great mage of Hasz. The so-called Master of the Dark Art. I understand that this ... lich is under your control?' The emperor continued without waiting for an answer. 'Well, my command is that you let it out. Let it out so that I might speak with it.'

Kelewulf's mind was a jumble of emotions. He could not believe what was being asked of him, but at the same time he understood the dire consequences of refusing to do what this ruthless ruler demanded.

He tore his eyes away from the wizened old ruler to look at Elafir, hating the implacable way she met his stare. With fear racing through him, he struggled to think of some solution to avoid carrying out this senseless order. But none came to him.

Eventually he straightened himself up to his full height and shot the trio what he hoped looked like a confident smile. 'What you command will not be easy, Your Imperial Majesty.'

Mamur met his words with a cold and stony look.

'I ... I will need a circle laid on the floor around me. The, er, price I've had to pay to entrap the lich inside this physical body has been very high – higher than I could even begin to describe. I would not have it escape now. So if I can have a circle of entrapment, preferably one of salt, I will try to do as you demand.' Even as the words left his mouth he could hardly believe he was saying them. His mind baulked at the mere idea of what he was being asked to do.

Kelewulf watched as Elafir summoned one of her shaven-headed attendants from the shadows with a motion of her head. He was intrigued by the item the slave was bringing: a large metal ring. The man rolled it upright before him, struggling to ensure it did not escape his control. With a grunt, the man laid it on the floor and gestured for Kelewulf to step inside as the two guards moved away.

'Silver,' Elafir said to Mamur in a loud voice as Kelewulf took up his place inside the ring. 'Salt circles are all very good, but there is no finer material than silver for an entrapment ring. It seems our young necromancer was right when he said he had much to learn from the Hasz'een.'

'Get on with it,' Mamur growled.

Kelewulf, staring down at his feet, felt panic rise up inside him again. The pain, both physical and mental, that he'd endured to take control over the lich had almost killed him more than once. But despite the appalling cost, he'd gained control and subjugated Yirgan. To let the lich have even this amount of freedom could undo everything he'd worked so hard for. It was almost too much to bear.

Lost in his thoughts, Kelewulf had failed to notice Elafir descend the dais. The high priestess approached him and dropped to one knee, pretending to adjust the position of the silver circle.

'The emperor grows impatient,' she said, quietly enough that her voice would not carry up to the man sitting on the throne.

'Does he know what he's asking?' Kelewulf asked, keeping his own voice low.

'Consider this a demonstration of your trustworthiness. Emperor Mamur has asked this of you as a display of … dependability.' Her face softened a little. 'You can't refuse him, and you can't back out now even if you wanted to. If you did, your life would be the price.' The high priestess stood. Stepping back, she held his eyes with her own and gave an almost imperceptible nod of her head.

Kelewulf went to reply but stopped himself. The sorceress was right, he had little choice but to go along with the sovereign's wishes. Taking a shuddering breath, he gathered himself and concentrated, stretching out with his mind to the Art. Slowly and tentatively he reached into the dark centre of it until he had forged a connection between himself and that terrifyingly powerful force.

In Kelewulf's mind's eye, he was standing inside an old fishing hut near a lake. It was a place he'd been taken to once as a child. In the middle of nowhere, hundreds of miles from the nearest habitation, it was perfect for what he'd needed when he was struggling to build a 'mental prison' in which to confine the lich. He'd made a few modifications: the windows and door were gone, and there was a dim glow from the walls that warned of the enchantments placed on them.

It was the object on the floor in front of him that provided most of the illumination, however. The huge strongbox was made of a dark hardwood. The metal clasps and hinges on its corners and edges gave it a formidable appearance; but it was the heavy chain wound round it that really hurt Kelewulf's eyes to look at. Strong majik was woven into each of those links, and stronger still was the enchantment on the lock that

46

secured it. He hated to remember the time and effort he'd had to put in to make the thing, and he'd thought never to open it.

Raising his hand, Kelewulf traced an intricate and ancient symbol in the air with his finger. As he did so, the lock unfastened and fell away from the box, followed by the chain.

Shaking his head at the foolishness of this venture, he jabbed at the air. The lid to the strongbox flew open and, just like that, Yirgan's undead lich was freed. It hung in the air of the cabin with its back to Kelewulf, its movements sharp and panicky. Disorientated, it cranked its head about for a moment before turning and focusing its attention on its nemesis. One side of its face was almost entirely missing, revealing the skull beneath, but its expression of hatred was still clear to see.

'You!' it said, pointing a withered finger at Kelewulf. 'You will regret trapping me here like this. We made a pact—'

'A pact that you chose to renege upon. I warned you, lich. I told you what would happen if you betrayed our agreement. You tried to take over my physical body and use it for yourself!'

The lich seemed on the verge of answering back when it stopped. As wily and cunning as ever, it seemed to be considering the situation in which it found itself.

'Why have you released me?' it asked.

'Somebody wishes to talk to you.'

'Wh—?'

Abruptly Kelewulf cut Yirgan off and spun away from the cabin, returning his consciousness to the real world once more. Reeling from the wave of sickening dizziness that washed through him, and with the throne room spinning before his eyes, he almost staggered out of the silver circle. To do so would have been disastrous because Kelewulf could feel the presence of the Hasz'een mage's lich with him now; a terrible invisible force that was enclosed inside the small circular space with him. Slowly but surely his senses returned, and Kelewulf did what he was most dreading by giving Yirgan sway over his physical body, so the lich could use his eyes and ears to see and hear, his tongue to talk. He peered up through watery eyes as the old man on the throne began to speak.

'Am I correct in thinking that the last great mage, Yirgan, is here?' Mamur asked. The emperor narrowed his eyes and leaned forward; he could see that the foreigner before him was confused as to his whereabouts, despite having only closed his eyes for a few seconds. It seemed as if the young man were engaged in some inner turmoil that made it hard for him to concentrate. As Mamur watched, something like recognition finally dawned on the foreigner's face and succeeded in returning the emperor's gaze with a mixture of alarm and horror.

'Your Greatness! Yes, it is I, Yirgan. Imperial M-Majesty, I beg of you, help me.' Although the voice appeared to come from the young man's mouth, it was very different to the one he'd used moments earlier. 'This foreigner has imprisoned me!' he continued, gesturing down at himself. 'I ask for your mercy. I ask you, as a fellow Hasz'een, to free me from the captivity I have been forced to suffer at the hands of this ... this—'

'My, my,' Mamur rasped, a smile slowly beginning to form on his lips. 'Listen to the "last great mage". Begging.'

'Yes! Yes, I beg you. I—'

'Silence, you dog!' Mamur spat. 'I wanted to speak with you, yes, but not to listen to you whinge and moan. And not because I have any wish to *free* you.' A wheezy rattling sound drifted down to the silver circle as Mamur laughed. 'No. I wanted you to witness the blossoming success of the very thing you hoped to eradicate when you tried to end the imperial bloodline.'

'Wait, I—'

'You would have killed my great-grandfather, the Emperor Lundazh. Had you succeeded, neither my grandfather, father or I would have lived to rule. When you look upon me, you look upon your greatest failure. Oh, you covered your tracks well enough at the time, and they couldn't prove it was you, but my great-grandfather always suspected you were the one. It's why he found an excuse to banish you fr—' The old man stopped when a racking cough took hold of him, but he waved away offers of help.

'*That* is what I wanted you to see and hear, O mighty Yirgan. And now you are a slave. A slave to a boy!' The wheezy rattle started up again. 'How apt that the Hasz'een master famous for keeping more slaves than anyone in the history of our people should now be the chattel of another!'

'Please, Mamur, I am useful to you. I still have a great wealth of knowledge of the Dark Art. I could serve you.'

'Silence!' The old man looked stonily down from above. 'The history books say that you never served anybody but yourself, Yirgan. Your recent betrayal of the young man in whose body you are trapped suggests you have not changed. I had a mind to destroy you, but on reflection your enslavement pleases me more.' Mamur paused, as if considering this proclamation. 'Yes, much more.' Then, with a small nod of his head, he sat back and crossed his hands on his lap. 'Enough of this. Boy, come back, I am tired of this traitor's embarrassing pleading.'

The Hasz observers watched as Kelewulf's body went rigid and he screwed his eyes shut. His face twisted from one ugly grimace to another, his whole body violently jerking and spasming as if racked with pain.

'What's he doing?' Mamur asked his high priestess, who was still standing a short distance away from the silver ring.

'He's fighting for control over the lich again,' Elafir said. 'It will not be an easy battle for him to win.'

50

The emperor turned to the guards still standing on either side of the metal boundary. 'If he fails, cross the circle and kill him,' he ordered.

Elafir baulked at her emperor's command. Of all the people in the throne room, only she truly understood the intensity of the battle that the young necromancer was waging in his mind as he tried to regain control over the undead mage's spirit. She could also sense that he would not be able to keep up the struggle for long. Kelewulf might be a foreigner, but his death would be a waste when he showed such a natural gift for the Art.

Despite knowing that she risked inviting the emperor's displeasure by doing so, she felt compelled to question his order: 'Your Imperial Majesty, I think the boy's majik is powerful enough to make him a useful asset for us – I would not have suggested this meeting with him if I didn't. However, I do not think he has the strength to suppress the lich again after he's spent so much effort conjuring it up.' She studied the old man's face for any suggestion she had overstepped the line. 'With your permission, I'd like to try to help him.'

The emperor stared at the struggling boy.

Elafir knew Mamur was as likely to refuse her request as he was to grant it; he was cruel and notoriously fickle. She held her breath until he turned his one good eye in her direction and gave her the merest nod of his head.

The high priestess reached out with her mind to the boy.

It was like stepping into a tornado. A raging war of wills was being waged between the lich and the young man, and she marvelled at how the latter was still conscious, let alone fighting on.

'Let me help you,' she said, directing her thoughts to Kelewulf.

'I ... I'm losing. I can't control it!'

'You must ask for my help if you want it. Only with your permission can I gain access to your mind without damaging it.'

'Y-yes ... help me ... please.'

She felt a strange sensation, something like a snap inside her head, and suddenly another world was superimposed over the one she was seeing through her physical eyes.

In this other place she was sailing through a sky filled with dark, storm-riddled clouds, buffeted this way and that by their violent jostling. Then, through a small break, she saw an island in the middle of a lake. It was towards this that she felt herself plummet, drawn by some invisible hand.

She closed her eyes for a second and when she opened them she was in a dark, windowless hut. Kelewulf was there too. He had managed to wrestle the lich into a wood-and-metal box, but he could not secure the thing shut. The lich could be heard screaming and cursing from inside the box, the lid jumping up and down as the two opposing forces hammered away at it from opposite sides. As she watched, Kelewulf sank to his knees. He appeared dangerously close to collapsing altogether. He was trying to sketch something in the air before him, but his shaking hand would not form the shapes properly.

Elafir knew the symbol and the enchantment well. She threw her own hand up and traced the character.

The scream that came from the box just before the great glowing chain materialised hurt her ears and her mind. After the chain came a lock that snapped shut, silencing the lich and sealing it inside the chest.

'Thank you,' Kelewulf managed to croak, just before losing consciousness.

Elafir was alone in the hut. She hesitated for a moment. With Kelewulf out cold but their psychic connection unbroken, she had full access to the young man's mind. She could, if she wished, delve into it, discover if his reasons for being in Hasz were as straightforward as he'd made out. Not only that, but she could do so safe in the knowledge that he would never know she had.

The high priestess wrestled with the rights and wrongs of what she was about to do, eventually coming to the conclusion that she would only look at the things relating to Kelewulf and Hasz, nothing else. Hoping that she wasn't making a terrible mistake, she left the hut-prison that Kelewulf had constructed in his mind and went in search of answers.

* * *

Mamur watched the young man crumple to the stone floor.

'Was he successful in wrestling back control?' he asked Elafir.

The priestess seemed not to hear her emperor for a moment – as if she were distracted in some way – but finally she turned to look back up at the man on the throne. 'He was. He's stronger than he appears.'

Elafir felt uncharacteristically anxious as she ascended the steps of the dais again. The emperor was watching her approach, and something about his expression unnerved her. She was never certain if the old man had more experience in the Art than he let on. If he indeed did, he might have sensed what she had done in the few seconds after Kelewulf passed out.

'Is it wise to let this young necromancer into our trust?'

'He came of his own free will, knowing it could easily spell his death. He has no love for his people – quite the opposite, in fact. I will keep a careful watch on him and destroy him if I suspect he is lying to us in any way.' She glanced at Grad'ur. 'The Hasz'een have a history of taking not just slaves from foreign lands, but also individuals whom we recognise as being a possible benefit to us. Kelewulf could be useful for your war plans – he will have knowledge of geography, political alliances, the strategic thinking of his people. And who knows, if under my tutelage he becomes as adept at all aspects of the Art as I think he might, we could recruit him as a battle mage.' She gave a small shrug. 'If I am honest, I can see something of myself in the boy, and his skills could be useful, if polished and refined. I would also welcome the chance to see if any of the majik he learned through Yirgan is of use to us.'

Mamur considered her words. 'And Yirgan truly is reduced to an irrelevance?'

'He is. The boy has no love for the dead mage's lich.'

When Mamur next spoke, it was to order the guards to get Kelewulf to his feet.

'Have him taken back to High Priestess Elafir's citadel. I think our young Stromgardian has earned the right to stay in Hasz and learn our ways, for now at least. In return, we will learn what he has to offer us by way of information about the Rivengelds and the Six Kingdoms over the sea.'

Stromgard

3

Astrid and Lann crested the hill, pulling their horses to a halt so they could both take in the city below them. Even from this distance, the capital of Strom was every bit as impressive as Lannigon remembered. In size and grandeur it was about as different from the farm he grew up on as it could be, but even though he did not hail from Strom, it still felt like he'd come home.

He was about to say as much to Astrid when he saw the look of consternation on her face.

'What is it?' he asked, looking back at the city to see if he could make out what was bothering her.

'Something's wrong,' she said in a small voice. 'I can't put my finger on it, but I've had this feeling for a few days now. I know it's probably just me being silly, but I can't seem to shake it.'

'Then what are we waiting up here for?' With that he set his mount forward, urging it towards the city.

They entered the city walls through the Northern Gate. Being close to a marketplace, the streets were chock-full of people looking to buy from the traders who lined the large square not far from the royal longhouse. Nobody paid the two cloaked and hooded travellers much mind as they led their horses through the crowd.

It was an area of the city Lann knew all too well, and the square in particular held bad memories for him. It was here that he and the Dreadblade had fought the mercenary Frindr Oknhammer in a trial by combat to prove Astrid's brother Erik innocent of his father's murder. A shiver ran down Lann's back as he recalled that day: how the dark blade had judged the mercenary an evil that had to be removed from this world; how he had wielded the weapon against the giant, deflecting Oknhammer's brutal attacks before spilling the man's lifeblood on to the floor of the packed earth where people now walked and shopped.

Not wanting to draw attention to themselves, they tied their mounts up a little way away from the royal long-house and approached its doors on foot, only to be stopped by two of the king's guards.

'King Erik is in discussions at the moment. He will not be dealing with disputes or hearing entreaties today.'

'Not even from his sister?' Astrid asked, pulling the hood of her cloak back to reveal her face.

Lann almost laughed out loud as the man's expression went from shock to panic when he realised the young woman in front of him was indeed who she said she was. However, once the guard had recovered his wits, it was his next response that took Lann by surprise. The man hardened his features and pulled himself up to his full height, the spear in his hand still firmly barring the entrance. When he spoke, it was in the same officious tone as before.

'Princess Astrid. Despite the joy your return will undoubtedly bring to the king, he was explicit in his instructions. Nobody is permitted entry to the Great Longhouse until the individual with whom he is currently in discussions has left.'

Lann turned to his friend, noting how all trace of humour had deserted the shield maiden's face. Even more worryingly, the fingers of her left hand were creeping towards the pommel of her sword.

He reached across and placed a hand on Astrid's forearm before addressing the guard. 'Well, I think the situation is perfectly clear, and please accept our apologies for putting you in this uncomfortable position. I'm sure I speak for the princess when I say how encouraging it is to discover the king's personal guards taking their roles so dutifully.'

He turned his head in the shield maiden's direction, stressing each word. 'After all, the king is the king, and his orders must be obeyed … by every Stromgardian.'

Astrid kept her eyes fixed on the guard, the muscles at the edge of her jaw bunching and unbunching as she struggled to control her temper. Just as Lann thought he would have to bodily remove her, another voice a short distance away made her turn her head and seek out its owner.

A tall, blonde shield maiden was hurrying towards them. She was dressed in a warrior's traditional leather garb, but the golden clasp at her cloak signified she was also a member of the King's Guard. The excitement on her face was matched only by that on Astrid's, and the two were quickly in each other's arms, laughing and smiling and talking across one another.

Lann recognised the young woman. Maarika was Astrid's oldest friend, the two of them having joined the maidens at the same time. He watched with pleasure as they talked animatedly with each other. At the same time, Lann tried to ignore the less welcome emotions springing up, unbidden, inside of him. He was a little jealous of the bond they clearly shared. Growing up as he had on an isolated cattle farm, Lann had never had any close friends and certainly no one who would have welcomed him home like Maarika.

Astrid beckoned him to join them. As she did so, Maarika whispered something to her friend and playfully grabbed her forearm, causing Astrid to hiss in pain and screw up her eyes. The apologies that followed were as profuse and heartfelt as the welcome had been, and continued until Astrid insisted that Maarika be quiet.

Lann inspected the wound. Thankfully the stitches he'd put in place had not come undone.

'You'll have a fine scar,' Maarika said, now that she'd finally stopped fretting about her clumsiness. 'I hope you paid your opponent back with cold steel in their gut.'

'I'm not sure demons have guts, but yes, the creature paid a high price for marking me.'

'Demon? Then it's true what they say? That the traitor Kelewulf opened up the gates of hell and the two of you were charged with closing them again?' Maarika looked from her friend to Lann and back again.

Lann gave a little snort. 'I think that might be stretching it a bit.'

'Ignore him,' Astrid said, cutting across him. 'That pretty much sums up what happened in Vissergott, yes. I witnessed things that day, and in the days since, which I had only thought to see in nightmares. I might have been done for on more than one occasion had it not been for Jarl Gudbrandr here.'

'Then he is my hero!' Maarika said, surprising Lann when she enveloped him in her arms, hugging him close and kissing him on the forehead. All of a sudden, a troubling thought must have occurred to her because she let go of him and took a step back, straightening her cloak and uniform as she did. 'My apologies, Jarl Gudbrandr, I forgot myself for a moment there. I had no right to grab a man of your office in that way. I—'

'Please stop,' Lann said, hoping that the red he could feel rising to his cheeks was not noticeable. 'I am a jarl only because of what I did to save the king. I am as uncomfortable with the title and the office as is possible, so please … call me Lann. Or Lannigon if you must.'

'Thank you, Jar— Thank you, Lannigon,' said the blonde shield maiden sincerely, before turning back to Astrid. 'My, but we have much to talk about,' she said to her friend. 'I too have important news!'

'You do?'

'Yes! I am to be married!'

Lann's face split into a grin as he watched the pair embrace with joy again.

'Who is it?'

'Do you remember Ingridd? Tall, with long coppery hair?'

'She joined the maidens just after us? Excellent with a dagger?'

'Yes. You do remember her. Good!'

'When is the wedding?'

'Tonight!'

'Really? Then it is lucky we returned when we did.'

'Luck has nothing to do with it. The wedding could have been last week or next month or next year.' She paused and smiled at Astrid's perplexed look. 'I have been waiting for your return. I could not get married without you there to bless the event.'

'Then your wedding might never have happened,' Astrid said, gesturing down at her forearm.

'Rubbish. I don't care if it's a demon, some other creature from the Void, or Lorgukk himself, they are no match for a shield maiden like you, Astrid Rivengeld. Now if you'll both excuse me, I must get back to my duties.'

'Talking of which,' Astrid said, stalling her friend as she made to leave. 'Who is my brother seeing in the Great Longhouse right now?'

Maarika answered with a shake of her head. 'Somebody who trusted your father with their life, and who now trusts your brother in the same way. Do not ask me more, Sister, for I would not betray the king's confidence to tell you, even if I knew.' With that she moved away, addressing them over her shoulder. 'I will go now and try to get word to your brother that you are here and eager to see him.'

Lann stood and stared after Máarika a little while before turning back to Astrid. 'She's marrying young, isn't she?'

Astrid nodded, watching her friend as she made her way towards the building that was Stromgard's seat of power. 'The shield maidens dedicate their lives to fighting for their kingdom. Many do not live to see their old age. Because of this, it is not uncommon for many of the Sisters to wed when they are quite young. Before I took off after Kelewulf with you and Fleya, I was almost married off myself.'

'You were?'

She gave another nod. 'To a swordsman from a powerful family my father thought would make a good match.'

'Oh.'

The long pause that followed was thankfully broken when Astrid laughed. Then she took him by complete surprise by leaning forward and kissing him on the cheek.

'Don't worry,' she said. 'He is well out of the picture now.'

The pair turned at the sound of a man's voice demanding to know where the king's sister was, and soon after they were brought before King Erik through the very doors of the Great Longhouse that had been barred to them minutes before.

* * *

Although she had only been gone from Stromgard a relatively short time, the place felt different to Astrid. The Great Longhouse had been such an important part of her life when she was younger; a warm open space she'd loved to run around when business of the kingdoms was not taking place inside its walls. But today it felt ... *smaller*, and not just the longhouse, but Stromgard itself – as if the weeks she'd spent away from the capital had diminished it in some way.

Lann and Astrid walked side by side as they approached the dais topped by the ancient River Throne. Sitting in that great chair, looking extremely regal, was Erik, King of Strom, the most powerful ruler in the Six Kingdoms.

'He's put on weight,' Astrid said in a hushed voice. 'And if that's a beard he's trying to grow, it looks ridiculous.'

'Hush, Astrid. He'll hear you.'

'Yes, he will,' said Erik in a loud voice, getting to his feet and coming down from the dais with a look of unbridled joy on his face. 'But when has that ever stopped my beautiful sister from saying whatever the hell she likes?'

The siblings smiled at each other and embraced.

When they separated, Erik turned to Lann. 'We welcome you back to Stromgard, Jarl Gudbrandr.' He paused, and when he spoke again the sorrow in his voice was clear to hear. 'I am so sorry for your loss. We received news of the events at Vissergott from a messenger sent here by the new ruler of Vorneland. Your aunt was an extraordinary woman, and I owe my freedom and my reign to her every bit as much as I do to you.'

'Thank you, King Erik. She was very fond of you too.'

The king looked at Astrid. 'The same messenger brought news of how our cousin's foul majik had set loose a host of demonic creatures and that the pair of you were hunting them down. You cannot imagine how worried I have been for you both.'

'We are fine, brother. A little battered and bruised, is all.'

Erik scanned his sister's face as if he were able to read more there than in her words. Then with a clap of his hands he broke the spell and returned the smile to his face. 'I would like to hold a feast, tonight, in honour of you both returning to us! But with Maarika and Ingridd marrying it seems only fit to hold the two celebratory banquets together.'

Astrid frowned, as if she too could sense something that remained unspoken behind the king's joyful words. She reached out and placed a hand on her brother's arm. 'You look tired, Erik. What is wrong?'

'We have much to talk about, but I would really rather not burden you with worrisome matters just as you have both returned ...'

'What is it, brother?'

The king paused before answering: 'Trouble is brewing. It seems Hasz is planning war.'

'Kelewulf!' Lann exclaimed immediately. 'He planned to go to Hasz. No doubt he is there and responsible for—'

'He is in Hasz, yes,' the king said, cutting him off. 'But he is not at the root of this – although I doubt my hateful cousin is at all concerned to discover their plans. No, Emperor Mamur wishes to end his reign with a war against the only people who have defeated his nation, albeit a long time ago.'

'War? Are you sure?' Astrid shook her head in disbelief. 'Why, after all these years of peace?'

Erik covered his sister's hand with his own. 'It is not certain. Mamur is behind the times and still believes in the old ways of his people. But the Hasz'een are changing. They have lived without conflict for a very long time now, and many of them have no appetite for a return to death and bloodshed. Some are even changing their attitudes towards slavery, and refusing to be part of that disgusting practice. We must hope that these new minds find a voice and use it to stop Mamur before it is too late.'

Astrid sensed this information had something to do with why she had not been allowed to see him immediately upon her return. Narrowing her eyes at her brother, she demanded, 'Who were you with before you agreed to see us?'

'I cannot tell you that, not right now. It would not be safe for the person in question.'

'But—'

Lann cut across her. 'Do you know why Kelewulf wanted to travel to Hasz? He seeks Lorgukk's heart. If it is there, and if he succeeds in finding it, a war between our kingdoms and Hasz – or anyone else for that matter – will be the least of our worries. We will all become slaves of the dark god.'

'I know why he's there,' Erik answered in a flat voice. 'And I also know he's no nearer to finding the heart than he was before he left these lands.' The look Erik gave them was enough to remind Lann and Astrid of his authority. 'Please, Lann, I know your destiny and that of my cousin are closely entwined, and that you want nothing more than to rush off to Hasz to seek him out. But try to understand that as a king I must first look to protecting my people from any and all threats. Yes, Kelewulf presents a danger to us. He wishes to plunge us all into chaos. But answer me this: does war make it easier or harder for him to do what he wants?' He turned to Astrid, silently asking the same question of his sister. 'Kelewulf may not be the cause of the Hasz'een war plans, but it suits his purposes for it to go ahead. He has met with Mamur and he has told him that Strom and the Six Kingdoms are weak with me on the throne, and that an attack now is likely to be successful.' He noted their puzzled expressions. 'He believes that the chaos he created in Vorneland has destabilised us and that many of the creatures still abound. Thanks to the two of you, he is wrong in that, at least.'

'This information,' Astrid said. 'It comes from a source in Hasz, doesn't it?'

'It does.'

'And are you certain this person can be trusted?'

'I am.'

'Why? The Hasz'een are slavers and warmongers. Who is it?'

'I'm not comfortable talking about this. I have sworn an oath to keep the person's identity secret.'

'By the gods, Erik!' Astrid shouted, her frustration boiling over. Pushing Lann away as he attempted to calm her, she thrust her face into her brother's. 'Lann and I have been hunting monsters all across Vorneland to keep the people of the Six Kingdoms safe. We have done so in order to serve those kingdoms and you, our ruler. I'm not asking you to reveal your precious source's identity, I'm just trying to ascertain if you are being played in a deadly game that could result in the Hasz'een landing on our shores again without us being properly prepared!' Another thought occurred to her. 'Hasz can only be reached by crossing the Norderung Sea, and our countries have had nothing to do with each other for many, many years. This source of yours can't be sailing back and forth regularly without drawing attention to themselves.' She narrowed her eyes at the king. 'Unless you have another method of communication? Could it be that you're using Hasz'een majik to speak with this person?'

During the silence that followed, Lann looked between the pair and noted that Erik was somehow managing to remain calm, despite his sister's outcry. When the king spoke, it was in a tone that was as regal as it was firm.

'The Hasz'een source is one that our father established a working relationship with. He believed that sharing and receiving information was crucial in keeping a peace between the two nations. So yes, sister, I am willing to trust the individual of whom you talk. For now, at least.' He weighed his words again. 'Like you and Jarl Gudbrandr, I am doing my best to keep the people of the Six Kingdoms safe. I am sorry if my methods are a disappointment to you.'

His words seemed to strike home, and Astrid faltered before responding. 'Forgive me, brother – my king. I was wrong to talk to you like that.'

'How long do we have?' Lann asked. 'Before they are ready to attack?'

'If the emperor gets his way and war is declared, not long. The Hasz'een navy could launch with minimal preparation,' Erik responded. He turned and mounted the steps to sit in his throne again. 'There might, however, be a way for us to ensure no Hasz'een attack ever reaches these shores.'

Lann felt the Dreadblade stir at his side; a quiet murmuring noise in his head that was accompanied by tiny pins-and-needles sensations all over his body. He placed his hand on the pommel of the weapon.

King Erik continued: 'I will not prevent you from going off to Hasz, Jarl Gudbrandr. It would not be right of me to do so – not after everything you have done for me. I will arrange your passage to Hasz by the most expedient methods available to us. All I ask is that you make a stop on the way to talk, on my behalf, to a man.'

'What man? And how can it be "on the way" if I am aboard a ship?'

'His name is Brundorl. He has made his home on the Sölten Isles, which are situated almost exactly halfway between here and your goal.'

'Brundorl?' Astrid's eyes were wide. 'The marauder?'

'The very same. Except now he is the self-proclaimed king of the people that have made the isles their home.'

'What does he have to do with this?'

'Hasz can only invade by crossing the Norderung Sea. Brundorl's fleet is unmatched in both size and power.'

'It's not a fleet, it's a mishmash of pirate ships that operate as individuals.'

'Not true. Not any longer. Brundorl has organised them. Think about it. *If* Hasz was to attack, he could scupper the Hasz'een navy before it ever got a chance to approach us.

Without their ships, Hasz has no hope of waging their war.'

'Then why wait for them to reach the Sölten Isles?' Lann asked. 'You could simply have Brundorl sink the fleet while it is still at harbour.'

'That would be an act of aggression I'm not willing to make. As I pointed out earlier, I believe this might all be possible to resolve without bloodshed.'

'And what will you offer Brundorl for his help, brother?'

'Gold. And the opportunity to have the Sölten Isles recognised as part of the Six Kingdoms.'

'He's a marauder, Erik. A pirate. He won't stick to any such agreement.'

'Even brigands have a code, sister. I'm also betting on the fact that a king's emissary wielding a sword like the Dreadblade will influence the way the man thinks. A sword of the gods is a powerful political weapon.'

The king's words annoyed Lann, but he held his tongue. The same could not be said of the dark sword, which wailed its displeasure inside his head. It was odd for the blade to react to humans in this way, and Lann could only guess it disliked being used as a pawn in this affair – it would rather be about the business for which it was forged.

Welcome to my world, Lann thought silently.

'Will you do this for your king?' Erik asked, snapping Lann's attention back to the room.

The young jarl answered his monarch's question with a low bow.

'Good. Thank you, Lann.' Erik said, turning his attention once more to his sibling. 'Now, I would very much appreciate it if I could have a word in private with my sister here. We have some things we need to catch up on.'

Nodding his head, Lann left the pair and went outside for some much-needed fresh air.

The Great Longhouse was eerily quiet on the morning after the celebratory feasts. The smell of food and alcohol still hung in the air as Lann made his way towards Astrid's room. Maarika and Ingridd's wedding had been a riotous affair, and the shield maidens had made sure it was a night neither bride would ever forget. Lann had politely refused most offers to join in with the revelries, not really in the mood to celebrate, but he'd been happy to sit at the high table watching Astrid and her warrior Sisters dance and laugh together. He had never seen Astrid so happy. And neither had he seen her looking so striking. During their journeys together he'd become accustomed to seeing her in her studded leather armour. Last night, she had been in a long dress that clung to her figure in a way that made it almost impossible for him not to stare at her. She'd had something done to her hair too: it was cut into a new shape that was long on one side, whilst the other side was brushed back and braided close to the scalp in a new style he also spotted on a number of other women in attendance.

She'd caught him looking at her on one occasion; she'd beckoned for him to join her, but he'd shaken his head and diverted his stare to cover his embarrassment.

Having arrived at her door, Lann paused, gathering himself before knocking. He'd come to talk travel plans for the following day and he knew his news would not be easy to deliver.

When a sleepy-eyed Astrid opened the door he felt a little guilty for having woken her earlier than she may have wanted.

'Morning,' she said, her voice hoarse. She grinned at the sound of it, her hand going to her slender throat. 'Too much singing.'

'Did you have a good time?'

'Heavens, yes. You?'

He nodded. 'I didn't get a chance to say, but, er, you looked nice.'

'Nice? Is that the best you can manage?'

'Very nice, I mean. Lovely.' His blush turned an even deeper shade of red. 'I, um, I haven't seen you in a dress since you were queen.'

'Queen regent,' she corrected him. 'It was only ever a temporary role, thank goodness.'

'Nevertheless. It looked good on you,' he said.

'I hated it. But Maarika insisted I wear something "pretty" to her wedding.'

'Well, it's certainly that. As were you.' His heart did a weird bump-thing when he realised what he'd just said. 'I mean, er, your hair, and, um, jewellery and things. They were all pretty …'

'Thank you.'

The silence that followed was an uncomfortable one, and for the first time in weeks neither of them knew what to say to the other. Astrid eventually broke it.

'Don't think you can get out of sword training this morning just because we're travelling tomorrow.'

Lann gave a small shake of his head, his reason for being there returning to him. 'We are not going. At least, you're not.'

'What do you mean?' Astrid said, giving him a look that would have withered most people. It was a look he'd seen many times before on their travels together.

'When the ship leaves tomorrow afternoon, I'll be on it alone. Hear me out,' he said, stopping her interruption. 'Your brother needs the best military people around him in case the Hasz'een go ahead with their plans for war. Your place is here with our king.' He found it impossible to look at her now and set his eyes on the floor just ahead of his feet. 'I want you with me. After everything we've been through I can't imagine going out alone. But I also know how hard the last few weeks have been on you, and how you said you needed to be home now.' He thought again of how happy she'd been last night, how easily she'd laughed and joked with her friends and the other wedding celebrants. He had no right to take her away from all that so soon.

The silence that followed went on for what felt like an age. When he was unable to take it any more, Lann looked up, hoping to read something in Astrid's expression. Just when he was about speak again, she surprised him by lurching forward and pushing him forcefully in the chest, making him stagger back into the wall behind him and fall to the floor.

He stared back up at her in shock as she spoke.

'Do you really think you can come here and order me about like that, Jarl Gudbrandr?' she said, stressing his title in a haughty tone he hadn't heard before. 'As you have just pointed out, it was not that long ago that I sat on the River Throne of Stromgard. I am also a distinguished shield maiden of this city and sister to the king! I will go where I want, when I want, in the Six Kingdoms. And right now, I choose to go with you to the Sölten Isles.'

'But—'

'Do not "but" your recent queen,' she spat. 'That could be considered treason. A crime that is still punished with death here in Stromgard, jarl or no jarl. I am going to the

Sölten Isles, *not* because I am a spoilt and privileged brat who demands her own way, but because I want to be with you!' She glared at him, daring him to answer her back.

When he didn't, she nodded and leaned forward, offering him a hand and helping him to his feet. This time, when she spoke it was in the calm, low tones he was familiar with.

'You're an idiot,' she said with a little sniff.

'I'm sorry.'

'An idiot I'm very fond of, but still an idiot.'

'Again, I'm sorry.'

'We have been through too much together to suddenly break apart now, Lann.' She held a finger up to stop his interruption. 'I know I said I wanted to see home, and I have. Last night we celebrated my best friend's wedding, where we ate and drank and danced. I could not have asked for more. I have to thank you for coming home with me and giving me the chance to do those things. And tomorrow we will depart for Hasz via the Sölten Isles, to do our king's bidding and try to secure him a navy.'

'I never stood a chance of stopping you from coming, did I?'

'No, you didn't. But I know why you tried.' When she leaned forward and kissed him on the cheek, Lann felt his knees give way just a little, and the weird bump-thing returned, churning hard enough in his chest that he thought his heart was trying to burst free. For the second time since arriving at her door, he stared back at her in disbelief as she continued. 'My fate is intertwined with yours, and it seems that the gods have decided they are not done with us yet. We were always going to Hasz together, you and I. I want to hear you say that's still the case, and that you want me with you.'

'I want you with me.'

'Good.' She took a step back and looked him up and down. He was still wearing the fine clothes he'd worn to the wedding, having been unable to sleep at all last night.

'You looked nice too,' Astrid said. 'In your wedding finery.'

'Nice? Is that all?' he said, parroting her.

'Don't push your luck, Lann.' She ran her hand through her hair. 'Now go and get changed into your leathers. We have sword training to do. You've got thirty minutes. I'll see you on the training square outside the shield maidens' barracks.'

With that she turned and re-entered her room, shutting the door in his face.

Gematik's Citadel, East Hasz

4

It was Kelewulf's second morning in Hasz, and despite the exhaustion he felt from his encounter with the emperor he found himself awake before the sun had fully risen.

A strange mixture of emotions coursed through him when he thought about what lay ahead. It was to be his first day of training under Elafir's tuition, and even though the real reason he was here in this land had nothing to do with these studies, he was nevertheless both nervous and excited at the prospect of seeing how the Hasz'een taught majik. In particular, he was looking forward to studying with the high priestess. Her powers were undeniable, as had been demonstrated when she helped him subdue the lich. His only regret was that he'd been forced to ask for that help, and how he'd allowed her to see him in such a vulnerable state.

He started when there was loud knock at his door.

A short while later Kelewulf found himself being escorted by one of the priestess's silent servants deep into the citadel, twisting this way and that through a myriad of corridors until he had no idea what the way back might be. When they eventually came to a halt it was in front of a vast, metal-reinforced door that looked out of place inside the citadel, making him wonder what forces and dangers it was created to withstand.

Nodding in its direction, the attendant scurried off back in the direction he'd come.

The door was every bit as heavy as it looked, and Kelewulf found that he had to lean into it with his full bodyweight to get it open. Stepping inside, the young necromancer stared about him. The floor was made of blue interlocking wooden tiles that had symbols and hieroglyphs carved into them, only a few of which he recognised. But it was the walls that he could hardly take his eyes from. They seemed to be composed of a swirling, shifting smoke-like substance. Not only were they fascinating to behold; he could feel the power contained in them. Layers of majik were woven into their fabric.

Tearing his eyes away from the walls, he looked across at the person standing in the centre of the room. They had their back to him, but they were dressed in the dark purple attire that was commonplace in the citadel.

'Close the door,' the figure said, turning to face him for the first time. It was not Elafir, as he'd been expecting, but the young female acolyte who had discovered him that first night. He scanned his memory for her name: Alwa.

'Where is the high priestess?' Kelewulf asked, doing as he was bid.

'She has been called away on business,' the young woman replied. 'She told me to begin your tutelage in her absence.'

Kelewulf let out a derisive snort. 'You? A mere acolyte? *You* are going to teach me in the ways of the Art?'

'That is correct.'

'You *do* know that I have managed, single-handedly, to entrap the lich of the last great mage, Yirgan, don't you?'

'You've mentioned it. On a number of occasions,' she said, her voice dripping with sarcasm. 'High Priestess Elafir believes you need to learn the underlying principles of the Art, to make you stronger and less reliant on the undead necromancer.' She gave him a humourless smile. 'I understand you had quite a time with the lich when you had to reveal it to our Imperial Majesty.'

'She told you about that?' he asked, anger boiling up inside of him.

'The high priestess?' The acolyte shook her head. 'My mistress would never gossip. But the goings-on of the royal palace are often difficult to keep secret. These things have a habit of getting out.' She paused, never losing the mocking smile as she looked him up and down and gave a dismissive little sniff. 'We wouldn't want such an unfortunate event to happen again, would we? I'm told it was all rather … undignified.'

How dare she talk to me like this? The young woman's impudence caused a great wave of indignant rage to break inside Kelewulf. He felt the lich stir for the first time since he'd managed to subdue it with the help of Elafir, but he ignored it, instead letting his own anger take hold. Throwing out a hand in Alwa's direction, he summoned up the majik to painfully constrict her throat and put a halt to her insolence.

Acolyte Alwa was ready for him. With no more than a swipe of her own hand she swatted aside his clumsy attack. Then, with the same economy of effort, she flicked her fingers in his direction and cast her own spell.

The force of impact was like the god Og's axe hitting Kelewulf full in the chest. He felt his feet leave the ground as he flew backwards and crashed into the door, crumpling down on to the hard floor. No air would come to his lungs, and the more he tried to breathe, the more panic started to grip. His eyes bulging, he clawed at his chest and throat until, eventually, with a frightened gasp he sucked in a great breath. He blinked up at the acolyte. As he scrambled back to his feet he felt his anger returning, but before he could act upon it Alwa disappeared.

Only her voice remained, and it came at him from a number of directions all at once.

'Don't. You will lose,' was her warning, but there was a taunting tone to it.

'Where are you? Show yourself!'

She did so, blinking back into existence off to his right as quickly as she'd disappeared.

Kelewulf called upon the lich's vast knowledge of majik, and a terrible incantation formed in his mind. Curling his hands into fists, he looked down at them as they transformed into glowing balls of fire. But as he threw his arms out to release them in Alwa's direction, they simply sputtered out. At the same time, he was suddenly seared with mind-numbing cramps that seemed to go down to his very bones. He folded into himself, his face a rictus of pain as his hands and fingers curled into agonised claws. His legs too curled up beneath him and he dropped, pitching forward, unable to move his arms to break his fall even as his face crashed into those wooden tiles. The scream that threatened wouldn't come either. Tears sprang to his eyes and ran down his cheeks.

And then, as quickly as it had started, the agony was gone.

Alwa came to stand just in front of him, leaning forward so she was in his eyeline. Gone was the sneering mask she'd worn moments earlier; now her face was blank and expressionless. 'Yirgan was a great necromancer, but he was no battle mage,' she said, her voice softer than before. 'His majik is powerful in more studied situations.' She frowned as if weighing her words before continuing. 'When used in anger – in haste – it is easily countered. Do not get me wrong, I am in awe of what the great man accomplished when he was alive, and I doubt there are many here in Hasz who are capable of doing a fraction of what he was able to – particularly when it comes to summoning from the Void. In that, he had no match.' She met his eyes with a hard stare. 'Do you understand why we needed to do what we just did? Why I goaded you into acting in that way? What I was trying to show you?'

Kelewulf simply nodded.

'Are you ready for your lesson?' she asked.

Kelewulf wiped at his face and looked her squarely in the eye as he got back to his feet. 'Teach me,' he answered.

Kelewulf was exhausted. For more than an hour Elafir's acolyte had him fend off attack after attack, tutoring him in different ways to defend against her seemingly endless knowledge of battle majik until both his mind and body were battered and bruised.

At the end of a short break, a still sweat-drenched Kelewulf began struggling to get up from where he'd collapsed on the floor. Watching him, Alwa sighed and gave a little shake of her head.

'What now?' Kelewulf said.

'You.'

'What about me?'

'You're holding back. Not playing to your strengths.'

'Is that so?'

'It must be if a mere third-year acolyte like me is managing to dominate you like this. And no, this time I'm not being deliberately snide so that you'll lose yourself to your anger. It's just ...' She hesitated.

'No, go on ... please.'

'You have more than enough knowledge inside you to deal with the likes of me. You just seem afraid to use it.'

He looked across at her as the realisation of what she was trying to tell him slowly dawned. Alwa met his stare with her own.

'The lich?' he asked.

'The lich.' She nodded.

Kelewulf swallowed. 'Let's go again,' he said, nodding back in her direction.

Alwa attacked, using a variation of a powerful force spell she'd employed earlier. Remembering what she'd taught him, Kelewulf deflected her majik with a spell of his own, but this time, rather than come back at her with yet more battle majik, he dipped into Yirgan's vast knowledge of summoning and allowed the lich the freedom to help in a way that he had not done for some time. Euphoria filled him as the familiar dark majik flooded his being; the reaction was the lich's every bit as much as it was his own.

The demons appeared together, one in front of Alwa, the other behind. Both were the stuff of nightmares; the creature that materialised before the young acolyte actually made her stop in her tracks. It roared at her, its entire form ablaze with dark flames that let off neither smoke nor smell. It stood on two legs that ended in heavy, black hooves, and its upper body was heavily muscled and bull-like. Huge, curled horns protruded straight out from both sides of its head. The demon to Alwa's rear was altogether different. Although smaller than the first, it was still a head taller than Alwa herself. Its face, if it could be called such a thing, was a mass of writhing tentacles, each tipped with an eye that glared balefully down upon the young woman. As Kelewulf watched, this figure lifted up its left hand, the clawed fingers of which were balled into a huge fist, preparing to smite the acolyte.

The field of protective majik appeared just in time: a dome of fizzing, popping grey stuff that stopped the great fist just as it came down on Alwa's skull. Despite the defensive shield, the force of the blow was enough to send her to her knees and she let out a loud gasp. The demon raised its hand a second time.

'Enough!'

The voice behind him made Kelewulf spin around. Elafir had entered the room. Closing her eyes, she swiftly drew a symbol in the air in front of her, and both demons disappeared as quickly as they had formed. All that could be heard was the crackling of the dome covering Alwa, until this too vanished. The high priestess stood perfectly still now and seemed to be considering what she had just witnessed.

'I ... I'm sorry,' Kelewulf said, eventually breaking the silence.

He was not expecting the puzzled look Elafir gave him by way of a response. 'What for?' she asked.

'The demons. I summoned them.'

'Obviously.' She frowned, as if expecting him to continue. When he did not, she turned to her acolyte. 'Overall, I think that first lesson went rather well, don't you?'

'Yes, mistress.'

'Run along now, Alwa. You have studies with Master Larghal and you're already late. You know he hates it when you're not there for the start of his lessons.'

Kelewulf watched with his mouth open as Alwa left the room. As she passed, she gave him a nod that looked surprisingly like one of approval.

'You must be hungry,' Elafir said to him once they were alone. 'I know a summoning like that always makes me ravenous. Come with me, we'll see what the kitchen can rustle you up.' Without another word she turned on her heel and left.

His head spinning with questions, Kelewulf took one last look at the room before following the high priestess out.

The thick lamb stew was full of spices and herbs that he had not encountered before. Despite the fiery sensation it left on his tongue and lips, he found he liked it and wolfed down his first bowl, nodding eagerly when a member of the kitchen staff offered to refill it.

Kelewulf and Elafir were sitting across from each other on long benches that ran the length of the table. It was Kelewulf's first time in the refectory, where both the tutors and those under the tutelage of the high priestess ate. The noise from the kitchen as the cooks prepared lunch was oddly reassuring after the crazy morning he'd had.

'She is very good,' he said between mouthfuls. 'Alwa, I mean.'

'Yes, she is. She excels in the art of battle majik. That is why I chose her for your lesson.'

'Things got out of hand. I should not have—'

The high priestess raised her hand to stop him. 'Do not apologise for using the skills you have acquired. And besides, Alwa was not in any real danger. In fact, I think you might have done her a favour, in a way.'

'Me? How so?'

'Acolyte Alwa will be a great advocate of the Art one day, but she is headstrong and proud. She needed a small lesson in being more ... humble. Just as you needed one in discovering the many holes in your knowledge. I think it was good for both of you.'

Kelewulf, realising he would not be able to finish his second helping, pushed his bowl away and stared across at Elafir. 'You were watching the whole time?'

'I confess that I was. But please do not think I singled you out in any way. Every acolyte is subjected to a similar test during their first session. It allows me to get a sense of their raw skills and what they are capable of when they're pushed. Alwa did a good job in the pushing department, don't you think?'

'You must think I'm a fraud.' It was strange hearing these words come out of his own mouth. Nevertheless, he recognised the truth in them. Unlike Alwa, Kelewulf had not given himself up to the years of study and dedication required to master the Art, had not made the sacrifices she had. No, he had decided that he could sidestep all of that and steal the knowledge and power he sought. Consequently he lacked the discipline and control that the likes of Acolyte Alwa possessed.

Kelewulf frowned as he tried to make sense of the conflicting emotions that swirled inside him. He had come here thinking there was nothing he could truly gain from the Hasz'een; that their majik was meaningless to him and could be found through other means. Now he was beginning to wonder if that was true, and whether he might learn more from the high priestess than he'd thought.

He watched as Elafir reached over and picked a small piece of meat from his bowl, popping it into her mouth before meeting his eyes. 'Do I think you're a fraud?' She shook her head and offered him a sad smile. 'No. No, I think you wanted to know how it felt to wield power like your father did when he was a king. I think your mother taught you that true power does not always come from the ability to wield a sword or command an army. I think that finding the phylactery that housed the undead lich of Yirgan must have been difficult and dangerous, and I *know* it must have taken no small amount of courage and self-belief to allow such a creature to share your body, particularly when you knew you risked the lich taking control of you – as it indeed tried to. I think you are a complicated person with much to learn. But mostly, I think you need to find your place in this world and decide what legacy you will be remembered for.'

She gave him a brief smile and stood up, signalling that their conversation was over. 'You have a lesson with Master Zhu tomorrow morning. He wants to test your knowledge of elementals. I understand you have some experience with summonings of that type?'

'Indeed.' He paused as he too rose from the bench, his brow creasing for an instant. 'If it's OK with you I'd like to go to my rooms to rest. I'm afraid the efforts of this morning have quite taken it out of me.'

Elafir silently cursed herself as she watched him walk away, realising her error too late. Kelewulf's experience with elementals had been revealed to her when he'd asked for her help to confine the lich and given her access to his memories. The young man and the undead spirit inside him had summoned a creature to help create a huge portal between this world and the Void. Elemental majik was difficult, and performing it, even with a lich on board, proved again the young necromancer's aptitude when it came to the Art. Of greatest concern, however, was the insight she'd gleaned about Kelewulf's obsession with the dark god Lorgukk.

She resolved to tell the young necromancer, should he ask, that word of his portal had come from an overseas source, perhaps the crew member of a merchant vessel, along with the rumour that an elemental had been used to create it.

Besides, her biggest concern regarding the young necromancer was how she could steer him away from his intention to return the dark god to this world. Lorgukk's heart. That was the real reason that Kelewulf had beaten a path to Hasz: a path of assured destruction.

Lost in her thoughts, she started when someone lightly placed a hand on her shoulder. Turning, she stared into the face of her personal servant, Hrol. Smiling, she gestured for him to sit in the place just vacated by Kelewulf.

'How was your trip?' Hrol asked. He used his hands to speak, forming words and symbols with his fingers. He and Elafir had formulated the language together, before teaching it to all of the others in Elafir's employ who'd had their tongues removed by slave traders.

'It was hardly a trip. I merely used majik to appear in person to the Strom ruler.'

'That majik is just as exhausting as any voyage would have been. And as dangerous, should somebody discover what you are doing.'

The high priestess gave a little shrug. 'It went well, thank you.'

'What did they say?'

'Our friends in Strom are rightly worried about my news. The new king, Erik, seems to be cast from the same mould as his father, and I believe we can work together to stop this war. He has agreed to keep my identity secret until we achieve what we need to on this side of the sea. But it is hard to play both sides of the same game without drawing attention to oneself.'

'Well, I hope you can continue to do so. For all our sakes. The emperor would not take kindly to discovering his high priestess was acting as a spy for his greatest enemy.'

'I prefer the term "peacekeeper".'

'Mamur would not agree.'

The high priestess looked across at her servant, taking in the brand on his neck. It had been placed there by the same man who'd taken his voice. Hrol had been ten years of age at the time. Every attendant in her household had suffered at the hands of some loathsome flesh-peddler or other. Aware of her glance, he lifted his hand to the disfigurement, tracing its edges with tips of his fingers and offering her a sad smile. Elafir returned the gesture.

'We must indeed hope that our subterfuge goes undetected, old friend,' she said. 'If we do not, and another succeeds to the imperial throne instead of me, I fear we will never stop the disgraceful practice of slavery in our realms.'

'Even if you do become our next ruler, the Hasz'een people will take much persuading on that score,' he said, his hands effortlessly forming the words. 'Not everyone is as enlightened as you. Those of us who have found ourselves in your employ can only thank the gods we were not purchased by another. You have treated us more like family than slaves.'

'I think of you as family. You know that. My greatest regret is that I do not have the resources to free more from the slavers, and provide them with a better life too.'

'You always do what you can. And I thank the gods you found me.'

'Still, it enrages me that we must keep up the pretence that you are merely vassals. But do not worry too much about the Hasz'een people, Hrol. If there is one thing that they are known for, it's their absolute obedience to their imperial leader.'

Hrol looked off in the direction Kelewulf had just left. 'The boy. What is his role in all this?'

'He is a criminal accused of murdering King Erik's father. He could come in useful as a bargaining chip later on in this affair. I might be able to offer him over to the Strom king, in return for concessions beneficial to Hasz.'

She raised an eyebrow at the series of short, sharp huffing noises that greeted this announcement. It was a sound she knew well. Hrol was laughing.

'What?' she asked.

'I suspect you might not find it so easy to hand him over.'

'Why?'

'Because you've come to like him.'

She sighed, a smile briefly touching the corners of her lips. 'Yes. Maybe you're right.'

Kelewulf stood in his chambers, his mind racing.

Elafir's mention of the elemental was the cause of this turmoil, and he racked his brain to remember if there was anything he'd said to reveal this information to her. He was convinced he had not. But then how could she have known? Perhaps she did not; she had posed the possibility not as a statement of fact, but as question. Hadn't she?

Deep inside himself, he felt the lich stir. Summoning the demons earlier had meant engaging with Yirgan's majik, and as was often the case after these episodes, the lich seemed to have a greater presence in his mind than Kelewulf would have liked. His first reaction was to crush it back down, but two words rose to the surface of his consciousness that gave him pause.

She knows …

Against his better judgement, Kelewulf relaxed his control and allowed the lich to continue.

You were careless. When you sought to imprison me again after our meeting with the emperor.

'What are you talking about?' Kelewulf said aloud to the empty room, his question greeted by a cold, grim laugh that made him shudder despite himself.

You let her inside. When she offered to help you, she also helped herself. To our memories, our accomplishments, our secrets. She's not what she seems, that one.

'You never give up, do you? You never stop trying to find a way to take over. Why should I believe anything you say?' But even as he voiced the words, Kelewulf realised there might well be some truth in what the lich had said.

How else would she have known about the elemental, hmm? Do you think she guessed? No! When the lich spoke again it was in a calmer tone. *The important question is not what she knows about our past, but what she has discovered about your future plans.* The creature paused. *You're a good boy, Kelewulf. I would not wish to see you harmed in any way. Perhaps if you allowed me some more freedom, I could help you.*

Kelewulf shut the lich down, exerting his will and pushing it back into the darkness so that he would not have to listen to it any more. At the same time, he acknowledged the siliver of sadness he felt in doing so. Having the creature back in his head, even just for a short while, had given him a small degree of comfort. In this place, where everything and everyone was foreign, even the scheming machinations of the lich were a welcome thing.

He began to pace the room, still talking out loud to himself.

'If she knows why I am really here, why has she not had me imprisoned or used her majik against me? What purpose could there be in teaching me like she did today?' He felt the lich desperately trying to make itself heard, but he held firm and denied it the chance. Instead, he walked to the door and put his ear to it, convinced now that one of her servants or acolytes might be listening in on him from the other side. The rising paranoia was impossible to shake off, and he opened the door a fraction to peek out into what proved to be an empty hallway before closing it again.

'Stop it,' he told himself, moving over to the bed and throwing his aching body down on it. 'Stop it or you'll drive yourself mad. She doesn't know why you're here. She can't. There's some other explanation as to how she knows about the elemental. And don't listen to the lich. It is not your friend, you know that.'

Forcing himself to clear his mind, Kelewulf closed his eyes, knowing that sleep would be hard, if not impossible, to come by.

Stromgard

5

Lann and Astrid stood on the docks, their travel sacks at their feet. Erik had suggested he might accompany them to the quayside and see them off, but in the end they'd said their farewells back at the royal longhouse instead, brother and sister holding on to each other in a long embrace that said more than any words could.

Stromgard harbour was as busy as Lann remembered it being the first time he'd laid eyes on it. Everywhere he looked ships were loading and unloading their cargoes, the sailors eager to get the work done so they might either go ashore and spend their money enjoying the capital's many delights or get back to sea to earn some more. The briny smell of the sea filled his head as two brilliant white seabirds screeched angrily at each other from adjacent masts.

The blade at his side murmured something at the same instant Lann became aware of somebody's eyes on him.

97

He looked up to see a familiar, if not particularly friendly, face approaching.

'Captain Fariz,' Lann said, giving the man a nod.

Ignoring his greeting, Fariz stared back at him, his lips pinched together in a thin line, as if he were afraid of what might come out if he loosened them. Lann fancied he understood the mixed emotions going through the skipper's head. The last time they had spoken was after Fleya had raised a terrible monster from the ocean depths to destroy a pirate vessel intent on taking over the man's ship, the *Ra'magulsha*. Although her actions had saved the captain and his crew, everyone else on board, including Lann, had been left terrified by the things they'd seen that fateful day. His aunt had paid Fariz a small fortune to have his ship repaired, but they had not parted on good terms.

'I remember telling you that I hoped we would never meet each other again,' Fariz said eventually.

'You did.'

'You seem to take great delight in pouring salt into my honey. Imagine my surprise, my delight, when I was approached by a member of the king's own retinue to charter the *Ra'magulsha* to the Sölten Isles under the white flag of parley, offering to pay handsomely for the danger such a trip entails. Then imagine my horror when they said one of the passengers was a young man who carried a black-bladed sword, and that he was on an urgent mission. I knew it could not be a coincidence that they had come to me.' The captain stared at Lann, daring him to contradict him. 'I would have refused, but the king made it quite clear that was not an option – not if I wished to return to this port in the future.'

'Indeed, it was not a coincidence,' Lann said, unabashed. 'King Erik's men came with a list of the ships and captains in the harbour. As soon as I saw your name, I told the king you had to be the one.'

'Why?'

'I know you and—'

'You don't think my crew have suffered enough, is that it?'

'No, I—'

'Many of them refused to go back to sea after what happened the last time.'

'But some did not. And I would wager that they stayed on because they know you are a captain to whom they can entrust their lives. I saw how you handled the *Ra'magulsha* when the pirates attacked us. If it hadn't been for you, we would not have survived.'

'It wasn't me who sank that ship and killed every pirate on board. That … thing did, with your aunt somehow controlling its mind.' He closed his eyes and let out a sigh. 'My crew are not alone in their nightmares about that day. She should never have awakened such a terrifying creature.'

With this he looked about him, scanning the milling crowds on the docks. 'Where is she? Where is the witch?'

'She's dead,' Lann replied, his heart twisting.

Fariz must have seen the pain on Lann's face, and his own softened in response. 'How?'

'She too was killed by a monster. I couldn't save her.' He placed a hand on the Dreadblade's pommel as the sword let out a long lament inside his head.

The sword's reaction interested him. When he'd first been tasked with bearing the weapon, it cared nothing for the people Lann was close to; its only concern was removing monsters from this realm. Lately, however … it seemed to Lann that he and the blade were melding into something more unified, as if the thoughts and needs of both parties were becoming one. No sooner had this thought occurred to him than he remembered how the sword had endangered Astrid back when they'd faced the jurdlek, and he pushed the idea away as quickly as it had formed. Forcing himself to concentrate on the matter in hand, he addressed the skipper again, steering the conversation back to less upsetting matters. 'We need swift passage to the Sölten Isles. You're not just a great sailor, Captain Fariz, you're a good man. It's the main reason I asked the king to insist you take me. A message has already been sent by bird to King Brundorl. The pirate code will not allow your ship to be attacked while sailing under the banner of peace.'

'Lann is right, Captain Fariz,' Astrid said, speaking for the first time from beneath her hood.

'And you are?' Fariz asked. 'Let me guess, another witch.'

Astrid threw back her cloak and extended her hand. 'I'm the king's sister, Princess Astrid Rivengeld. It is a pleasure to meet you.'

Fariz opened his mouth as if to say something, then closed it again, looking from one of the young people to the other as if trying to ascertain if she was telling the truth or not. Eventually, with a tiny shake of his head and muttering in a foreign tongue, Fariz reached down and picked up Astrid's travel sack. 'Then we had better hurry. We are due to leave Stromgard in just over two hours and there is still much to do on board.' He flashed a humourless smile at Lann. 'If I remember rightly, you spent the start of our last trip hanging over the side, sick to your gills. I have something you can take to stop that happening this time.'

Gematik's Citadel, East Hasz

6

It was late evening when Kelewulf knocked at Master Larghal's door, having arrived there at the time specified by the academic. After a day full of lessons, his brain felt fit to burst with everything he'd been taught.

Hearing the academic bid him enter, he pushed the door open.

Larghal was perhaps the oldest living person Kelewulf had ever seen. So much so that he managed to make even Emperor Mamur look youthful by comparison. He was sitting behind a huge desk piled high with books and scrolls and scribbled notes of all kinds, peering down at whatever he was working on with piercing eyes that were set deep into a wrinkled and wizened face. Larghal wore robes of the same purple hue as Elafir's, but either the old scholar's had been fashioned for a man twice his size, or Larghal himself had shrunk to such a degree since they'd been made that great folds of spare fabric were now bunched up around him. But Kelewulf knew from asking around the citadel's scholars that what Larghal lacked in youth, he made up for with his almost limitless knowledge of the Art.

The books in the master's quarters were not confined to the desk. All about the room were floor-to-ceiling shelves that held hundreds and hundreds of volumes, most of which looked even older than the academic. The books that could not be housed on shelves were piled up in stacks so higgledy-piggledy that Kelewulf doubted anyone could know what was where. In addition, there was a separate area high up and out of the way where Larghal kept the tomes that were out-of-bounds to students. These were secured by chains and, no doubt, majik – in case anyone was stupid enough to risk fooling around with them without the necessary permissions.

The academic was so focused on the notes he was making that he had not looked up once since Kelewulf had entered the room. Eventually, not knowing what else to do, the young man cleared his throat. 'I, er, I made an appointment to drop by?'

'Indeed. And what can I do for you?' Larghal asked, still not looking up. The man's voice reminded Kelewulf of somebody pulling their fingernails across old and weathered leather.

'I was wondering if you had any works on Trogir and his battle with Lorgukk?'

The academic paused, then finally put down his quill. He raised his eyes in his visitor's direction. 'You too? It would seem that is a popular subject all of a sudden. I suppose it is inevitable, what with all these rumours coming from our spies in the Six Kingdoms.'

'Rumours?'

'That the Dreadblade is back. That the sword has found another champion to wield it in its battle with the creatures from the Void. Preposterous, of course. The sword is gone. Destroyed, like the god who once wielded it.' Larghal shook his head and waved his hand in the air, as if swatting the idea away. 'Vorneland.'

'I, er, beg your pardon?' Kelewulf said, frowning as he struggled to keep up with Larghal's sudden changes of topic.

'The latest supposed sighting was in Vorneland, but the reports are misleading. Some say the blade is wielded by a furious god with fireballs where its eyes should be, others that a snow-giant from the icy north has the weapon, whilst yet others claim that a mere boy carries the blade. A boy! Ha. Preposterous! As if a human lad could wield the Bane of Lorgukk! That, by the way, *The Bane of Lorgukk*, is an excellent book. I have it here somewhere …' The old man continued prattling on, but Kelewulf wasn't listening any more.

Larghal's revelation had struck the young necromancer like a physical blow. Because it occurred to him now that he might have actually *seen* the legendary weapon. And recently. While he too had been in Vorneland! He thought back to that fateful day when he'd opened the portal at Vissergott, remembering the boy he'd watched charge down a hill into the horde of hellish creatures that had managed to get through from the Void. Yirgan's lich had told him a young man would be coming and that he was carrying a dread blade, but for some reason Kelewulf hadn't for a moment thought it was *the* Dreadblade.

He remembered too how the sword the stranger was brandishing had triggered an unnatural feeling of disquiet in him: a cold, creeping unease that wormed its way into his psyche and solidified into fear when a voice had started up inside his head. Though he did not understand the words the voice used, he was sure it was screaming in anger at him for allowing those creatures into this world from another.

The terror had been so great he had fled that place, leaving the young man and his sword to their fate.

Was it the Dreadblade? Had the boy been successful in facing down the hellish horde? If so, perhaps the Six Kingdoms might not be in the dire state of chaos Kelewulf was counting on ...

'The sword. Is it black?' he asked, already knowing what the answer would be.

'From tip to pommel. Fashioned by the creator Og himself from a substance now lost to the world.' The academic gave a sniff and returned to his notes, screwing up his face and taking up a large magnifying glass. 'Behind that ladder to your left, third shelf up.'

'Pardon?'

'There are a number of texts on Trogir and Lorgukk there.'

As much as the academic's news had rocked him, Kelewulf forced himself to return to his original purpose for coming here. He moved towards the titles Larghal had indicated, while addressing him over his shoulder. 'I was more interested in the aftermath of their battle. When Lorgukk was banished through the Nemesis Arch?'

'Uh-huh?' Larghal's attention was on his work now and he paid the young man little mind.

'It's a fascinating part of the old gods' story, don't you think?'

'Hmm, for some maybe. I, however, have never been a great fan of ancient legends and folklore. There are more than enough mysteries in this world without getting fixated on old wives' tales.'

'I'm particularly curious about what might have happened to the dark god's heart.' The sound of Larghal's scribblings stopped. 'The legends say Lorgukk tore it free from his own body, throwing it back into the human realm before he was bundled through the arch. So that he could one day return. Don't some say it was found by the people of the West? The people who later became the Hasz'een?'

'Some say that, yes.'

A long silence stretched out between the two of them.

'What do you think, Master Larghal?'

'I think the heart, like the Dreadblade, is as you say: the stuff of legends. If it were in Hasz, it would have been discovered by now, and to my knowledge it has not.'

'I wonder if—'

'Some things are better left alone.' There was a coldness to Larghal's voice suddenly. 'Now, that might seem strange, coming from one who has dedicated himself to knowing all he can about the Art and its many inscrutabilities, but mark me, boy, if the heart was meant to have been found, it would have turned up by now. The lich that inhabits your body was once the soul of a man who dedicated his life to the Dark Art. Yirgan sought the heart, he searched for it in Hasz after he became obsessed with the idea it was here, right under his nose, but it remained hidden even from him.' The master sniffed, and gestured towards Kelewulf. 'Take the texts on Trogir and Lorgukk. Read them well, and see the danger the dark god posed to the world before he was banished.'

Kelewulf did as he was bid and took the books. On his way out he paused in the doorway. 'Maybe Lorgukk was not the embodiment of evil he has been made out to be. Perhaps it is mankind, with its wars and its slavery and its cruelty, that needs to be expelled from this world. My father was lauded by many as a good king, but I saw the callousness he truly represented. He treated me like I was nothing. And because of him my mother killed herself. The old gods forced Lorgukk and his armies into the Void and allowed mankind to prosper and grow. But who is to say that the bigger evil was not allowed to remain?'

Kelewulf didn't wait to hear if the academic responded to this outburst. Clutching the books to his chest, he was already striding back to his room.

The door through which Kelewulf left had no sooner shut than another, at the back of the room, opened, and Elafir entered.

'Well?' she said.

'He is determined to find the heart. And he believes it is here in Hasz.'

'Then he will be disappointed.' She pursed her lips, small lines creasing her forehead as she studied Larghal for any hidden reaction. 'Or am I wrong? Do you know more?'

'If I did, would I tell you?'

The pair locked eyes, then Master Larghal broke into a wheezy chuckle that quickly turned into a nasty-sounding coughing fit.

'No, you would not. And if I am completely honest, neither would I want you to.'

The academic gestured to the door through which Kelewulf had left. 'He is beyond help, Elafir. His hatred for his father consumes him, and he has allowed it to grow so large he wants to punish the world. Teaching him more about the Dark Art can only be a bad thing.'

'But he already knows a great deal of majik thanks to Yirgan. Perhaps the best we can hope to do is to show him that it doesn't have to be used for evil. I think I can break through that shell of hate.'

There was a loud rap at the door and the pair turned to see Alwa standing in the opening, with two of Elafir's household guards behind her. One look at the young acolyte's face was enough to tell the high priestess that something was seriously wrong.

'It's the emperor,' Alwa said. 'He has been poisoned.'

Stromgard

7

E rik sat nervously on the ancient River Throne and
fiddled with the large jewelled ring on his left hand.
Having demanded he be left completely alone, posting his
men outside the doors to the Great Longhouse, he was
now struck by the eerie quiet of the place. He was so rarely
by himself these days, and he took the opportunity to
reflect on many of the things that had happened to him
since he'd ascended to power. Inevitably, his mind turned
to his father. Mirvar Rivengeld had never given the impression that the demands of the crown were burdensome.
Instead, he had made everyone around him, from his most
trusted advisor to the humblest farmer, feel that they had
his full attention. And he was as wise as he had been kind.
Memories of this sort were double-edged for Erik; the
powerful feelings of love he had for his father were always
sullied by the loss he felt at his demise and the knowledge

that his death had come at Erik's own hands. It made little difference to Erik that he had not been in control of his own mind at the time – that he'd been used as a puppet by his cousin Kelewulf and the evil lich inside him.

And now here he was, about to meet with the woman sheltering the real killer.

He forced himself to push these thoughts away, resolving, as he always did in moments like this, to make amends for that terrible deed by becoming the ruler his father would have wanted him to be.

The fire pit in the centre of the room spat loudly and Erik looked up as a spark leaped clear, the fiery ember glowing brightly in the air for a moment before falling to the ground. In its place, standing in the exact spot the ember had landed a split-second before, was Elafir.

The high priestess was wearing her usual deep purple robes and her glossy black hair was held back with a silver ring. He was once again struck by her handsome looks and the feelings she stirred up inside him. His heart beat a little faster. When she acknowledged him he stood up, staring at her as if she were really there and not the majikal projection he knew her to be.

'King Erik,' she said, a faint smile touching the edges of her lips.

'I did not anticipate seeing you again so soon.'

'Indeed.'

There was something about Elafir's demeanour that put Erik on his guard. 'What brings you here?'

The priestess seemed to scan his face closely, as if she were trying to glean something from his features. 'Somebody has attempted to kill Emperor Mamur.'

The revelation sank Erik back down into his throne, his mind racing as the reason for the high priestess's visit struck him. 'You can't think it's me?'

'It would make sense. For you, at least. It would, in the short term, avoid war.'

Erik took a moment to quash the annoyance her accusation had stoked up in him. When he spoke, it was in a calm and considered tone. 'I gave you my word. My father trusted you, and I put the same faith in you when you asked it of me. Our nations have been estranged from each other for a very long time, and as a result mistrusts and animosities have been allowed to ferment. That is in neither nation's interest. Knowing all this, why would I say one thing to you and then do another?'

'You're a king.'

'And what is that supposed to mean?'

'Rulers have a habit of doing precisely that. Their word is not always what it should be.'

'That might be the case in Hasz, High Priestess, but in the Six Kingdoms a person's word is an inviolable thing, be they a monarch or a pauper. I said I would not act against the emperor and I have not.'

Elafir stood perfectly still, stony faced. Then, just as suddenly as she had appeared in the spark from the fire, her demeanour changed. She let out a sigh and offered Erik a sad smile that he took to be an apology.

'In truth, I did not think it was you. But I needed to hear it from your own lips and look you in the eye as I did. I came here to keep you abreast of the situation. To let you know how things stand in Hasz.'

'I take it the assassination was unsuccessful,' he said, sitting back in his throne a little easier now. 'You used the word "attempted".'

'It was. The emperor lives, but only just. My people are helping to try and restore his health, but the poisoning has taken its toll on someone of Mamur's age.'

Erik twisted the ring on his finger again. 'Last we spoke, you told me how you thought you'd convinced enough people of influence to support your bid to take over from the emperor should he die. How does this change things?'

'It has created a toxic environment in the imperial palace. Many people among the household staff have been beheaded for their incompetence in letting an assassin infiltrate the palace. The executions continue as I speak.' She looked off to her right, as if her real self could hear these terrible events taking place. 'Those closest to the emperor

113

are looking with suspicion at everyone who has shown any interest in taking over the throne of Hasz. The people I thought I could rely on to back me are understandably nervous, and some are talking of changing their allegiance.'

'They suspect you?'

'They suspect everyone.'

'Could my cousin Kelewulf have been responsible?'

Elafir nodded thoughtfully. 'I considered that. Mamur almost killed him when they met, and I know that Yirgan's lich had Kelewulf use poison to kill your own father. But no, he is in my citadel, not the imperial palace. He has not had an opportunity to get close enough to Mamur to do such a thing.'

'He could have—'

Elafir interrupted him. 'Trust me, Your Grace, Kelewulf can do nothing in Hasz without my knowing about it.'

Another silence stretched out.

'Why bother trying to save him? The emperor,' Erik asked. 'Why?'

'Yes. Surely his death would open the door for you.'

Elafir sighed. 'As I said, I am still short of the supporting votes to guarantee my bid, and Grad'ur of Rishtok is still favourite to take over. And yes, before you ask, it has occurred to me that Grad'ur may be responsible for the attempt on His Imperial Majesty's life.' She frowned. 'But I still think I can manipulate this situation to my advantage and achieve my goal. I just needed to be certain that you had nothing to do with the murder plot. If that were the case, and anyone in Hasz found out, I could never hope to thwart the war efforts currently under way.'

Erik nodded, feeling a pang of guilt about how he was deliberately refraining from telling her about Astrid and Lann's mission to the Sölten Isles. He hoped that peace with Hasz could still be achieved, but he needed the insurance of knowing the Six Kingdoms could call on Brundorl and his pirate fleet if the high priestess failed in her attempt to gain power. The decision did not sit easily with him, however. In the course of their talks together he had become fond of the Hasz'een woman. He had even thought of offering her his hand in marriage if she was successful in succeeding Mamur. Doing so would certainly ensure a lasting peace between Hasz and the Six Kingdoms.

'Are you quite well, King Erik?'

Her question brought him out of his reverie. He smiled back at her and nodded his head. 'Fine. You, however, look tired.'

The high priestess raised an eyebrow, a look of mock indignation on her face. 'Some women might take that as an insult, Your Grace.' She laughed softly as he went to apologise, halting his words with a gesture of her hand. 'But your observation is a fair one. Keeping up this projection of myself is in itself exhausting, so I will take my leave of you.'

No sooner had Erik nodded his head than the image of Elafir winked out of existence. He was left staring at an empty space once again, wondering over the wisdom of the path he had set out upon. His gambit in the Sölten Isles could backfire terribly if Elafir found out about it. But not having Brundorl's navy would mean he had little chance of stopping the Hasz'een forces should Mamur recover and go ahead with his plans to attack.

As the concerns about his decisions crowded in on him, he recalled a conversation he'd had with his father when Mirvar was on the River Throne. The then Prince Erik had asked him what the hardest thing was about being king. His father's words had stayed with him: 'As a ruler, I am forced to do many terrible things in order to keep our people safe. The hardest thing I have to rule is my conscience. Of all my many subjects it is the most vexing, and the most difficult to appease.' Mirvar had ruffled his son's hair and smiled. 'It is also a king's greatest asset. Never ignore it, Erik. Sometimes your conscience is the only light you have to guide you through the darkness that is doubt.'

Remembering his father's words, Erik rose from the throne, reassured that he was doing the right thing in sending Lann and his sister on their mission. He only hoped Brundorl would accept his offer and help protect the Six Kingdoms if Hasz attacked.

The Sölten Isles, Ilfinstur

8

Despite taking Captain Fariz's concoction to stop seasickness, Lann's second journey on a ship had been as miserable as his first, and he spent the entire trip looking decidedly green-faced whilst hanging over the edge of a gunwale.

When the lookout high up in his basket on the mainmast cried, 'Land yonder!' and pointed ahead, Lann was able to forget his roiling stomach for long enough to raise his head. While he was struggling to make out more on the horizon than an indistinct smudge, the shout had spurred the crew of the *Ra'magulsha* into action. The captain's first order was for two flags to be hoisted: one the Rivengeld banner, the other a huge plain-white pennant that was the recognised symbol of parley. No ship, be it a pirate vessel or otherwise, would attack another that sailed under the white flag until the two captains had had a chance to talk.

The Sölten Isles were comprised of two main land masses known simply as the Nord and Sud Isles, and it was not long before the smudge had transformed into these towering twin stacks of rock. Looking out at them, Lann wondered how anyone could have made their home on the unforgiving and bleak islands, whose cliffs rose dramatically from the sea as if thrust violently out of the water in a fit of anger by the gods themselves. They did have one thing going for them, however: an abundance of natural harbours that allowed protection for the vessels that hid there from the authorities who sought them out on the high seas.

It was to the larger and more populated of the two – the Nord Isle – that the *Ra'magulsha* headed, and before long the ship was sailing between towering cliffs that rose up steeply on either side, the grey rock stained white in numerous places thanks to the seabirds that had also made this place their home. The first thing that struck Lann was the sound. After being in the vast open sea, where the wind snatched away all but the loudest of noises, the claustrophobic passage seemed to echo their very breaths back at them in a way that was strangely unsettling.

'This passage leads to Ilfinstur, the largest bay,' the first mate explained to Lann and Astrid. 'At the back of the bay, in the cliff walls, are a series of interconnected caves that are like a labyrinth. They're easy to defend, even for a community as small as the one that lives there. That's where Brundorl's court is.'

'How do you know all this?'

The man hesitated, as if considering whether to reveal more. 'I used to live here. I was a marauder for seven years.' He nodded and gave a short humourless snort. 'Best days of my life.'

'Does Captain Fariz know you were a … marauder?' Astrid asked.

'Most of the *Ra'm*'s crew were, at some point or another. Think what you like about the pirates of world, but you won't find better sailors.' The look Astrid gave him elicited a largely toothless grin before he turned his attention to the opening at the end of the passageway, which had just come into sight ahead. 'We're nearly there,' he said. 'We'll drop anchor and they'll send out a boat to take you to shore.'

'And the *Ra'magulsha*?'

He gave them a long sideways look. 'Fariz's orders were to bring you here, but he'll not anchor in the Sölten Isles. Even sailing under the white flag of parley, this is no place to bring the *Ra'm*. She'll be seen as a prize sailing vessel, and good ships are always at risk of being seized by Brundorl and his kind. My understanding is that we will get you ashore and then sail just beyond the Isles, awaiting a signal to come and fetch you and take you on to Hasz.'

'You know him? Brundorl?'

'I do. But he wasn't the "Pirate King" back then – he was just another brigand like me.'

'What kind of man is he?' Lann asked.

The first mate sucked at his teeth. 'He's cold. Cold and dangerous.'

'Can he be trusted?' Astrid asked, thinking of how her brother was putting his faith in the man to help him stop a war.

'If he gives you his word, yes. He might be a ruthless cut-throat, but he's a cut-throat with an honour code.'

Later, Lann sat in the longboat sent out from the harbour to transfer them to shore from the *Ra'magulsha*, lost in his thoughts. Astrid, next to him, hardly said a word either, and he wondered if she too was mulling over the position in which they found themselves. The first mate had been correct: the captain of the *Ra'm* would not drop anchor in the pirate port. Despite Fariz's assurance that he and his crew would be waiting not very far away for the signal to come and get them, Lann couldn't shake the nervous feeling that hearing the sailors' shouts to haul anchors stirred up in him. It wasn't just the departure of their ship that was bothering him, however. This mission, one that could decide the fate of a nation if Erik's worst fears were true, was not the kind of thing he'd ever imagined himself capable of. A farm boy, even one who had experienced the things he had of late, should not be acting as an emissary for a kingdom like Strom.

By the time they pulled up to the jetty, the *Ra'm* was already under way. Fariz had not even spared them a backward glance. Lann reached across and placed his hand on the scabbard at his side when the blade let out an anguished groan that perfectly reflected his own feelings.

'I know, I know,' he muttered under his breath.

'Hmm?' Astrid said.

'Nothing. I'm just glad we're going to be back on firm ground again.'

The caves where the brigands had made their stronghold were surprisingly warm and well lit, with passages connecting the larger spaces into a maze-like complex. Although it was past midnight, it appeared Brundorl was insistent upon seeing the visiting emissaries from Strom as soon as they were ashore, and the pair were escorted by the brigands who'd manned the rowboat, their guards walking along beside them in silence. It was in this way that Lann and Astrid were brought before the king.

Brundorl's throne was a huge piece of driftwood that had been carved in the likeness of an octopus: four of its appendages snaked downwards to create the throne's legs, two more made up the armrests, and the last two rose up at the back to curl forward again over the occupier's head. Brundorl himself was a figure of contrasts: his cracked, weather-distressed leather armour spoke of decades at sea as a marauder, while the polished silver band of interlocking crab claws he wore around his head appeared to be pristine and newly fashioned. Sporting a fine black-and-grey beard that curled into his lap, he glowered down at the two young people brought before him. Even by the standards of the Volken people, the pirate king was a huge man.

Lann and Astrid bent their heads in Brundorl's direction. The gesture was not returned. Indeed, their presence here seemed positively unwelcome.

'Imagine my surprise when I received a messenger bird from the new King of Strom to say he was sending his own sister here to make me an offer I'd be unable to pass up. And not only a princess. A jarl too – one who carries a mysterious and powerful weapon.' Brundorl's voice did not match that of a man who was happy to parley. It was laced with menace. But it was the manic look in the pirate king's eye that caused Lann the most unease. The man seemed positively unhinged.

Astrid took a step forward. 'I am Astrid Rivengeld. This is—' She stopped when Brundorl held up his hand. Somewhere outside, the low mournful note of a horn being blown could be heard. The sound seemed to visibly shake the man on the throne, and he stared over his visitors' heads at the entrance they'd come in through.

Lann and Astrid exchanged a glance. 'This … this is Lannigon Gudbrandr … Jarl Gudbrandr. We are here to—'

'You come at a bad time. I am in no mood to barter for favours with anyone right now. You should leave these isles and return from whence you came.'

Lann and Astrid turned as a small group entered. All of them looked exhausted, and were covered in mud and sand, as if they'd been out hunting or foraging. One of the men stepped past Astrid and Lann without waiting to be called forward, and approached the throne, whispering something in the marauder king's ear and shaking his head nervously when asked a question in an equally quiet tone. Whatever had been said seemed to increase Brundorl's agitated state, his expression becoming a mixture of desperation and anger as he gripped the arms of his great chair.

Brundorl cast his eye over the newly arrived men. 'Go back and try again,' he said. The group hurriedly left.

Astrid looked at Lann once more: her confusion perfectly matched his own. Brundorl wasn't even pretending to pay them any attention now. The ruler was staring down at his hands, the muscles at the sides of his jaw bunching and unbunching. Astrid took a breath and continued. 'We have been sent here to impress upon you the benefits of listening to our king's proposal. We offer not only gold, but a chance for you to have your islands recognised by Strom as a part of—'

'MY SON IS MISSING!' the man bellowed, standing up out of his seat as if he'd been forced out of it by the wooden creature itself. He glared down at them, his hands balling into fists. 'You are here to talk about money and concessions and matters of state. But my son has been taken from me! Do you think I care a damn about your parley? About your gold? Do you? My little Sebastien has disappeared! *That* is all I care about right now!' The man hammered his hands into his thighs. 'One of my enemies has taken him – snatched my little boy from under my nose. And by the gods, when I find them, when I discover the people responsible for this deed, I will kill them so slowly, using every foul and hideous method imaginable, that they will beg me for their death!'

The Dreadblade at Lann's side had come alive at the pirate king's outburst, but it was not a reaction to any anticipated threat. Instead, it seemed to Lann that it was the news of Brundorl's son's disappearance that had awakened the sword and set it to whispering in its strange tongue inside his head. Most of the words were unrecognisable to him, but one stood out; one he'd heard as a young boy listening to stories of terrible creatures he'd always thought were merely things of the imagination.

Draugr.

'How old is your son?' Astrid asked.

'Ten years of age. But he—'

'Where was Sebastien last seen?' Lann asked, keeping his voice as steady as possible, despite the increasingly loud droning of the sword's words in his brain. The dark blade was sure the boy's disappearance was linked to a monster, repeating the same words over and over.

Nir-akuu. Draugr. Es ek trundr et Murrke! Nir-akuu. Draugr ...

As fearful as Lann was for the boy's safety, there was a small part of him that felt thankful that his presence here might not be the utter waste of time he'd thought it would be. Perhaps now he could do some good. He might not be a statesman, able to broker peace deals with brigand rulers for the promise of recognition and rewards ... but monsters and demons? Thanks to the blade he knew about *them*. Knew about them and knew how to deal with them. He took a step forward, fixing the king with his stare. 'Please, King Brundorl, it is important.'

'Why should I tell you? Strangers. What do my affairs have to do with you?'

As if she too were able to hear the blade's words, Astrid glanced at the scabbard hanging at her friend's side before answering. 'We might be able to help.'

The pirate glared back at Lann and Astrid, his expression a mixture of anger and desperation, before suddenly slumping back into this throne. They watched as tears filled his eyes. He did nothing to staunch them, letting them fall down his cheeks and into his beard.

'He was last seen in the gardens next to his living quarters, at the top of the cliffs above these caves. He was out there alone that night, having asked his maidservant to leave him be for a short time. At this time of year, a particular flower Sebastien loves smells its sweetest.' He glanced up at them through red-rimmed eyes. 'I've had great sections of the gardens planted with night-scented plants, just for him.'

'He was in the garden at night?'

King Brundorl narrowed his eyes at Lann, as if he were weighing the young man's words for some hidden inference. 'It is always night for Sebastien.'

The realisation struck Lann like a slap, and with it came a flood of emotion. 'He's blind,' he whispered, remembering the time he himself had been sightless: how he'd had to learn to use his other senses to make sense of the world, and how, even when he'd come to terms with a permanent darkness, he had still been filled with fear or panic when he was taken out of his realm of familiarity. Sebastien would be experiencing those same feelings now, the terror of his abduction made exponentially worse by not being able to see where he had been taken or by whom.

'You didn't know?' Brundorl said.

'No.'

126

'My son has been blind from birth.' The king's own voice was little more than a whisper.

'Where is Sebastien's mother?' Astrid asked.

'Dead. My son is all I have left.' He wiped a hand across his face, drying the tears.

'I'd like to see this garden. To see the place Sebastien was taken from,' Lann said. 'If it pleases Your Grace.' Sensing the man's reluctance, he looked him unflinchingly in the eyes and added, 'What do you have to lose?'

Brundorl's fear for his son's safety was etched into every line of his face as he stared back at him. Whatever he saw in Lann's face seemed to make up his mind. Rising from his throne, he came down the steps, two of his marauders emerging from the dark shadows behind the throne as he did.

'Come with me,' he said to his visitors.

Brundorl led them out of the cave complex and to a series of roped walkways and ladders that wound their way up the cliffs, eventually coming out on to an area right at the top. They were in front of a small, squat house. 'My son has always refused to live in the caves,' he explained. 'He says that it is bad enough living in his own darkness without knowing he is surrounded by it too. He loves nothing more than feeling the wind in his hair and the sun on his face, so I had this place built for him.' He gave a sad shake of his head. 'You would not believe how difficult it is to create and maintain a garden here on these isles. Nothing wants to grow here. I had experts brought in from all over to make it happen.' He gestured to a walled area adjacent to the house and led them to it.

Bathed in the afternoon sunshine, the gardens were indeed beautiful. The smell alone made Lann's head spin – sweet and fresh notes from a host of plants combined with the musty, earthy soil to make an intoxicating perfume. The whole space had been designed to suit Sebastien: the walkways were lined with waist-high ropes and filled with soft chips of bark in case Sebastien should trip and fall. A fountain burbled and rippled somewhere, its sound reminding Lann of the stream that ran close by the house where he'd lived with Fleya throughout his own blindness. He'd loved the noise of that stream during his time in the darkness, not only for its calming music, but also because it gave him a constant point of reference for his surroundings whenever he became disorientated.

No sooner did he set foot in this garden paradise than the Dreadblade started up a harsh cry in his head that was impossible to ignore, try as he might. He addressed the king. 'Sebastien was taken from this garden. The creature that came here knew him and forcefully removed him.'

'Creature? What creature?! What are you talking about?' The king's voice cracked when he asked this last. He grabbed a handful of Lann's cloak and pulled him close.

'This is no time for fantastical nonsense. I demand to know what you mean.'

Draugr, the blade whispered, stretching the word out so that it resonated eerily with the breeze stirring the leaves around them.

'I know why I am here now,' Lann said, his voice low as he disentangled himself from Brundorl's grasp. 'Why Astrid and I had to stop here on our way to Hasz.' He paused, doing his best to think above the dark blade's noise and to find the words that would not alarm the king too much. 'Forgive me for asking this, but how do marauders ... how do you ...' He paused again. There was no way to pose his question delicately. 'How do you dispose of your dead?' Lann was hardly able to meet the king's eyes. 'I'm sorry to ask, but it's important.'

One of the guards answered for his ruler. 'If we are at sea, we return them to the water, to the god Morinar.'

'And those not at sea? Those that might be here on the Sölten Isles?'

Brundorl looked away, his face set in a grim mask. The implication of Lann's question was not lost on the marauder king, but he remained silent.

The guard continued: 'Some of us whose homelands have a tradition of burial are laid to rest over there.' He gestured in the direction the king was staring. 'We use stone to line a boat-shaped excavation in the ground and place the dead into it, along with the items they wanted to take through to the next world with them. A wooden structure goes over everything, which in turn is finally covered with earth and turfs.'

'A burial barrow? Like the Neshian people have?' Astrid asked. In Strom the dead were cremated, but Lann knew she had seen similar tombs in Nesh when she was a young girl and that they had fascinated her.

'Yes.'

'These barrows,' Lann said, looking off in the direction the man had indicated. 'Are they far from here?'

Brundorl spoke now, his voice small and flat. 'Where the land falls away into the sea about half a mile away, another isle rises up close by. A rope-and-wood bridge connects this isle to that other. It is there that the dead are interred.'

Draaaauuugggrrrrr …

'You think my Sebastien has been killed and taken there?'

Astrid, who had been watching Lann closely throughout, waited as he closed his eyes and tilted his head a little to one side. It was a gesture she had seen many times during their time together over the last months: the Dreadblade was doing its best to make itself understood to the young man who wielded it. When he opened his eyes again, he gave her a tiny nod of his head.

130

'I do not think your son is dead. Not yet,' Lann answered the king. 'Astrid and I will go to this burial site now.'

'Not alone you won't. I'll have a group of my men accompany you.'

Lann shook his head. 'If you wish to send your own men, I cannot stop you. These are your islands and you are king. But the more men you send, the more likely that the creature who has Sebastien will do something foolish that endangers him further. Not only that, but I ask you this: are you willing to risk none of them returning, dead at the hands of a monster they have no hope of killing?'

'If that is the case, what hope is there for you? What *are* you?' Brundorl asked, narrowing his eyes at Lann. 'A witch of some kind? Tell me.'

Lann reached across his waist and drew the Dreadblade from its scabbard. As he did so the two guards cried out in alarm and sprang forward, raising their own weapons.

Astrid's sword too was in her hand, but neither she nor Lann made any move forward. If Brundorl's men were unsettled by the humourless smile that crept over the shield maiden's features as they brandished their weapons in her direction, they hid it well.

Knowing his friend was more than a match for the two marauders, Lann looked unwaveringly back at the king. 'This is the Dreadblade. It was fashioned by the first god Og and given to me by Rakur. I alone can wield it. The dark blade spells death for any creature not of this world. If I cannot defeat the monster who has taken your son from you, nobody can.' He paused, taking in the man's distress. 'I believe I was sent here by the gods to help your boy.'

The king let out a small sigh before gesturing for his men to sheathe their weapons. 'This ... creature ... that has my Sebastien ... what is it? And how can you know?'

Lann considered his response, not sure how best to explain his relationship with the sword, let alone how it communicated with him. 'Your son was taken by an undead thing – a draugr. I know this because the Dreadblade told me. I understand how hard that is for you to believe – I have struggled to come to terms with these things myself. But this dark weapon was put on this world to rid it of such creatures, and I have to trust it is correct. King Brundorl, let us get your son back.'

The king turned to look at the night garden as he collected his thoughts. When he turned back to Lann it was clear he'd come to a conclusion. 'You have my permission to go to the barrows to see if this monster has taken my son there. But Haldirk and Lorgen here –' he gestured at the two guards – 'will accompany you. They are my most trusted men and they know Sebastien. If he is where you think he is, and you find him, it will be good for him to hear a voice that he recognises.'

Despite his misgivings about having the men along, Lann could not argue with the ruler's logic.

Brundorl reached out and hooked Astrid's elbow in his hand. 'If you and your friend manage to return my boy to me unharmed, I will help your brother Erik do whatever it is he sent you to parley for.'

Astrid looked into the stricken father's face and smiled back at him. 'As Lann said, we are here because we were meant to be, and we were meant to be here because a creature that has no place in this realm has taken your son.' She gently removed Brundorl's hand from her arm. 'There will be time to talk about those other matters, later, after we have returned Sebastien to you.'

Lann nodded at the pirate king before turning to the two men who would accompany them. 'We leave immediately. As much as I would love to wait for tomorrow and not face this thing after the sun sets, I fear for the boy's safety. Let's go.'

Hasz

9

Since the assassination attempt on the emperor, the atmosphere in Elafir's citadel had become very different. The sharp looks Kelewulf received as he walked along the corridors and passageways reinforced his suspicion that people had begun talking about him behind his back. It was understandable. He was a guest in a nation that harboured deep, long-seated suspicions of his homeland, and the timing of his turning up on these shores just as there was an attempt to murder its beloved ruler was bound to reinforce people's mistrust of him.

So it had come as no surprise to Kelewulf when the royal guards knocked on the door of his room that morning, just giving him time to dress before they hauled him off to be interrogated by a thin, dangerous-looking man who'd questioned him over and over about his whereabouts on the day Mamur had been poisoned. His airtight alibi – that

134

he was in lessons with various teachers inside the citadel – seemed to matter little. Things had started to take a nasty turn, with his interrogator taking pleasure in describing the Hasz'een torture methods used to extract the truth from criminals who were reluctant to speak, when Elafir came barging into the small room. Wearing a furious expression, she pointed out that her young charge had answered all of the inquisitor's questions in full and demanded he be released. The man's fear was palpable. Apologising profusely, he turned his prisoner over to the high priestess without argument.

The freedom Elafir had won Kelewulf was short lived, however. No sooner had he returned to his rooms in the citadel than there was another loud knock on his door. He opened it to find more guards, this time with a demand that he accompany them to the imperial palace.

But despite the new dangers of this foreign land, Kelewulf was finding he quite liked it here. The climate was so different to his homeland on the other side of the sea that he still found himself donning numerous layers of clothing before going out, only to quickly shed them again.

The biggest surprise, however, were the people. Despite the suspicions some clearly held about him, he still struggled to recognise the Hasz'een from the tales he'd been told about them when he was growing up. It was true that the older generation, with their adherence to the practice of slavery and the dreadful treatment of their serfs, reinforced his beliefs about the terrible things humans were capable of. But in contrast to these diehards were others, like Elafir. She treated the people in her household more like family, even though they'd been sold to her as slaves. They were well fed and cared for, and even given time to pursue interests of their own. And it wasn't just her slaves … She had accepted him. Accepted him in a way that nobody had since … since his mother.

His mind was a jumble of thoughts and emotions, and he was struggling to keep his focus on the *real* reason he was in Hasz. His earlier investigations and searches for clues as to the whereabouts of the heart had been extensive, and he'd been happy to dig ever deeper in an effort to find it. Now, however, enjoying his studies under the high priestess's tutelage, he could feel his resolve weakening, and the fact that he seemed no nearer to knowing anything about the heart or its whereabouts seemed less important than it had …

All of these thoughts went through his head while he was being marched through the streets surrounded by Mamur's guards.

The summons to the imperial palace was unexpected, and despite already confirming his alibi numerous times that day, he could not help but wonder if he was being led towards the same fate as the people whose ghoulish, fly-covered faces followed his progress from the spikes on the city walls above.

Kelewulf was brought to the throne room, but it was not the emperor who stared down at the young foreigner from the seat of power. Instead it was Grad'ur of Rishtok, his face devoid of emotion.

At Grad'ur's signal Kelewulf's escorts left, so that only the two of them were left occupying the vast space that was the Imperial Hall. It was odd how the departure of these heavily armed men made Kelewulf more, not less, nervous about why he'd been brought here. Remembering one of Alwa's battle spells, and preparing his mind to be able to cast it quickly should he need to do so, he bowed deeply from the waist, as was the custom in these lands. With his head down like this, it struck him that he had no idea how he was supposed to address the nobleman. Rather than risk offence, he opted for a general term he hoped would suffice. 'Your Excellency,' he said as he straightened, watching the man's face for any sign that he'd insulted him.

Instead, Grad'ur gave him the tiniest nod of his head in return. 'You are no doubt wondering why you have been brought before me.'

'I am a guest in your country. As such, it is not my place to wonder such things. You sent for me, I am here,' Kelewulf answered.

Grad'ur waved his words away. 'Your father was a king, is that correct?'

'Yes.'

'Then you understand that matters of state must continue to be dealt with while His Imperial Highness recovers from his recent *illness*.' Grad'ur let that last word hang in the air, as if daring the young necromancer to question it. 'We must prepare for the possibility that Emperor Mamur's period of convalescence might be longer than we would hope.'

Be careful of this one, he is as devious as he is ambitious, the lich said inside Kelewulf's head.

'Be quiet,' he answered under his breath. 'I didn't give you permission to speak.'

'What was that?' Grad'ur asked from the dais.

'Nothing. I was just offering up a small prayer for the emperor's swift recovery.'

'Hmm, quite. We, all of us, must continue to pray for that,' Grad'ur carried on, 'but if the unthinkable should happen and our beloved emperor should *not* recover, it is only wise for the people of this nation to consider who will take the throne.'

'If I might be so bold: Your Excellency seems to fill the chair perfectly.'

If Grad'ur was annoyed at all by this response he hid it well. Instead, he pretended to brush at something on his cloak. 'What do you think of the high priestess?'

The question caught Kelewulf off guard. 'I'm sorry? In what way?'

'You don't have an opinion about her?'

'She is a powerful practitioner of the Art.'

'You like her?'

'I have no personal opinion on her. She has agreed to teach me, that is all.'

'Indeed. Does she seem content with her ... position?'

Kelewulf's mind raced as he tried to understand what was going on here.

'I have no—'

'Does she crave power? Perhaps a desire to rule?'

And there it was: the reason Kelewulf was standing here right now. Grad'ur wanted to find out if Elafir was a threat to him and his own aspirations to the throne.

He considered the question. Why would Grad'ur think the high priestess was considering a move against him? And why would he ask Kelewulf, of all people – someone who, in the eyes of the Hasz'een, was as lowly as a foreigner?

'Well?' the nobleman pressed.

Kelewulf knew even without the lich's warnings that he had to be cautious. In Strom, when his own father sat atop a throne, he'd seen people conspire to wrestle his power away for themselves. These coups never ended well: death or banishment were the usual results, not only for those directly involved but for anyone associated with them.

Somehow Grad'ur clearly believed Kelewulf was closer to the high priestess than he really was.

'I have no idea. However, perhaps I could help Your Excellency by keeping a check on her and reporting anything suspicious back?'

'You would spy on your mentor?' Grad'ur said, one eyebrow raised. Despite the man's big show of pretending that this idea was new to him, it seemed obvious to Kelewulf that this was what he was hoping for all along.

'As I have said, I have no personal relationship with the high priestess. And I have no particular interest in the machinations of the Hasz'een imperial court. I would be happy to help.'

The nobleman studied his face as if searching for something hidden there, the silence stretching for an uncomfortable time before he gave a single nod of his head. 'Do that. But let's be careful to keep this between the two of us, eh?'

'He asked you to spy on me?' Elafir asked, shaking her head in disbelief and pressing her lips together in a tight, thin line.

'Well, "spy" might be a bit of a stretch, but yes, that was the gist of it,' Kelewulf responded.

'That snake. That low-bellied, scheming snake!'

The pair of them were sitting in the deep, high-backed

chairs that faced the huge open fireplace in the high priestess's personal chambers. Kelewulf had asked for a private audience with her as soon as he'd returned from his meeting with Grad'ur. After he'd described everything that had transpired between him and the nobleman, they'd sat gazing at the flames licking up from the logs, Kelewulf occasionally glancing over at the high priestess, who seemed lost in her thoughts. The only other person present was Hrol, Elafir's personal attendant, but the man stood in the shadows and seemed to pay them no attention.

'Thank you for coming straight to me with this,' she said eventually.

'I thought it best to do so. I have the impression you would have found out about the meeting anyway, assuming you had not already done so.'

Her expression remained impassive. 'Nevertheless, the gesture is noted.'

'Is it true?'

'Is what true?'

'That you wish to become empress?'

She answered his question with one of her own. 'Is Hasz what you expected it to be?'

'You know it is not. To be honest, I find it hard to recognise it from the things I was told as a child.'

'Exactly. The same was true for me when I first visited

141

the Six Kingdoms. We were told that the Volken peoples were all bloodthirsty, seagoing murderers – savage marauders and pirates who ransacked all the lands they came across. We were led to believe that they were uncultured heathens who worshipped the dark one, Lorgukk, and still had the god's heart hidden somewhere.' She gave him a smile and shook her head.

'Our view of you is no less inaccurate,' Kelewulf replied. 'The Hasz'een are spoken about as nothing more than warmongers and slavers. There are tales of how you rampaged across this continent, destroying the indigenous people on your way from your original lands far to the west, and of how you ate the livers of your enemies to take what power they had.' He paused. 'We too were told that the Hasz'een were worshippers of Lorgukk and that *they* still had the god's heart somewhere.'

Elafir spread her hands and gave a shrug. 'See? Neither of us are what the other believes them to be. Nevertheless, the mistrust and hatred continues.'

'And if you were empress, what would the future opinions of our respective peoples be? How would new generations view our nations?'

'I'd like to think that they would tell of how we found a common and lasting peace. That we put our racism and hatred aside for the betterment of all. That we learned that, despite our bloody history, we are not really so different from each other.'

Kelewulf gave a small nod of his head. 'And what of the heart? Where do you think the truth of those differing legends lies?'

He'd dropped the question into the conversation casually, but Elafir could sense the tension behind the young necromancer's words. What surprised her was the sadness she felt that he'd asked it.

'Who knows? The best we can hope is that neither is correct, that the thing either never existed or that it has been destroyed forever.' She watched as he gave a little shrug, but the gesture was impossible to interpret.

'I could help you ... with Grad'ur,' he said.

'How?'

'He thinks I am spying on you and that any information I give him will be to his benefit. But now you know that to be the case, it should be easy for us to tell him things that are for *your* benefit.'

'A double agent.'

'I did not know that was the term, but yes, if you like. I could be your double agent in the imperial court.' Kelewulf matched her stare, all too aware that she was scanning his face for any sign that he was lying.

Eventually she took a deep breath and sat back a little. 'Grad'ur is from a region of Hasz far to the west of here.

The Rishtoks are derided by some as gruff and unfriendly people. Some say they are unrefined and lack the social graces possessed by those Hasz'een who live closer to the capital. But the Rishtoks' warring prowess has always been greatly admired, and Grad'ur's grandfather was a famed military man. Grad'ur too started out as a soldier, and he has done well for himself in rising up, first through the ranks of the Hasz'een army, and then continuing on through the imperial hierarchies of the state. Of course, he has certain other attributes that lend themselves particularly well to ruling.'

'Such as?'

'He is ruthless.'

'And would you say that is a quality essential in a ruler?'

'I would say that it helps.' The wry look she gave Kelewulf made him smile in response.

The high priestess rose from her chair and stood with her back to the fire. With the dancing light behind her he was struck, not for the first time, by her splendour and the force of her character.

'I want you to tell Grad'ur that you have heard nothing of me wanting to become empress,' Elafir said, 'and that right now I'm solely focused on identifying the poison used on the emperor. Tell him I'm close, and that once I know, it should enable me to discover who was behind the plot.'

'And *are* you close?' The stony look with which Elafir met his question suggested he should not have asked it, but just as he was about to apologise for his insolence, she replied.

'If I am honest, I am struggling to identify the toxin. All I know is that fellden root is its main ingredient. It makes the whites of the victim's eyes turn a horrible orange colour, so it's not too hard to detect.'

Kelewulf felt Yirgan's lich stir inside him at the mention of the plant stuff, but he pushed the creature into the background for fear that Elafir would sense its presence. Standing up, he nodded his thanks and started towards the door. 'I'll do as you bid, mistress. And I hope whatever I say to Grad'ur will help.'

The Sölten Isles
10

Astrid hunkered down against the icy wind that was blowing in off the sea as the four of them approached the rope bridge. The sight of the crossing, suspended as it was between the two towering cliffs, sent shivers through the shield maiden. Beside her, Lann was shivering too. Haldirk and Lorgen were up ahead, leading the way. Neither man had said so much as a word since setting off. Astrid glanced up at them, noting how they craned their heads left and right, looking for something that wasn't there.

At least not yet, it wasn't.

Astrid's bangle was sending tiny pins and needles shooting up and down her upper arm, the sensation getting stronger with every step. But, like Brundorl's men, she didn't really need the trinket to know something sinister was afoot. There was a presence in the air, a feeling of danger so thick she could almost reach out and touch it. It was something she had experienced on a number of occasions when she and Lann had been in Vorneland hunting Kelewulf's escaped monsters: a creeping sense of menace that made the hairs on her neck stand on end. She knew it was worse for Lann, with the sword talking to him constantly, demanding to be about its business. She turned to look at him, offering him an encouraging smile that he struggled to return.

'Well, that looks perfectly safe,' she said, nodding in the direction of the bridge.

Lann looked up ahead, and this time he couldn't help but crack a half-smile at his friend's sarcasm. Just wide enough for two people to walk side by side, the crossing spanned a gap between two cliffs that was at least twenty arm-spans in length. The drop below it was easily three times that. Something had loosened over the years to make it sag in the middle, and in places the wooden boards appeared to be cracked and split.

The four of them gathered at the point where the land stopped and the wood-and-rope creation began, pausing to take in the grey seas below, where seabirds skimmed the surface looking for food. A weather front was coming in fast from the south, bringing the smell of rain ahead of it.

'The Sleeping Isle,' Lorgen said, nodding towards the land mass on the other side of the crossing. 'There is not much to recommend the place, I'm afraid.'

'You don't have to come,' Astrid said. 'Lann and I can go ahead and look around the barrows. If we need help, we'll come back for you.'

'We have our orders,' Haldirk replied, 'and King Brundorl is not a man to accept disobedience lightly. Besides, we aren't here simply because we were commanded to be.' The rough-looking man glanced at his feet, as if embarrassed. 'The boy is a good, gentle person.' He gestured at Lorgen. 'The two of us are often around him when his father is away, and we have come to like him. We want to see him brought back safely if there is any way it can be done.'

Lann nodded. 'All right. Then lead the way, and let's hope we find him before this weather hits us.'

Brundorl's men turned and started out across the bridge. As sailors used to being aboard vessels that pitched and yawed at sea, neither man seemed to need the chest-high ropes on either side for stability. The same could hardly be said for Astrid and Lann, who had taken no more than a few steps before they were forced to throw both arms out and grab on, feeding the rope through their hands as they gingerly made their way across the swaying, shifting thing. When they'd finally traversed it, they ignored the smirks of the two islanders.

'Neither of you would make it as a seafarer,' Lorgen quipped. But the comment only lightened the mood for a moment. He pointed ahead of him. 'The burial sites are just over that ridge.'

There were perhaps fifty barrows spread out across the landscape atop the Sleeping Isle. To the casual observer they might have looked like little more than a series of regular-shaped mounds covered in the sharp-edged band-grass that grew so readily here. Many were no bigger than a rowing vessel, some were much larger affairs, but all had been constructed in the unmistakeable oval shape of an upturned boat.

No sooner had they crossed the bridge and set foot on firm ground again than the Dreadblade's voice started up its unforgiving cacophony inside Lann's head. Now, with the burial site before him, he screwed his eyes shut and gritted his teeth at the din.

Nir-akuu! Monsters!

Draugr.

NIR-AKUU!

Lann was filled with strong and conflicting emotions when the sword was like this. The fervour of the weapon to be about its business stirred up a similar passion inside him, but at the same time he was aware of the need to keep the thing in check and curb its desire to rush into danger. The sword was made to be wielded by a god, and Lann often wondered if it knew or cared that its new bearer was a mortal thing of flesh and blood.

Lann allowed the noise to wash over him as he turned his head slowly back and forth. As he opened his eyes he saw the others were all looking at him, worried expressions on their faces.

'This way,' he said, striding out ahead of the others and leading them between two barrows in the direction of one of the largest a short distance away. 'It's that one,' he said, pointing.

Although Lann was oblivious to it, Astrid picked up on Haldirk and Lorgen's anxious murmurings as they followed him up the path. 'What is it?' she asked, her own voice little more than a whisper.

'That barrow,' Haldirk said, nervously eyeing it. 'Brundorl's wife, Latva, lies there.'

'Sebastien's mother?'

Haldirk nodded. 'It was almost one year ago to the day that she was placed inside that thing, but …'

'But what?'

'There have been stories. Men claim to have seen her ghost wandering the caves at night. They say they can hear her weeping.'

'Sailors are known for their superstitions and stories.'

'That's true enough. But the boy also claims to have heard his mother's voice of late. He says she has spoken to him in his dreams. And here we are, heading directly for her barrow. Her death was—'

Whatever he was going to add was left unsaid. Lann had come to a sudden halt, his body tense as he stared out ahead of him. The others moved up to be by his side. 'What is it?' Astrid asked.

'The mouth of the barrow,' he answered.

They peered ahead and saw the gaping hole that had been made in the thing. The earth and grass that had once covered it was strewn around the opening in great clumps, and the wooden structure behind had been smashed. Splintered timbers, some as thick as an arm, jutted outwards in their direction.

'Someone broke in,' Lorgen whispered.

'No,' Astrid said with a shake of her head. 'They broke out.'

Something moved in the shadows just inside the opening, causing both the marauders to unsheathe their swords. At the same time, Astrid reached across to her quiver, nocking an arrow to her bow in one swift motion. Only Lann's weapon remained undrawn. The four spread out into a line facing the barrow, and as they did so the rain started: heavy drops pelting down on them, quickly soaking them to the skin. The sun was already at the horizon and the dark clouds choked what little light was left in the sky.

'Lann,' Astrid said, her eyes never leaving the darkness inside. 'That barrow – it's the resting place of Sebastien's mother.'

'No it isn't,' Lann said. 'At least not any more. Something else resides there now.'

'This draugr. Can it be killed?'

Lann turned to look at his friend. The strange half-smile on his lips, coupled with the wild look in his eyes, made her shudder a little. 'I think we're about to find out.'

Placing his hand on the pommel of his sword, Lann had taken no more than two steps towards the mound when a terrifying creature showed itself in the entrance. It stopped the four of them in their tracks as they stared back at it in fear and disbelief.

It was the dead queen, and yet it was not. The clothing the woman had been wearing when placed inside the burial mound was torn and ruined, the once-white fur trims caked in mud and mould. The long, bejewelled dress was ripped from the shoulder on one side so that the front hung open to reveal much of the upper torso, including a long gold chain draped around the figure's neck. That it had once been human and female there was no doubt, but now it was a thing of horror. Decay had robbed the body of its flesh in many places and what was left was putrid and mouldering.

Bathed in shadows, the creature stood regarding them through eyes as black as the tomb behind it.

'Who comes to this place?' the draugr asked. The dull, flat tone of its voice was as terrible on the ear as its appearance was to the eye.

'We ask the same question. You are not the person who was entombed here a year ago,' Astrid said.

The creature gave a grim chuckle. 'What would you know of such things? I am her and I am more.' The monster gave a little jolt as it uttered these last words.

'Where is the boy Sebastien?' Lann asked.

'Ah, my beautiful son.' Although barely noticeable, there was something different about the voice now: emotion, previously absent, was woven through it.

'Queen Latva!' Astrid said, seizing on this subtle change. 'If you can hear me – is Sebastien safe?'

They watched its fingers clenching and unclenching, as if the creature and the original inhabitant of the body were undergoing some desperate internal conflict. 'He is not safe as long as he remains on these isles. I promised Latva we would take Sebastien away from danger. Away from *him*. I intend to keep my promise.'

'Him?'

'One of Brundorl's captains, Tengredd. The murderer. He killed Latva.' From the corner of her eye, Astrid saw the pirate king's men react to this. 'But I have brought her back. I have given her life again, I have given her back her son!' There was something in the voice, an anger that the

153

draugr was struggling to contain. 'The queen and I made an agreement.'

'Tengredd killed the queen? Why?' Haldirk asked in a small voice.

'She discovered he was Brundorl's illegitimate son. She threatened to reveal his identity along with his plans to usurp his father.'

Astrid glanced at Brundorl's men. It was clear from their expressions that this news was as much a shock to them as it was to her.

Lann began to speak, but whether it was to his comrades or to himself was unclear. 'The draugr can only exist inside a host that died believing a terrible wrong was done to them.'

The draugr shot a glance towards the darkness of the barrow, as if something from within had called upon its attention. When it turned back to them, all agitation seemed to have leached out of the creature. It cast its black eyes over the four of them before turning to look at the last sliver of sun at the precise moment it slipped below the horizon. A sick grin crept over the creature's face. 'You're too late,' it said. 'We are leaving.' With a quick backward step, it disappeared into the shadows of the tomb.

Lann reacted first, throwing himself forward, but the sodden ground beneath his feet caused him to stumble. He would have fallen if Astrid had not stopped to grab him. It was in this way that Haldirk became the first to launch himself into the darkness after the monster, ignoring their calls for him to stop.

His agonised scream was as short-lived as it was dreadful.

Lann let out a curse and turned to the remaining brigand. Lorgen was visibly shaking, his sword tip dancing in the air before him as he struggled to hold the weapon steady. 'Stay here,' Lann called to him, already moving in the direction of the barrow. 'Don't come after us unless we shout for you.' He shot the man a glance. 'Lorgen, did you hear me?'

The man managed a tiny nod, his eyes never leaving the opening.

'Ready?' Lann asked Astrid as she came alongside him.

'No. Not really.'

'Neither am I. Let's go.'

With that, they entered the barrow.

They hurried forward as best they could, but the darkness meant they could not go as quickly as they would have liked. Just as their vision was adapting enough to make out the slumped figure of Sebastien on the floor ahead of them, a strange light appeared at the back of the barrow. Except it wasn't light. It was a lack of light that was somehow even greater than the darkness around it; a terrifying void that Astrid and Lann both recognised. They had first encountered it when Lann had stood before a wall of foul blackness, hacking and stabbing at the creatures who dared to pour through the Void after one of them had killed his aunt.

'Come, Sebastien,' the draugr hissed and it grabbed hold of the unconscious boy, draping him over its shoulder as it approached the void.

'It's a rift!' Lann shouted. 'It means to escape through it!' The Dreadblade's voice filled Lann's head now, a storm of fury that was directed at the hideous creature.

Forgoing all thoughts of caution, the pair ran forward, Astrid abandoning her bow and drawing her own sword instead.

Neither one of them noticed the hunk of wood in the draugr's other hand until it was launched in their direction. It caught Lann full in the head, sending him crashing to the ground with the world spinning sickeningly about him. There was no doubt he would have blacked out if it hadn't been for the Dreadblade, the sword somehow lending Lann its power so that a feeling, like a galvanising current, coursed through his veins. Dazed, he shook his head to clear it, and looked up to see Astrid was almost upon the creature. He watched her raise her sword, then lower it again, unwilling to swing the weapon for fear of striking the child. Instead, she grabbed the boy, looping an arm around his waist as the draugr roared back at her in anger and frustration. Stumbling over his own feet, Lann rushed to her side.

'Grab Sebastien!' she cried, throwing her sword down to the ground and reaching for the short dagger she always carried in her belt.

As he encircled the boy's waist with his arms, trying to wrestle the youngster free from the monster's grip, Lann caught a glimpse of her raising the weapon. What happened next would haunt him forever. Realising it couldn't hope to hang on to the boy, the draugr pushed the child at them instead, sending Lann sprawling to the floor with Brundorl's son still in his arms. The creature swung at Astrid with all its might, ignoring the dagger as it sank into its shoulder and catching her a blow to the jaw that made the shield maiden's legs crumple beneath her. Grabbing her as she fell, the draugr threw itself towards the rift.

'ASTRID!' Lann stared in disbelief at the shimmering void through which the pair had disappeared.

The Dreadblade was screaming now, a strident caco-phony of noise, the meaning of which Lann, still in shock, couldn't discern until he saw how the portal had started to flex and buckle, as if it were on the verge of collapse. Scrambling to his feet, he shouted back over his shoulder for Lorgen and was relieved to see the outline of the man appear in the opening to the barrow.

'Over here, now!' Lann yelled, lifting the blind young boy up from the floor before handing him over into the safe arms of the marauder, who was staring in horror at the pulsating thing of darkness a short distance away. 'Lorgen, listen to me. LORGEN!' The man finally tore his eyes away and focused them on the young man with the black sword in his hand. 'Get Sebastien safely back to his father. Tell him what you heard and saw here, especially about the danger Tengredd poses to Sebastien.'

'What about you?' Lorgen asked.

But Lann had already set off at a run in the direction of the portal, praying for the gods to be with him as he dived headfirst at that terrible hole which led from one world into another.

Hasz
11

Kelewulf's concentration was so complete that he hardly noticed the sweat that ran down his face, forming into drips on his nose and chin before falling into his lap. The heat he was generating as he sat cross-legged on the floor inside the training chamber was made worse by the large fold-out screen he had been forced to sit behind, separating him from the rest of the space. His confines also concentrated the strange smell in the air – a harsh, coppery tinge that tickled the back of his nose and throat. Both the heat and the smell were by-products of the majik he was performing.

Beyond the screen, standing in the centre of the room were two figures: Master Shintal was one; the other was a tall woman wearing a long, beautiful gown, her hands and neck adorned with fine jewellery. Only one of these figures, however, was real.

Shintal was one of the younger scholars, a small, thin man who specialised in majik of deception. His lessons were always tough and his criticisms harsh. Of all the scholars Kelewulf had met in the citadel, he suspected that this man held him in particularly low regard.

Shintal leaned in towards the woman, his face close to hers as he studied her features. 'Better,' he said. When he reached out a hand, the woman stepped back, the smile never leaving her face, despite it being clear that she would not allow herself to be touched by him. Shintal's lips twitched a fraction.

'Where did you say you were from?' he asked her.

'Southern Bantusz,' she answered, her accent confirming her response. She reached up to replace a lock that had fallen loose from her ornately styled hair.

'Ah, the Ruby Lands. I am told that the Bantusz kingdom is very beautiful, as, it would seem, are its inhabitants.'

'You're too kind.'

'I love the accent of your people. It makes our own tongue sound clumsy somehow.'

'I'm not sure I agree with you. I think your way of speech is rather lovely.'

Shintal smiled briefly at the compliment, then his brow furrowed slightly, as if he were trying to recall something. 'Didn't a former queen of the Six Kingdoms come from the Ruby Lands? Married off to one of the Rivengelds, if I remember correctly.'

'I think you are referring to Elenor of Lynt.'

'Did you know her?'

A strange look crossed the woman's face but she quickly replaced it with a smile. She shook her head.

'Hmm. They say she went mad and threw herself out of a tower somewhere.' The woman's smile fell. 'Some say she tried to kill her child at the same time.'

The woman's face contorted into an ugly mask and she flickered once, briefly, then more dramatically as she winked out of existence altogether to reveal, standing in her place, a life-sized humanoid figure fashioned entirely from straw and fine wire. What couldn't be seen – right at the mannequin's centre, where a human's heart would be – was the small, walnut-sized ball that Kelewulf had planted there, fashioned under Shintal's tutelage using hair, fingernails and dead skin from his own body, along with other objectionable excreta like spit and snot and earwax. It was this object, not the straw figure, which was the real focus of the majik that made the gölem possible.

'No!' Shintal bellowed. 'No, no, no!' He shoved at the mannequin and sent it crashing to the floor, then strode across the room and pulled the screen back to reveal the young necromancer glaring back up at him. 'What happened?'

'You insulted my mother! You know those things aren't true and yet—'

'Stop!' Shintal threw his hands up and shook his head. 'Why, when I could have picked any race of people, do you think I asked you to muster up a gölem in the shape of a Bantusz woman? Could it possibly be that I knew it would be harder for you to maintain the deception if I spoke of things that were personal to you, things that would cause you to lose the intense concentration necessary for this form of majik? Do you think your enemies would not talk about you or your past to a figure like this? Do you think you will not hear objectionable things through the ears of your illusion?'

'You had no right to—'

'I have every right to show you your limitations and teach you to overcome them. *You* have no right to question my methods, just as you have no right to be here in Hasz learning our ways!'

Kelewulf went to stand up, a baleful expression on his face.

'Sit down,' Shintal said, pointing to the floor. 'Sit. Down.' There followed a long moment when each of them glared at the other, the tutor eventually nodding when his pupil did as he was bid and sat.

Taking a deep breath, Shintal collected himself. 'Now, I might not like the high priestess's decision to allow you to study here, and I might not like the way you have circum-vented the criteria necessary to do just that. But I am sworn to serve Elafir.' He gestured to the prone straw mannequin. When he spoke again his voice was perfectly calm. 'You need to understand that the gölem is a powerful weapon against your enemies – a figure that can be made to look like anyone you choose, that can talk and react to those around it, and which will allow you to see and hear through it for as long as it remains untouched. Using such a device can create havoc in the right situations.' Shintal paused. 'The mage Welgur the Majestic was a master of this form of majik. It is said that, many years ago, he had four – yes, four – gölems in the royal court of Vorneland when they were deciding on who would take the throne, and that his majik was pivotal in the ruling.' The master shook his head. 'Do you imagine that one of the demons you are so adept at summoning could do such a thing? Do you?'

'I am sorry, Master Shintal. I will try harder.' Kelewulf looked towards the door as a gong sounded four times somewhere in the citadel: mealtime in the refectory. He went to stand again.

'Yes, you will. Sit back down. You and I will work until I am satisfied you can keep your concentration at a level necessary to maintain the deception that is the gölem even when provoked. I always find hunger is a great way to focus the mind.'

Doing his best to ignore the rumblings in his stomach, Kelewulf returned to the floor and crossed his legs.

'Good. I think we'll have a common beggar this time. A Hasz'een native. I want you to create someone who will make me sorry for their plight. Perhaps some terrible disfigurement?' Shintal nodded at the young necromancer. 'Begin,' he said, pulling the screen back across.

Kelewulf felt the heat stir the air around him as a filthy, bearded figure with a withered hand got to his feet from the floor in the middle of the room.

'Where were you at mealtime?' Alwa asked. The acolyte had caught up with Kelewulf in one of the many corridors that wound through the citadel.

'Master Shintal,' he said by way of a response.

'Ah. He can be a real pain sometimes.'

'He hates me.'

'Shintal hates everyone. Except Acolytes Mee'an and Frunk, that is. They both want to become shadow mages like him, so he goes easier on them. What do you have next?'

'Arcane Knowledge with Larghal.'

'So do I. Come on, we'll go together.'

'Larghal,' Kelewulf said. 'The name doesn't sound right in my Eastern ears.' He repeated it, stressing the middle three consonants in the same way the Hasz'een people did. 'It sounds like somebody clearing their throat.'

Alwa laughed at his description. 'Trust me, it sounds like that to everyone, Eastern ears or not!' Still smiling, she fished around in the pocket of one of her robes, and when she pulled out her hand she was holding a red apple. 'Here,' she said, tossing it in the air for him to catch. 'I stole it from the refectory when I saw you weren't there.'

'You did? For me?'

'Uh-huh.'

Kelewulf narrowed his eyes at her and tried to keep a straight face. 'You're not a Master Shintal gölem, are you? Sent here by him to torment me further?'

Alwa laughed and punched him playfully on the arm.

Kelewulf stared down at the fruit in his hand. Despite his jesting, he didn't understand why the young woman walking at his side would have taken it for him. The obvious conclusion did not sit easily with him. Did Alwa consider him a friend?

Back in Strom he'd never had any friends. Except Erik, when they were young. But that was years before Kelewulf had allowed Yirgan's lich to kill Erik's father and then frame the young prince for the murder. The memory was unbidden and unwanted, one he'd buried as deeply as he could in the dark recesses of his mind. It caused something to clench inside him, as if something had taken a tight grip on his heart.

Stop it, Kelewulf told himself. Because to think about it was to resurrect the terrible feelings of despair and guilt he'd fought so hard to overcome. It wasn't enough to tell himself that he had been battling with Yirgan for control of his mind and body at the time, or that all he'd really wanted to do was scare members of his family – to show them they were not as indomitable as they thought. His uncle had died a horrible, painful death, and Erik – the only friend he'd ever had – was almost hanged as a result.

As all of this unravelled in his mind walking along next to Alwa, he was unaware of the small sob that escaped him.

'Are you OK?' she asked.

'What? Y-yes, I'm fine.'

Everyone I've ever been close to gets hurt. Or worse, he thought.

He handed the apple back to Alwa, coming to a stop in the middle of the passageway and facing her as other students and household staff continued around them. 'I don't need you to steal food for me. And, just so we're clear, I'm not your friend. I don't need you or anybody else to look out for me, so please, do both of us a favour and keep your nose out of my business.'

He ignored the hurt expression on her face as he strode off towards Master Larghal's rooms.

* * *

The lesson passed slowly. Master Larghal, sitting up at his high desk, prattled on about passages he'd recently discovered in some old book or other, while the students did their best to look as though they cared. After their spat in the corridor, Alwa had taken a seat as far away from Kelewulf as she could, and although he did his best to avoid looking over at her he could feel her cold eyes on him.

When the lesson was finished and the rest of the acolytes hurried for the door, Kelewulf hung back until he was alone with the old scholar. Larghal, his head buried in the heavy tome open before him, remained oblivious to his presence until a loud cough got his attention.

'Hmm? What is it?' He stared out at him through rheumy eyes, before slowly and reluctantly setting down his magnifying glass and closing the book. 'Acolyte Kelewulf. You seem to want something … again.'

'Actually, I'm returning these to you.' Kelewulf placed several books on the edge of the desk. 'The works you let me have on Trogir and Lorgukk?'

'And? I assume that you're not hanging around after what was – if the reaction of your fellow students was anything to go by – a rivetingly interesting lesson simply to tell me that.'

Kelewulf smiled. Despite Larghal's extreme old age, he was as sharp as any of the academics at the citadel. 'No, I did not. I wanted to ask you about something I discovered in this.' He held up a small, ancient book.

Larghal peered through the viewing device at the thing in Kelewulf's hand, his face distorting into grotesque caricature through the magnified glass.

'Ah, Losterian's *Scourge of the Dark God*. An often overlooked work, in my opinion. Did you know that Losterian had all of the fingers of her right hand cut off when she—'

'In particular, I wanted to ask you about this passage,' Kelewulf interrupted, knowing he didn't dare let Larghal start on one of his long and tedious stories. He turned to the pages he'd marked. 'Here.' He pointed to the section. 'This bit about the Black Shield.'

Larghal peered down at the passages. 'Hmm. Yes, interesting in a purely conjectural sense, I suppose.'

'Because?'

'I believe we had this discussion the last time we spoke, acolyte. For this majik to be of any use, one would have to believe that the Dreadblade has returned to the realm of men again. As it has not, this is purely an abstract notion of no consequence to anyone.'

'But it exists? The spell? And it could be used to protect someone against the dark blade?' Since discovering the reference to the spell, Kelewulf hadn't been able to get it out of his head. He couldn't believe it was coincidence that rumours of the black blade appearing in the world again had *just happened* to coincide with his and Yirgan's lich's plans to return the dark god. And if these rumours were true, and if he *had* seen the Dreadblade in the hands of the young man that day in Vissergott, he would need to minimise the risk the sword represented to his future plans. It would be no use his locating the heart, only for it to be destroyed by that weapon.

Larghal waved his fingers in the air in a strange fluttery motion that Kelewulf took to indicate frustration. 'The spell exists. Of course it exists. But merely as a piece of obscure frivolity. Really, Acolyte, I would have thought somebody of your age would be more interested in love charms or spells of attraction.' He peered at Kelewulf and puffed out his cheeks resignedly when he gave no reaction. 'I have a scroll containing the Black Shield spell in the library somewhere, I think.'

'Could I see it? Purely as a lesson in frivolity, of course.'

Larghal wrinkled his nose and set the magnifier down again. Just when Kelewulf had become convinced that his request would be refused, the master made a small grunting noise and nodded to himself. 'I suppose I could try and find it. Come and see me tomorrow and I should have it for you. Really, though, there are much more interesting things you could be spending your time on, you know. For instance, this book I'm reading here tells of the murgen-volk, the tiny people believed to be ...'

'Yes, fine,' Kelewulf said, already backing out of the room. 'Thank you. I'll, er, come back tomorrow.'

He had almost closed the door when he stopped at the sound of a bell – a low, bass tolling sound that affected him at some deep-seated level. When he looked back into the room at Master Larghal, he noted the look of disquiet on the old man's face. 'What's that?' he asked.

'The Ölumbell. The emperor is dead.'

The Rød

12

Lann started to regain consciousness. The first thing to register in his brain was the dreadful pain. It emanated from every muscle and joint of his body, as if he had been in a terrible battle with some huge, powerful foe – and lost. He was lying on his side with his eyes closed, and for those first few seconds he had no recollection of where he was or how he had come to be here. Then it all came back to him: the burial barrow, the draugr, the rift. Along with the pain and the slow return of his senses came something else: a horrible feeling of dread that seemed to creep over and through him, like a poison infecting his soul.

It kept him pinioned to the ground, that fear. It was like a physical force, pressing down on him.

Reluctantly, he opened his eyes and saw the Dreadblade. It had been torn free of his hand when he'd crossed between the realms and was lying a short distance away.

The desire to hold it was so strong Lann could think of nothing else. A small grunt escaped him as he stretched out and used his fingertips to hook the sword towards him until he was able to curl his hand around the grip. As soon as he did, he felt the dark blade's power course through him, pushing back at the pain, but even more importantly at the dread and fear that had been threatening to overwhelm him.

'Astrid?' He called out her name, his voice sounding weak and insignificant.

Gathering himself, he got to his feet, but the world spun and lurched sickeningly, and he almost fell down again.

'ASTRID!' he shouted, ignoring the odd nausea and staring around him properly for the first time. There was no sign of his friend or the creature that had brought her here, but the sight of the terrifying world laid out before him made him gasp.

The sky seemed to be on fire. Cold, black flames rolled and boiled across the firmament. Lann fancied he caught glimpses of terrible objects in those raging clouds: faces and creatures that formed at the edge of his vision and then disappeared as soon as he turned his full gaze towards them.

Forcing himself to tear his eyes away from this apocalyptic lightshow, he took in a bleak and desolate topography that was every bit as bizarre. He was standing at the edge of a vast vista that, although solid enough beneath his feet, appeared more like a seascape than land. As far as the eye could see was a fine red sand that shifted and moved in a slow, yawing motion like a lazy ocean. Strange stalagmites of the sand – easily as tall as he was – were popping up randomly all over, suddenly thrusting upwards out of the mass and staying in place for a few seconds before collapsing down and disappearing again. As strange as the sandy spikes were, odder still were the huge, black rocks made of a lustrous, glassy material. It took Lann a second to process that they were moving incredibly slowly across the red plain. The mechanism that made this movement possible, along with their purpose, was a mystery.

Fearful of the lack of any clue as to where Astrid might be, he spun around to see if she might be behind him somewhere. Lann gasped in marvel at what he saw.

Stretching up and out on both sides of him, with a hint of a curve to suggest it described a vast half-globe, was a silvery-white barrier. The relief Lann felt merely by looking at it was almost painful: the shimmering, lustrous radiance danced in front of his eyes and made him want to throw himself into it; because he knew, instinctively, that the world he'd left was on the other side, a world that at some level was demanding his return. Without consciously knowing he was doing so, Lann found himself raising his arm to reach out towards that beautiful iridescence ...

Nir!

The dark blade's voice inside his head was so loud that it instantly wrenched him back to his senses. He snatched his arm away, but his desire to touch the dome remained undiminished, so much so that he had to force himself to turn his back on it and return his attention to the red desert plain. The first thing he noticed was how several of the weird, land-sailing rocks had changed their direction and were now slowly approaching him from all sides.

Where could Astrid be? Had she entered this world at a different point to him? If so, where? Lann was about to call her name again when he felt something on his ankle. He stared at the long, thin, tendril-like thing that had stretched its way out from the base of the closest rock to snake its way over his foot and wind its way up his shin. The slightest touch of the Dreadblade's tip was enough to make the black shoot instantly withdraw, but not far enough to convince him it wouldn't creep back again. Indeed, as he raised his foot to take a step, the thing shadowed the movement. He dared a look away from it. More of the ugly tendrils were approaching, not just from the closest megalith, but also from those further out. There was no way he could stay where he was. He had to find Astrid! Strengthening his grip on the dark blade, Lann set off. Going back through the barrier was not an option, so right now straight ahead seemed as good a direction as any.

He'd taken no more than four or five steps when he heard the warning cry. He stopped and stared up at the sky in the direction it had come from.

High up in the air, flying almost directly overhead, was a woman, beautiful black-feathered wings beating at her back. Her muscular frame was clad in red leather armour and fine red chainmail the exact colour of the sands beneath Lann's feet. She pointed her sword down in his direction and shouted out, 'Stay where you are! Do not move.'

Doing as he was bid, Lann tried not to flinch when she hurtled out of the sky towards him, coming to a controlled stop no more than an arm's length away and kicking up a cloud of sand that made him squint his eyes shut as she folded her huge wings behind her. He couldn't help staring. The woman towered over him. The muscles on her arms and legs looked as if they'd been carved from wood and, now she was up close, he could see that they were covered with a host of symbols and pictograms, tattooed directly into her skin, as if she were a living canvas that some artist had decided to paint upon. She was like nothing he had ever seen before.

She stared back at him through almond-shaped eyes of a startling purple hue that would have looked out of place anywhere but here. 'Where do you think you are going?' she asked, speaking with a strange accent that made it difficult for him to understand her.

'Please, I need your help. I need to find someone. My name is—'

'I didn't ask you who you were. I asked you where you were going.'

'You're a vælkyrie,' Lann whispered, not trying to conceal his amazement.

'And that is the second time you have refused to answer my question, Lannigon Gudbrandr.'

'I'm sorry, how do you know who—?'

'Your aunt, the witch Fleya, visited us shortly after her death.' The vælkyrie said this as if it were nothing out of the ordinary. 'She told us you would come here. But your visit here is much sooner than we expected. Nevertheless, you are welcome.' She lifted the sword she was carrying, holding it straight up before her in what Lann guessed was a salute.

'We?'

Her eyes still glued to his, the woman gestured towards the sky and Lann looked up to see two more of the fantastic creatures in the air high above them. He had not seen them arrive, but he was certain they had not been there moments before. One was blonde, like his interrogator, and the other had short black hair. Both were keeping a watch, scanning the land and skies for some unseen threat.

Lann realised the tendrils from the rocks had stopped their advance.

'They will not approach while I am here,' the woman said, as if reading his mind. She pointed to an intricate tattoo on her left forearm. 'The ward of Xo.'

Lann stared at some of the other figures she wore on her skin. 'They are all protective symbols?'

She nodded. 'Runes and ancient shields. We would not be able to exist for long in the Rød if we did not have them. Nothing can.'

Lann glanced at the black tendrils. 'Maybe I should get some?' he joked.

The vælkyrie nodded sternly towards his sword. 'You carry yours in your hand.'

Lann lifted the Dreadblade, the weapon making a cat-like purring sound inside his head as he did so. There, along its length on both sides, and shining with a fierce white light, were tiny pictograms similar to those worn on the vælkyrie's skin. Lann wondered at them, turning the blade this way and that as he took them in. He'd always known there were marks or inscriptions on the sword, but they had always resisted inspection, blurring from sight whenever he'd tried to look upon them. But that had been in the human realm. Here, they glowed with a ferocity that spoke of the power they contained.

'The dark blade,' the vælkyrie said, the words whispered in an almost reverential tone. 'Never did I think I would

177

lay eyes on it. It does not belong here.' Her eyes returned to his. 'And neither do you.'

He remembered the stories he'd been told about these fabulous creatures. 'You were of the human realm once.'

'That was a long time ago, when your world was new. When Lorgukk was banished to this place, we were sent here by the gods.' She stood up straighter. 'We exist in the Rød to stop the creatures of the Murrke crossing between this world and yours.' She paused as if weighing her words. 'We failed in that recently, and for that failure we owe you an apology, Lannigon Gudbrandr.'

'Why?'

'When the young necromancer, the young man known as Kelewulf, opened up a portal between your world and this one, we failed to control the rush of creatures eager to use it.' The vælkyrie shook her head at the memory and gestured towards the shimmering barrier behind him. 'Usually, the holes, when they appear here, are small. My sisters and I are largely successful in stopping most of the creatures that try to cross through these rents. But that day the opening was too large. Creatures poured from the Murrke, and try as we might, we could not stop them all.'

'Do you have a name?' Lann asked.

'I am Sigrun.' Without looking away she gestured towards the vælkyrie overhead. 'They are Hildur and Göll.'

'Then I thank you, Sigrun – you and the others. I don't for a moment doubt that what I had to face on that day would have been much worse if you had not done what you could on this side.' He lifted the Dreadblade and did his best to copy her saluting gesture, and as he did so the dark blade spoke inside his head.

Tsh el agmon. Tsh el förter. She is a warrior. She is strong.

'The blade, it says—'

'I know what it said.'

'You can hear it?' Lann was surprised. In the human realm, nobody could hear the blade, let alone understand it. Astrid had told him she could often sense *when* it was speaking to him, but claimed never to have heard the actual words and strange utterances the thing made.

'Of course. We are vælkyrie,' Sigrun said with a shrug. 'Now, for the third time, tell me what you are doing here and where you think you are going.'

'I am here to find a creature that has returned here from my realm. A draugr.'

'Why would you follow it here?'

'It has brought a girl with it. Someone I'm very fond of.' As these words left his lips Lann saw the first real sign of emotion on the vælkyrie's face.

'Another human is here? With a draugr?'

'Yes. She's—'

'Enough talk,' Sigrun said, cutting him off. 'Come.' She beckoned him towards her. 'We must find this girl and return her to your realm as soon as possible. Every moment she is here in the Void is like poison for her.'

Lann recalled the sickening terror – almost like a physical thing – that had gripped him in his first moments here. Picking up the dark blade had countered that dread, but how could Astrid, with no such help, survive it? He remembered the bracelet she wore on her arm. It had been left for her by Lann's real mother, and like the Dreadblade it was a thing of majik. He could only hope it was helping Astrid right now.

A new, even more sickening thought struck him. 'If the draugr meant to kill her, it could easily have already done so.'

'It doesn't mean to kill her. It means to become her.'

'Wait. What do you—?'

'Enough questions for now!' The vælkyrie cut him off. Turning her back on Lann and sheathing her weapon, she opened her wings, displaying her broad shoulders and back to him. At the sight of the lustrous black feathers Lann was reminded of the crow form his mother, Lette, had sometimes taken back in the human realm. Sigrun dropped to one knee, looking back over her shoulder at him as she did so. 'Get on my back,' she said, signalling to her friends overhead.

'What? No, I don't—'

'Get on. Now. Wrap your legs around my middle and link your feet together at the ankles if you can.' Lann reluctantly followed her instructions. 'Put your arms over my shoulders. You can grab a hold of my cuirass if you must –' she gestured to the leather body armour that covered her upper torso – 'but do not put them around my neck. I do not wish to be strangled if you panic. Is that all clear?'

'Wait a minute. I'm not sure I—'

The rest of his words were lost as the vælkyrie leaped into the air and began to beat her wings with a low *thwump-thwump-thwump*, trying hard to gain some height. Even to Lann it was clear that his extra weight would make flight impossible, but just as he was about to shout out for her to put him down again, they suddenly swept upwards at an astonishing speed.

When he looked up, he saw why. Sigrun had reached out to grab the ankles of the other two vælkyrie. With all three of them carving at the air with their massive wings, they quickly rose up into the sky.

They were flying. Lann, filled with fear and exhilaration in equal measure, couldn't bear to open his eyes for the first few moments, and when he finally did he saw that they'd already climbed to a terrifying height. The wind whistled in his ears and made his eyes stream. Blinking to clear his vision, he summoned up the courage to peer out over the vælkyrie's left shoulder at the landscape stretched out below them. It was in this way that he finally understood what Sigrun had meant by the Rød and the Murrke.

The world below seemed to be made up of distinct zones. The Rød he'd just taken off from was the outermost and smallest of these, its red sands giving way to a much larger landscape, the nature of which was impossible to make out, obscured as it was by the ominous grey mist hanging over it. What small breaks there were in the mist – and there were precious few – allowed him glimpses of a bleak, swamp-like place. Beyond this, way off in the distance, was an inky nothingness, the mere sight of which was enough to send knives of unease lancing down Lann's spine. He wondered at this seemingly irrational reaction, but when he tried to force himself to look into it again, the sheer weight of terror and panic it induced in him quickly made him tear his eyes away once more.

'That terrible nothingness is the Blakk,' his ride shouted back at him, showing that uncanny ability to read his mind again. 'Do not stare into it unless you have to. It is where all the creatures of the Void originate from. It is also where the dark god is confined.'

Sigrun's revelation struck Lann like a blow. Lorgukk was here, in this place! With this realisation came understanding. Somehow, Lann *knew* it was the dark god himself that was the source of the terror he'd felt in his first moments here: a poisonous corruption leaching out to infect everything in this realm. How could Kelewulf be willing to allow such evil to escape? He could have no concept of what this realm was really like.

Lann shook his head, as if clearing these thoughts and distractions from it, trying instead to focus on what had brought him here.

'All of the mist-covered region below us, that's the Murrke that you mentioned?' he asked, eager to change the subject.

'It is known by many names, but yes, that is what we call it. The mist never lifts, so it is where those creatures not confined to the Blakk like to hide. They wait for a hole to open up in the curtain at the edge of the Rød.'

'The rifts ... they only occur in the Rød?'

'That is correct. And as soon as one does, those creatures nearest will try to make their way through to the human world before it closes again.'

'Why don't the creatures just take up a position in the Rød and wait there? Why hide in the Murkke?' he asked, gesturing downwards.

The vælkyrie looked over her shoulder and gave him a fierce smile. 'Because the vælkyrie are the guardians of the Rød and we deal death to most anything that enters it without our permission.'

'How often do you give that permission?' Lann asked, already knowing the answer.

'Never.'

Sigrun nodded her head in the direction of her companions, but her smile was already falling away. 'Our numbers are not what they once were, though. We have lost many sisters, and there are none to replace us. Because of that, creatures like your draugr have been more successful recently, managing to evade us and make the crossing.' He saw the way she clenched her teeth at the thought of this. 'However, your monster made a mistake.'

'What was that?'

'It came back. With a human. And now it will be made to pay.'

Although the vælkyrie were deep into the zone known as the Murrke, they were flying high enough that the thick blanket of fog remained below them. 'We're not far away now,' Sigrun shouted to Lann. 'The Murrke is split up into distinct regions, each of which is favoured by a particular creature, for reasons known only to them. The area we are about to cross over is known as the Stil. It is a dank and terrible place. Your draugr is not far beyond it.'

'How do you know?' Lann shouted over the wind whilst peering down at the swirling grey. There was nothing to suggest what was down there or where Astrid and the draugr might be.

'The human female, like you and your sword, does not belong here. Now we know what we are looking for, we can "feel" her. But we must get to her before it's too late.'

'Too late? I thought you said the draugr did not intend to kill her.'

'The draugr are usually only able to possess the corpses of the dead, but what they desire, more than anything else, is to enter the body and mind of a living thing. They can only do so by entering the person the split-second before they die, and they can only do it here, in this realm. That is why the creature brought your human friend back, and it will not have long to wait before it gets what it wants.'

The thought of anything happening to Astrid in this place filled Lann with horror. He should never have agreed to let her go with him to the Sölten Isles. This was all his fault. He should have been the one taken by the draugr, not her.

He was suddenly brought back to the present by loud shouts from Sigrun and the other vælkyrie.

A pair of leathery-winged creatures flew up at them out of the miasma, quickly followed by three more. The lead creature, its lips pulled back in a hideous snarl, was carrying a crude-looking spear, its arm cocked in readiness. The cry had no sooner left Sigrun's lips than the creature hurled the weapon in their direction. The missile narrowly missed the tightly packed group, and the dark-haired vælkyrie known as Göll returned fire with her crossbow, the bolt lodging in the thing's neck and sending it plummeting back downwards through the mist. When a second spear flashed past Lann's face, close enough for him to feel the air of it passing, he was about to thank his lucky stars when he heard it find a home just above him, the ugly head of the weapon deep in Göll's flank, just beneath her wing. The vælkyrie's scream was terrible. The force of the blow twisted her about in the air and caused Sigrun to lose her grip on her friend's ankle.

Their attackers had retreated back into the mist, but the damage was done. Without Göll, the remaining trio couldn't hope to maintain their height, and they'd already begun to drop down towards the grey sea below them.

'Sister!' Sigrun called out. 'You can make it back home. Go!'

Her words were met with a shake of Göll's head.

'Please! Magorlana can fix your wound, you know she can! You must leave us.'

'No,' her friend called back, offering her a sad smile. 'I'll never make it, not like this. We both know that.' She gestured back towards the mist. 'We're about to cross into the Stil, and the drishte that live there are not as cowardly as our winged attackers were.' She winced as a fresh wave of pain racked her, then hardened the set of her face. 'So I'll take the fight to them and buy you some time.' She shook her head to stop another interruption. 'I am a vælkyrie. A protector. It is my duty.' With that, she let go of her crossbow, reached across and pulled the spear free. With blood now flowing freely from the wound, the vælkyrie drew the sword hanging from her hip. Armed with both weapons, she gave them one final salute before plummeting down into the mist ahead of them.

'Go well, sister,' Lann heard Sigrun whisper as she watched her friend disappear. Despite the dread she obviously felt, Sigrun somehow found the strength of mind to take charge of the situation. Her voice was filled with emotion as she barked out instructions to the remaining vælkyrie. 'You must summon the others, Hildur. Together you must fly as quickly as possible to where the human girl is and save her from her fate at the hands of the draugr. Our sister Göll's noble act must not be for nothing.'

'What about you?' Hildur cried out.

'The boy and I will have to take our chances in the Stil. We will go on foot. Do not wait for us, Hildur! Do not come back for us. Your mission is to save the girl, do you understand?'

'Sigrun, no!'

'It's our only hope. Please, sister, do as I say.'

Hildur hissed in frustration, but the look that passed between the two was enough to make her reluctantly nod her head. 'Then may the gods lend you both good fortune.'

'And you, my friend.'

With that, Sigrun released the grip she had on Hildur, sending both herself and Lann plunging down into the fog that had engulfed Göll only moments before.

'Hold on tightly!' she shouted back at him. 'I'll slap you on the leg, like this, when you need to jump.'

'Jump?'

The world around Lann had become a blank, grey nothingness, the air wet and cold. Somewhere overhead he heard a long, mournful note as Hildur blew the horn that had been hooked on to her belt.

They were gathering speed rapidly.

'And do your best not to tense up too much when you hit the ground. But above all, try to remain silent. If you're hurt, don't cry out. Noise is not our friend in the Stil.' Even though she was having to yell to be heard, the significance of this last sentence was not lost on Lann. No sooner had the words left her lips than he sensed that the mist around them was thinning.

'Get ready, Lannigon Gudbrandr,' Sigrun hissed as the ground came rushing up to meet them. The vælkyrie grunted as she tried to level them out, thrashing wildly at the air in an effort to slow their descent and lessen the angle of entry.

Lann's mind raced as he wondered how fast they were going and how hard the ground below him was. Were there trees? Or rocks? But these thoughts had no sooner formed in his mind than he felt Sigrun's left hand slap his calf a split-second before her right one unhooked his ankles from around her middle. Offering up his own prayer to any gods that might be listening, Lann leaped from the vælkyrie's back.

Right before impact, he remembered her instructions and tried not to tense up. When he hit the soft and boggy ground he lowered his head and let his shoulder drop below him, in a move that Astrid had shown him many times in unarmed combat, rolling over and over in a loose ball until he came to a painful stop against something hard and unyielding that knocked all of the air out of him in one explosive *whoosh*. Winded and unable to breathe, panic gripped him, until suddenly his lungs sprang back to life and he gratefully sucked in one enormous breath after another.

Shaking all over, he gingerly got to his feet, amazed that he was not gravely injured. Lifting a hand to the right side of his forehead, he felt out the most painful of his wounds: a gash just above his hairline that was leaking blood down the side of his face. Happy that it wasn't too deep, he applied pressure to it and cast his eyes about for Sigrun, spotting her struggling to her feet a short distance away.

Something was clearly wrong with her left wing. Unlike its mate, it wouldn't fold up neatly behind her any more, and he noticed the painful grimace on her face as she moved it. He also saw how her left boot was dark with blood. High up on her left thigh a piece of wood had become lodged in the flesh. He watched as she reached down, carefully exploring the area, but she made no attempt to remove the alien object. Lann was on the point of calling over to her when she turned to face him and shot him a fearful warning look, placing a finger to her lips. The vælkyrie carefully drew her weapon, nodding for him to do the same.

He did so as slowly and quietly as he could, taking the opportunity to assess his surroundings for the first time.

The grey miasma overhead did not make it all the way down to ground level, but hung instead just above their heads, giving Lann an uncomfortable feeling of claustrophobia – as if it might press down and swallow him up at any moment. There was a muddy, swampy stench to the place that made Lann's stomach churn. Though the mist blocked out the sky, it was not completely dark, thanks to the strange, dimly glowing plants that grew here, one of which Lann had to thank for stopping his hazardous tumbling. He stared at it. The tree – if that's what it was – grew up just into the first layer of mist. Its short, fat trunk was topped with bulbous crowns about the size of a person's head, from which sprouted thousands of fine and delicate hair-like tendrils that hung down to the floor, emitting a sickly green glow as they swayed gently to and fro. The light from the plants dotted here and there was meagre, however, and did not radiate very far. Lann found himself straining to make out any details in the shadowy emptiness between him and where Sigrun stood.

The Stil was as eerie as the Rød had been bizarre. The silence that pervaded the place was unsettling. Despite their efforts, their crash landings had made a considerable din, but so far he could see no obvious sign of the danger the vælkyrie had alluded to.

Movement at the edge of his vision made him turn to look back at Sigrun. Bathed in shadows, the vælkyrie silently pointed ahead before setting off in that direction, limping badly on her injured leg. She'd taken no more than a few steps, however, when she tripped and fell, catching her damaged wing as she did. Her cry of pain was the first spoken sound Lann had heard since they'd landed in the Stil and it triggered an instant response.

The thing that attacked the vælkyrie appeared suddenly out of the darkness behind her, moving with a terrifying ruthlessness and speed. Pale and thin, the creature appeared to have no eyes, just two huge pointed ears that almost met above its head, and it made no sound as it ran straight for Sigrun, its mouth open in a silent scream that revealed rows of deadly teeth. It swept out a hand, aiming to rake its claws across her chest and throat, and would have done so had the vælkyrie not twisted away at the last second. Instead, the creature's talons swiped the vambrace she wore on the forearm of her sword hand, causing her to lose her grip on her weapon.

Whilst she'd avoided that first attack, the vælkyrie was now at the creature's mercy. It turned back towards her, both taloned hands stretched out. Lann was already running, the Dreadblade alive in his hand, and he was surprised not to hear it screaming in his head to be about its business. For once, he would have welcomed the noise. Nevertheless, his heart soared with the familiar feeling of exhilaration as the ancient weapon's power surged though him. Leaping forward, he thrust at the thing with all his might, burying his sword into its torso up to the hilt. The creature groped blindly at the blade jutting out of its front, pawing at the dark metal before collapsing. Lann reacted to a silent warning from the dark blade. Almost as if the sword were moving his arms, he spun on his heel and issued a small grunt as he swung the weapon in a short chopping arc that carved an ugly wound through the midriff of another oncoming creature. A gout of dark blood spattered his face. Blinking and swiping away the gore, he cleared his vision in time to see Sigrun, back on her feet now and reunited with her sword, dispatch the last of the monsters, her blade scything through its shoulder in a diagonal strike that almost cut the creature in half.

The vælkyrie turned to stare back at him, her chest rising and falling with the effort of the silent battle. A half-smile formed on her lips and she raised her weapon in the now familiar salute, nodding as Lann echoed the gesture. Without another sound they set out across the Stil.

Hasz

13

Kelewulf struggled to contain his frustration as he made his way back up the steep stairs from the underbelly of the citadel, pausing near the top to wipe some of the grime and cobwebs from his face and clothes. It was a national day of mourning in Hasz, during which the emperor was to be interred in the crypt beneath his palace. Knowing the citadel would be as good as empty, Kelewulf had feigned illness and stayed put rather than going out into the city with everybody else. A simple shadow-blend spell that he'd picked up from Master Shintal – in one of the few lessons the man had not been droning on about gölems – had made it easy for him to slip past the few guards and household members left, and he'd used the time to finally explore the citadel properly.

He was on the lookout for anything that might suggest where the heart could be. He'd ransacked rooms he'd been told never to enter; searched a few of the masters' personal lodgings and their possessions; and finished by taking in the caverns beneath the stronghold, squeezing through dark and dingy spaces that were filled with discarded piles of junk and in which rats and worms and spiders had set themselves up as the exclusive residents.

He'd found nothing.

Moving through the empty refectory, he sat down at one of the benches to gather his thoughts.

How could there be no clue as to the whereabouts of something as precious and powerful as the dark god's heart? It wasn't possible. In this place, a place that prided itself on keeping and guarding the secrets and knowledge of Hasz, there should be *something*.

He'd been told the thing was here in these lands some-where, but it was becoming clear now that the lich had lied, and the heart had never been in Hasz. Why had Yirgan deceived him and brought him here? Could it have been with the sole purpose of freeing himself from Kelewulf and finding a way back to his people? Could the lich have been so cunning and conniving that it had been plotting to do so from the moment they'd met? But if that *had* been the plan, then it had been undone at the first stroke, when Mamur had made it clear there was no place for the former mage here in Hasz.

Since freeing the lich that day, Kelewulf's power over the sorcerer's undead soul was not as strong as it had been, and using Yirgan's summoning powers against Alwa had only loosened the chains further. He could *feel* the thing, eager to be given more freedom, at the edge of his mind. And that mental itch, an itch he was trying so hard not to scratch, was muddying his thinking. Just this morning he'd wondered if he should talk to the lich and ask it why it was so adamant the heart was here. Thankfully, his distrust of Yirgan had overruled his frustration, and he'd dismissed the idea. Even so, his own shortcomings in finding clues as to the whereabouts of the heart weighed on him.

Was his failure to find the thing he sought really the true source of his vexation, though? And why had he started to have feelings of doubt about everything he thought was wrong with the world? Why had he started to harbour these uncertainties – questioning his motives, his will and, most importantly, his desire to find the object. Was he truly committed to obtaining the heart? And if he did, was he capable of using it to bring Lorgukk back to this realm?

Or could he make a life here, in Hasz? Elafir had accepted him. Why shouldn't he continue his studies and create something new for himself?

Sitting on the bench, his mind swirling with these questions and emotions, he felt the anger rise up in him. The anger was good – it was a fiery, righteous reaction that felt so much more familiar to him than the self-pitying, querulous feelings it replaced. Kelewulf knew that the anger was not entirely his own, and against all his better judgement he gave the furious lich its voice:

If you give up now, what was the point in everything you've sacrificed to be here? Look at what you have sacrificed already! You turned away from your family, your place in society, your very happiness. If you stop searching for the heart, all of that work will have been squandered. And for what? For her? Elafir? For a few parlour tricks – some spells that you might have been able to master from a book somewhere? Would they be worth all that?

'No.'

We have come too far together. Think of what you've had to do to become the person you are now. You poisoned your uncle and tried to have your cousin, your only friend in the world, hanged for the crime. You almost killed yourself with the effort creating that portal in Vorneland. You have risked life and limb getting to this damned citadel. Why? What did you want?

'A new start.'

Yes! A new start, but not just for you. You – we – wanted a new start for this world. A cleansing. That was what we discussed. That was what we agreed! This world is a bad place, and it needs purging. And the people need to be purged along with it. Humanity is responsible for everything that's bad about the world, and they need to be made to see that. And if some of them have to perish in order for that to happen,

197

so be it. That was what you said to yourself after your mother died. Do you remember?

'I do,' he said, speaking the words aloud to the empty room.

You can't give up. We can't let the world win.

'We? I don't think of us as we any more, lich. You tried to take me over.'

I made a mistake, a terrible mistake. But I will make things up to you, if you let me. I know what I did was wrong. Just as I know that you are the master, and I am your ...

'My what?'

Your slave.

'No. Not that. I have seen what it is to be a slave during my time here.'

There was a pause and then the lich spoke again. *A partner then. Not an equal partner.* The lich let out a sigh inside Kelewulf's head. *Please, give me one last chance to show you that I can work with you. Let me—*

'Be quiet!' Kelewulf pushed the lich back down into the darkness in the depths of his mind.

Getting to his feet, he wiped his hands one last time against his purple robes and headed off to Master Larghal's rooms to pick up the book the old man had promised to find for him. Perhaps the heart wasn't here in Hasz. But even if that were true, there were things he could take from this place that would help to make his vision for a new world come true. And one of those things was a spell that might be advantageous to him should he ever encounter the Dreadblade again.

The library was its usual chaos of books and manuscripts, but it felt oddly smaller without Larghal sitting up at his high desk in the centre. Kelewulf made his way over to the two crates that sat beside it: one for requested resources, the other for returns. Sure enough, in the first crate was a small scroll, along with a square of parchment bearing Kelewulf's name. Grabbing the document, Kelewulf turned to leave when the lich's voice, small and submissive, whispered in his head.

Look at the book in the returns crate.

He did so, scanning it for anything unusual. A hefty tome, it only just fitted inside the box. The outer cover was plain black leather with a motif stamped into the spine, but there was no title to suggest what it was about.

'What am looking at?'

I recognise that book. Look inside.

Kelewulf was wary. 'What are you up to? I warned you—'

No tricks. I'm not up to anything. I'm just trying to show you how I might be a useful partner. That's all.

Kelewulf hesitated, then took the volume out of the box, cradling its weight in one arm as he opened it with the other. 'It's a book about potions and poisons …' Even as the words left his lips, he was wondering about the significance of them. He peered down at the cream-coloured pages, the slightly musty waft of them filling his nose.

The ribbon that marks a page – where has it been placed?

Frowning, Kelewulf closed the book and turned to its top edge to see that a black ribbon had indeed been positioned between two of the leaves. Resting the book on the floor, he flipped the pages until he found it. The first thing he noticed was the orange-brown smudge on the edge of the right-hand page. He dabbed at it gently and tentatively sniffed his fingers, wrinkling his nose at the bitter smell.

That smudge mark is fellden root. When ground down into a powder, the stains it leaves behind are almost impossible to get out. Take a look at the full recipe. Not only is fellden root an ingredient, but some of the other components are rather interesting.

'In what way, interesting?' Kelewulf remembered Elafir identifying the root as one of the components in whatever had been used to poison Mamur. Suddenly intrigued, he scanned his eyes over the rest of the ingredients.

Redian arogo? There, towards the bottom? That only grows in one place as far as I'm aware.

'And where is that?' It was unusual for the lich to be silent at any time he gave it a voice, but it remained so now. 'Yirgan?'

Why should I tell you?

'What do you mean?'

Why should I do anything to help somebody who treats me the way you do? A prisoner with no rights. We had something special between us, Kelewulf, we had—

'If there was anything "special" between us, it was you who wrecked it when you broke our bond and tried to take this body over for yourself.' Kelewulf was unable to disguise the tone of regret in his voice.

A strange sound, like a long sigh, filled his head. *I did, and I was wrong to do so. I say that not just because I am now in the position I am, but because I have come to understand what might have been, had I not been so foolish. My only defence for what I did is that I have spent an eternity inside that phylactery waiting for somebody to free me. When you finally did I chose to ignore the sacrifice that you'd made, and instead sought to recapture the power and the glory I once had as a living creature. I ruined the chance I was given because I forgot that I have already had my time in the living world. Forgive me.*

The lich's tone, plus the genuine feeling of remorse that permeated through Kelewulf as the undead sorcerer's spirit spoke, took the young necromancer by surprise.

'Where is Redian arogo found, lich?'

Rishtok. The Rishtoks used to dip their arrows in the stuff when waging war.

Kelewulf's mind spun at this news. Rishtok was the region of Hasz that Elafir had spoken to him about recently. It was where Grad'ur's family originally came from; where his grandfather had been a military leader.

'Grad'ur poisoned the emperor.' Kelewulf whispered the words, shaking his head as he tried to take this in.

It would seem so.

What do we do now?

We? I thought there was no 'we'?

Kelewulf could hardly believe what he was about to say. 'You asked for another chance?'

I did. I do.

'Well, I am offering that chance to you now, lich. Wait,' he said as the lich went to respond. 'There will be no tricks and deceits this time. We are *not* partners, but neither are you my slave. You will serve me, not yourself, do you understand? In return I will give you the freedom you desire and stop shutting you away. I am offering you the opportunity to be a part of whatever the future holds for me, nothing more. That is the new deal I am offering you. And with it comes a dire warning: try to take control again, try to wheedle your way into my mind when I'm asleep as you did before, and I'll put you back in that phylactery I found you in, and burn it.'

No tricks.

'Think carefully before you respond, Yirgan.'

I understand the terms of your offer and I accept them.

'Welcome back.'

Thank you.

'What should I do about this?' Kelewulf said, gesturing down at the page again.

We need to be strategic, find a way to use it to our – your – advantage. Do not act too impetuously.

Weighing the lich's warning, Kelewulf got to his feet, clutching the book to his chest. 'I need to tell Elafir.'

The high priestess sat across from Kelewulf and listened to his news. When he'd finished, she remained in her seat, staring out into space with an expression that was impossible to read. She stayed like that long enough for Kelewulf to squirm a little in his seat.

Eventually she rose and moved to stand in the coloured light coming in through the stained window of her rooms. 'I will have him arrested and demand that a trial is held as soon as possible.'

'It's only a smudge in a book. Is that enough evidence to have him—?'

'Grad'ur will try to wheedle his way out of the charges,' she went on, as if she had not heard him. 'The people who support his bid to take the imperial throne will do everything they can to move the blame on to somebody else.' She turned her head in his direction. 'You will have to testify.'

'Me?'

'Of course.'

'Why? All I did was find a book that contained a recipe to make a poison.'

'A poison that was used to kill the emperor.'

'That's not certain.'

The high priestess waved this away. 'As a foreigner, your evidence will not carry the same weight as if you were Hasz'een, but I will speak to the court on your behalf and vouch for your character.'

'Elafir, please, I don't think I'd be—'

'I don't care what you think, Kelewulf. Your testimony in this matter is not up for debate!'

Elafir was staring at him in a way he had not seen since that first night he'd been brought before her, and he did not like the dangerous edge to her voice.

He answered her with a small shrug. 'What will be the sentence? If Grad'ur is found guilty?'

'He'll be flayed alive.' She turned her back on him and stared out of the window once more. 'It is the traditional punishment for anyone found guilty of murdering or conspiring to murder a member of the imperial family.'

'Flayed? Y-you mean he'll be skinned? While he's ... still conscious?' Kelewulf tried not to imagine the horrors of such a death, but a shiver ran through him nevertheless.

'Afterwards his skin will be hung over the entrance to the imperial palace for everyone in the city to see.'

'Does he have any recourse to a quicker death? Something that satisfies justice without a punishment like … that?'

The high priestess shook her head. She signalled that their meeting was at an end by moving to open the door. 'I will send someone to fetch you when the time for the hearing is set. Hopefully it should be no more than a day or so.' She paused, then added, 'Until then, I think it would be best if you stayed in your rooms. I'll post a guard outside to make sure you're not disturbed and arrange for your meals to be brought to you.'

Kelewulf fancied he understood the hidden message in her words. 'Am I in danger?' he asked.

'We're all in danger right now.'

The Murrke

14

There was almost nothing by which to gauge time or distance in the dark mist-covered world that Lann and Sigrun were making their way through. They walked quickly and in silence, making every effort not to step on or bump into anything that would give their position away. The going, however, was anything but easy. The air was wet and cold, soaking both the land and those who ventured through it. Their clothes stuck to their skin and their sodden hair hung down into their faces.

It was only when their surroundings gradually began to change from boggy marsh to sparsely populated woodland landscape that Lann noticed the vælkyrie's demeanour shift. A short time later Sigrun blew out her cheeks and turned to him, speaking for the first time since their fateful arrival.

'We have left the Stil. Those things, the drishte, will not follow us here. This region is inhabited only by draugr.'

Lann glanced behind him. 'They … they didn't have any eyes.'

'No. Drishte hunt by sound alone. We were very lucky to encounter only the few we did. I suspect many of them had been deliberately drawn away.' She cast her eyes downwards, a grim look on her face.

'Göll.' He remembered the vælkyrie's final words to them, and how she said she would create a diversion. 'Do you think you'll ever see her again?'

She turned her face away from him. 'You saw how deadly the drishte were. We two were doing our utmost to be silent, and we almost perished at their hands. Göll was alone, and doing her best to attract their attention.'

He offered Sigrun a sad smile as his thoughts turned again to his own friend and her rescue. He wondered if Astrid was OK, and if she was as scared and bewildered as he was. Once more, he silently scolded himself for letting her accompany him and putting her in danger in the way he had. He would never forgive himself if anything—

The vælkyrie reached out a hand and placed it on his shoulder. 'Back there –' she gestured in the direction from which they had just come – 'when I was at that creature's mercy … You saved my life. I will not forget that, Lannigon Gudbrandr.'

Embarrassed, he gave a little shrug and turned the sword in his hand, looking at those strange symbols on the surface of the blade. 'I had some help. How is your wing?' he asked, pointing at the limb that was still folded at an odd angle behind her back.

'It is broken. But it will heal in time. My leg is worse.' Lann joined the vælkyrie in looking down at the large shard of wood that was still buried deep in her thigh. Blood continued to ooze out around the foreign object, but he knew how much worse the bleeding would be if she tried to remove it. 'It is likely to get infected in this miserable place. I can only hope—'

The sound of a horn stopped her words. It was a high, sharp note that, to Lann at least, seemed to come from everywhere at once in the weird acoustics of the Murrke. Sigrun, however, seemed to have no trouble in homing in on its source. She stared directly ahead of her, into the trees.

'My sisters have found the draugr. Come!' With that, the vælkyrie sprang forward, somehow ignoring the pain of her injury and stretching out her long legs to run-limp at a pace Lann found difficult to match, ducking beneath low-hanging branches and jumping over exposed roots that seemed intent on reaching up and grabbing his feet and ankles.

It was not long before the vælkyrie raised a hand, slowing down and signalling for him to do likewise.

The mist seemed to lift a fraction as they entered a small clearing in the trees. At the centre was a huge stump, its top perfectly flat, as if it had been cut with one colossal blow from an enormous blade. Lying across this crude altar, her hands and feet secured by rope to iron rings set into the wood, was Astrid. She was deathly pale and unmoving. Lann's heart clenched hard inside him until he spotted the tiny up-and-down movements of her chest beneath her clothing.

Around her were six draugr who had arranged themselves in a tight circle facing outwards. The formation had been chosen so they could see the vælkyrie, who were creeping slowly towards them from all directions through the edge of the clearing.

The mere of the draugr filled Lann with revulsion and fear, although he did his best to stifle this latter emotion, knowing he would need to if he was to be of any use to Astrid.

The dead human bodies the creatures had taken possession of back in the human realm were in various states of decay and dishevelment. But all were horrifying to behold. Torn and ruined clothing still hung from some of the bodies, whilst others were almost naked. Of the six, only one appeared to have been young – perhaps a few years older than Lann – when its corpse had been possessed. The draugr that had taken over the dead body of Sebastien's mother was among them, Astrid's dagger still buried in its shoulder.

Lann noted how the ground – particularly that around the altar – was churned up, as if a struggle had recently taken place. Scraps of clothing littered the area too, but of most interest was the dismembered arm that lay among the detritus. Another glance at the creatures revealed that the limb had only too recently been attached to one of the draugr.

'They have been fighting over the spoils,' Sigrun said in a low voice. 'They all wish to be the one to possess your friend's body at the moment she passes.'

'Then they will all be disappointed, won't they?' The Dreadblade made a baleful sound in its wielder's head, and Lann felt the familiar energy of the weapon course through him anew.

'Remember, Lannigon Gudbrandr, the bodies these draugr inhabit were already dead back in your world, so do not expect they can be killed in the usual way,' the vælkyrie warned. 'Not only that, but the Murrke is a place of ancient power and they can feed off its strength.'

Lann kept his eyes fixed on the particular draugr he'd followed here, noting how the creature kept glancing round behind it at Astrid, an ugly and greedy look on the parts of its face that still remained.

'We do not have long,' Sigrun said. 'The draugr can sense it too.'

It seemed to Lann that a fight with such depleted, rotting creatures could only be a short-lived one with the might of so many of Sigrun's allies at hand, and he wondered why the vælkyrie were being so cautious in their approach.

As if on cue, at some unspoken signal, the vælkyrie gave a collective shout and ran forward. The fastest of them had nearly closed the distance between herself and the nearest draugr, her twin swords raised to strike, when something extraordinary happened. Lann stared in fear and fascination as the monster quickly started to grow in height and bulk. Its bones seemed to thicken and stretch, and where any flesh remained on its body muscle began to form until it had almost doubled in size. With a roar, the draugr stepped forward to meet its attacker.

Sigrun's battle cry filled Lann's ears at the same time as the Dreadblade's flooded his mind.

Nir-akuu!

All of the draugr were growing now, their dead, black eyes staring out at the vælkyrie in an unvoiced challenge, a challenge that was taken up by the guardians of the Rød, who swarmed towards them as one.

The dark sword's power surging through him, Lann took up the call to arms, angling for the monster with the dagger in its shoulder. But as the creature's eyes met his, he almost faltered at the darkness he saw there. He had felt that same terrifying nothingness when he'd dared look out at the Blakk whilst riding on Sigrun's back – and with the recognition came an understanding that it was Lorgukk's influence that was giving the draugr the power to transform. Pushing back at the fear as best he could, he continued forward. There was no time for thought now, no time for alarm. Not when Astrid was close to death!

Latva's draugr waited until Lann was almost upon it before it swept out a hand, clawing the air in front of his face and making him twist and dip to avoid the black talons. But the swiping blow had only been a feint. Stepping forward and bringing its arm up, the creature smashed its elbow flush into Lann's jaw, sending him staggering. His ears rang as the coppery taste of blood filled his mouth, and the world dimmed as he struggled to push back the grey curtains of unconsciousness. To his left, he was aware that Sigrun had moved forward to draw the draugr's attention and give him the precious time he needed to recover his senses.

Shaking his head clear, he spat red on to the ground and rejoined the fight.

Sigrun's injuries were hampering her ability to move properly, and it was obvious to Lann that she was trying not to put too much weight on her injured leg. The draugr saw it too. It feinted an attack, and as the vælkyrie brandished her sword in a defensive parry the creature wrapped its hand around the blade, heedless of the damage the honed edge was inflicting as Sigrun tried to yank it free. A severed finger flew into the air, but the creature seemed to feel no pain. Lann cried out a warning as he watched the beast kick out, but it came too late. The draugr's foot connected with Sigrun's wounded leg and the shard of wood that was buried there. Her scream of pain was horrible to hear.

With Sigrun's sword blade still locked in its ruined hand, the draugr used the other to grab her hair, wrenching her head back to expose her neck.

'NO!' Lann bellowed as he hurried to her aid.

He was almost upon the creature when he remembered Sigrun's warning. Originally intending to stab forward with his sword, he instead changed his grip on the Dreadblade, lowering it to his side with the tip almost grazing the ground as he ducked beneath a clumsily aimed blow. Tucking and rolling, he ended in a crouch behind the creature and brought the blade round in a sweeping motion to sever the tendons at the back of the creature's legs and send it crashing down on to its knees.

'The head!' Sigrun shouted. 'You have to remo—'

Her words were cut short when the Dreadblade, almost moving of its own volition now, swung round to carve through the rotten flesh above the shoulders and send the draugr's head tumbling. No blood came from the horrendous wound, and the decapitated body had returned to its former withered and shrunken state even before it collapsed into the dirt.

Helping Sigrun back to her feet, Lann glanced about him at the numerous skirmishes taking place. Two more of the draugr had already been killed, and the vælkyrie, more organised in their support of each other, clearly had the upper hand. But even outnumbered and surrounded on all sides, the dire undead creatures refused to surrender.

'Your leg,' Lann said to Sigrun, staring at the blood that was now pouring from the wound. He moved to see if there was some way he could stop the flow.

'Leave me,' Sigrun said, shrugging him loose and staring in Astrid's direction as if she could sense something he could not. 'Go to the girl. She is close to death! The moment they have been waiting for is near. Any one of the remaining draugr will try to enter her body in her last seconds. Cut her loose of that altar and get her away from here!' These last words were shouted to him because Lann was already moving towards his friend. One of the remaining draugr moved to intercept him, but Hildur saw and barrelled into the beast, her shoulder crashing into its legs as she tackled it to the ground and out of his path.

'Go!' Hildur shouted. She was joined by Sigrun, the second vælkyrie jumping on to the creature to help stop it from getting back to its feet.

Lann cut the ropes securing Astrid's legs, but she remained unmoving on the wooden platform. It was as he leaned across to cut the ties on her arms that he heard

214

the ugly rasping noise come from her lips. It was a noise he'd heard often when his aunt had taken him to attend the sick on their deathbeds. Fleya had called it the *siste pusht*, the last breath, and the sound was greeted by a roar of triumph from the remaining draugr – a signal that it thought its moment had come.

'No. Astrid! ASTRID!!' Lann put his hand to her face, not knowing what to do as he watched the life ebb out of her.

It was the Dreadblade's voice filling his head that brought him back from the brink of despair. The harshly shouted instruction was so loud that he struggled to understand it at first: *Din ir mae förtur! DIN IR MAE FÖRTUR!*

Grabbing his friend's hand, he laid the dark sword flat across her body and wrapped her fingers around the handle, holding them there with his own, blinking away the tears that came to his eyes. 'Help her,' he whispered. 'Please!'

The words had no sooner left his lips than the pictograms on the sword flared so brightly that Lann was forced to turn his head to one side as a spasm shook the Strom shield maiden, her body bucking violently as if it had been struck by a fork of lightning. Stumbling a little, Lann looked down at her again. Astrid had her eyes open impossibly wide, staring straight up into the mist overhead as she sucked in a great gasping breath of air. Somewhere

215

behind him he heard the last remaining draugr's roar cut short with what must have been the death blow from a vælkyrie blade.

A strange quiet – like the sinister silence of the Stil – followed. Not knowing what else to do or say, Lann returned his hand to rest over his friend's, and this time the contact seemed to register with her. Her eyes slowly lost that dreadful faraway stare and turned to focus on him instead. Reaching out with her free hand, she traced his features with her fingers.

'You brought me back from death, Lann,' she said, her voice little more than a whisper.

'I had some help with that,' he croaked in response.

The familiar feeling that had started as soon as he'd pressed the dark sword into Astrid's hand was growing inside him. It was the roiling fear that he'd felt in those first few seconds in this realm, when the dark blade had been out of his grasp. But now it was worse – as if great icy worms of panic were writhing inside of him, filling him up. It was so insidious that he cried out in alarm when Sigrun appeared at his side.

'You two must leave this place and return to your own realm,' she said, peering at him with concern. 'The blade is shielding Astrid as long as she holds it. But the protection it gives cannot be shared – you are the one in danger now. We must get you both to the Rød. Then we must get you home.'

Astrid gingerly got to her feet, still clutching the sword awkwardly in front of her with both hands, keeping the tip pointed at the ground between her feet as if she had never held a weapon before. Pale and exhausted, she wavered on the spot like a drunk.

Along with the dread he was experiencing, rolling waves of physical pain had begun to rack Lann's body now, making it hard for him to concentrate on anything but remaining upright. When his legs gave out beneath him, he would have fallen to the ground had Sigrun not caught him around the waist. Orders were shouted, and the vælkyrie hurried in their preparations to evacuate Lann and Astrid back to the Rød. Despite all of them being wounded and exhausted, they quickly formed a chain that would enable them to carry the two young people up into the sky.

Lann drifted off into oblivion just as his body was lifted from the ground, and the feeling of weightlessness was the last thing he remembered.

Hasz

15

The court hearing to judge Grad'ur's guilt or innocence was held in a large hall within the imperial palace. It was almost as impressive as the throne room, Kelewulf thought. It felt ironic that the last time he had talked to the nobleman, Grad'ur had been sitting on the imperial throne itself, free to interrogate Kelewulf about the high priestess and her own ambitions to occupy the seat. Now he was in a cage, and to judge by the cuts and bruises on his hands and face, he had not gone into it willingly. The accused's clothing was bloodstained, and his hands were bound with leather thongs that bit into the flesh of his wrists. Most shocking was the ugly, metal-and-leather contraption around the lower half of his face that forced his mouth shut and stopped him from speaking.

Kelewulf was the third witness to be called. The previous two were members of the royal court who had testified as to how Grad'ur had moved up through the ranks of the elite, and how he had made no secret of his wish to become the next emperor. They had delivered their statements in a way that suggested the man was a ruthless manipulator of people who craved power at all cost.

The caged nobleman glowered at Kelewulf as he was called up to take his place in the witness box. Entering the small wooden stall, the young necromancer took the opportunity to cast his eyes out over the great throng of people gathered to watch the proceedings, noticing how so many of them were dressed in the fine clothing of the city's wealthy elite.

'You are new to these lands, I understand?' the chief inquisitor, a tall, thin man dressed in long grey robes, asked him after he'd been introduced to the judges and the court.

'I am.'

'And you had never met the accused before coming to Hasz, is that right?'

'It is.'

'So you have no axe to grind with this man?'

'I'm sorry, what do you mean?'

'You have no hidden agenda, you bear him no … animosity.'

'I do not.'

The man nodded and crossed to a table, picking up the black book Kelewulf had found.

'You are responsible for discovering *this*, are you not?' the chief inquisitor asked, holding the item aloft so the crowds could see it.

'I was.'

'And where did you find it?'

'In Master Larghal's library, at the citadel.'

'You just happened to find it by chance? A lucky discovery? Some people might find that a little hard to believe.'

Kelewulf had to suppress the anger the man's tone and manner stirred up in him. Instead, he tried to remember the advice Elafir had given to him just before he had been brought to the courtroom: simply to tell the truth, nothing more.

'I was in the library collecting a manuscript that Master Larghal had left for me. I saw the book and started to flick through it.'

When questioned about how he knew that the book might contain the instructions to make the deadly poison, he answered that he had not known, and that he'd merely moved to the last marked page and discovered the recipe and the smudge.

'This page?' the man said, opening the volume and turning it so that first the judges, then the crowd, could see it. 'And this ... smudge –' the man pointed to the orange-brown smear at the bottom of the page – 'alarmed you. Why?'

'I had overheard the high priestess saying that the poison used on His Imperial Highness Mamur had contained fellden root. When I saw the smudge on that page, I realised it had been made by a powdered form of that ingredient.' It was a small lie, telling the man he'd overheard Elafir talking about the fellden root, when in fact Kelewulf and the high priestess had talked about it freely. But they'd agreed it was best that people didn't know how open she'd been with a person under her tutelage.

'Some people in this court might think it odd that something as unremarkable as a brown smudge led you to report your concerns to the high priestess.'

'It wasn't just the mark on the page. The other ingredients that are needed to produce the toxin caught my eye and made me think I needed to tell somebody.'

'Hmm. Please tell the court what specifically it was in the recipe for this terrible poison that made you do just that.'

'The Redian arogo.'

'And why is that unusual?'

'It is only grows in one place. Rishtok.'

A sly and humourless smile crept over the inquisitor's face. He turned away from his witness and addressed the crowd. 'Rishtok! The region that the man in the cage behind me would call "home". An ingredient that can only be obtained in that place.' He turned back to Kelewulf and excused him from the witness stand.

Kelewulf returned to his seat. He knew that his evidence was not enough to find Grad'ur guilty. It was, at best, circumstantial. The only link between the recipe and Grad'ur was an ingredient that happened to come from his birthplace, and whilst it *was* an uncommon plant stuff, it wasn't impossible that someone else might have obtained it. Kelewulf's inclusion in these proceedings did not sit well with him, and, as the next witness was called, he found himself wishing he'd never managed to become embroiled in the whole affair.

The young woman was one of Grad'ur's servants. When she took her place in the witness box her hands were visibly shaking and she was unable to make eye contact with anyone in the room, let alone the man in the cage. Instead, she kept her eyes fixed on a patch of floor in the centre of the space while the inquisitor asked her questions about her time in the nobleman's household and how long she had been in his service. Seemingly satisfied, the inquisitor walked back over to the table of evidence. Taking his time and enjoying the theatre of the proceeding, he made a show of looking for something there. Finding it, he nodded an apology to the judges. This time he lifted up a garment. It was folded neatly, but even so it was clearly an expensive and lavish costume, something only a person of means could afford to wear.

'Do you recognise this robe?' he asked. 'You will need to look at it, young lady.'

The servant raised her eyes and nodded. 'Yes.'

'And who does it belong to?'

'M-my master.'

'And how can you be certain it is the accused's garment, and not a similar one that belongs to somebody else?'

'It has his family crest on the collar.'

'Ah! Indeed it has,' the inquisitor said, pointing out the intricate embroidery work to the court. Then, with a flourish, he shook the garment out to reveal it in its entirety.

The gesture drew a collective gasp from the assembly. The hubbub that followed went on for some time, until one of the three judges loudly banged a wooden hammer and demanded quiet.

Kelewulf was staring at the tunic too. The orange-brown stains on the front and sides, as if somebody had wiped their hands down it, were unmistakeable.

'Where did you find this robe?' the inquisitor asked the servant. The young woman was now on the verge of tears.

'In a bag of things that my master had –' she paused, trying to gather herself – 'had ordered me to dispose of.'

More gasps rang around the place, and once more the judges were obliged to bring the court to order.

Kelewulf glanced across to where he thought Elafir had chosen to sit, only to discover the high priestess seemed to have left. He scanned the court, hoping to see her face somewhere in the crowd, but there was no sign of her. Why would she not have stayed here to lend him her support? It was, after all, her idea that he testify at all, and the two of them had prepared at length for how he might be questioned and what his responses could be. He tried to quash his disappointment and returned his attention to the proceedings.

After the servant girl's testimony, the inquisitor made his case against the nobleman, explaining how the pieces of evidence against him, if taken individually, could be viewed as incidental, but that, when considered together, they proved without doubt that Grad'ur was guilty.

Kelewulf watched the caged nobleman throughout the man's summing-up. He continually twisted his head back and forth, his muffled groans escaping around the edges of the gagging device. When the inquisitor reminded the court of how the nobleman had asked his servant to dispose of the garments, Grad'ur slammed his forehead into the bars of his cage hard enough to break the skin, so that blood ran down his face and started dripping from his chin.

The three elderly judges left the courthouse to consider their judgement. They were not gone for long. When they returned to their seats, they peered down at the caged nobleman with pitiless expressions that Kelewulf thought could not bode well for Grad'ur. The judge in the middle seat announced their verdict.

'Grad'ur of Rishtok, having heard all the evidence against you, we find you guilty of the murder of our Imperial Majesty, Emperor Mamur.' The man gave a little sniff and turned to his partners, nodding to each in turn, and Kelewulf watched as they performed the bizarre ritual of tying lengths of white cloth around their eyes. Once they were all blindfolded in this way, the head judge spoke again. 'The punishment for this heinous crime is grave: you will be flayed alive and your treacherous pelt hung from the doors of the royal palace as a warning to others. The punishment is to take place immediately.'

Even though all those present knew the price that would be paid for the crime, cries still echoed around the court. Grad'ur was to die a terrible death at the hands of the people he'd hoped to rule. As the judges removed their blindfolds, the guilty man was hauled from the cage.

Kelewulf had no desire to watch the horrors to which the nobleman was about to be subjected. Pushing his way through the crowds, he made his way outside and stood on the steps of the palace, breathing deeply of the fresh air and watching the last of the daylight fade away. It was like this, leaning against the sun-warmed wall, slightly obscured in shadow, that he spotted Elafir's personal servant, Hrol, slip out of the courtroom and hurry away.

Somebody seems rather nervous, don't you think? the lich whispered inside his head.

It was true, the man looked decidedly on edge, glancing about him regularly. He was dressed oddly for the weather too; his hood was pulled low over his face and he was wearing gloves, as if he were going out into the cold, not a balmy evening's warmth. Kelewulf's interest was piqued, but it was more than that. There was something about the whole affair surrounding Grad'ur and the murder of the emperor that bothered him. 'Damn it,' he whispered under his breath. 'I'm going to follow him.' He started to walk in the direction Hrol was hurrying in.

Careful.

'Of what?'

Like you, I feel uneasy about this poisoning business. It's clear that our mute friend has no desire to be spied upon. Use the shadow-blend spell you did back at the citadel that day.

Kelewulf hesitated when he remembered how exhausting it was to maintain a shadow-blend for any period of time. The spell required much of the person who cast it.

Do you want to follow this man or not? the lich said inside his head.

When Hrol took a turn into a small passageway, hurrying between tall buildings on either side, Kelewulf realised he

226

had no choice but to do as the lich suggested if he wasn't to be spotted. He cleared his mind and intoned the words of the spell, drawing on memories of darkness and shade as he drew the symbol he'd been taught in the air in front of him. The spell had dramatic and immediate effects. The first was a combination of things: a strange feeling of becoming 'thinner', almost as if he were suddenly occupying less space in the world, accompanied by a dimming of his vision, so that now he stared out on to a duskier version of the scene that had filled his eyes moments before. The second side-effect was even less welcome: a sudden, horrible shortness of breath, as if the air in his lungs had become as insubstantial as he himself had.

Kelewulf was a short distance behind the slave when he had good reason to be grateful he'd listened to the lich's advice. Hrol came to a stop, turning his head to peer behind him as if suddenly aware he was being pursued. Kelewulf stood perfectly still as the man's eyes passed over him, the servant pausing for just a moment as if trying to see something that wasn't there. Then, with a sniff and a shake of his head, Hrol turned his back and resumed his journey.

They had only gone a little distance further before the slave made a sharp right into one last, even narrower, backstreet, and finally came to a stop in front of a dilapidated old building that looked as if it had once been used as a food store. With one last look around, he entered through a ramshackle door and disappeared inside. The noise the door hinges made as they swung shut was enough to tell Kelewulf he had no hope of following him inside undetected. Besides, he was now so short of breath that his lungs were aching with the effort of pulling in air. The discomfort was so great that he had little option but to abandon the shadow-blend majik. Despite the terrible stink in the air of these poverty-stricken streets, the first deep breath he sucked in was nothing short of wonderful.

Scanning the building's walls for any kind of opening, he saw a thin window high up to one side that he thought he might be able to reach with the help of an old crate lying not too far away. Careful to be as quiet as he could, he clambered up on to his makeshift platform, hooking his fingers over the sill so he could pull himself up to peer inside.

Hrol was there with someone: a tall figure dressed in a cloak, the hood of which was pulled down to cover their face. The person in the robe was moving their hands anim-atedly, and Kelewulf watched as the servant started to wave his hands back in the unique, coordinated way he'd seen several of the attendants inside the citadel do. He knew it was a form of communication for those of them who'd had their tongues removed.

An exasperated sigh escaped the hooded figure. 'Take those damn gloves off, I can hardly understand what you're trying to say.'

Kelewulf's breath caught in his throat. The voice was unmistakeably Elafir's. But what was she doing meeting up with her slave here, in a rundown shack in the paupers' quarter? He watched as Hrol peeled off the gloves, revealing the ugly brown colour of his hands and fingers.

It was a stain Kelewulf knew well. And so he should; he had just testified about it in the court. It was the same colour as the hand-shaped marks found on the discarded garments of the man currently being flayed alive not more than a stone's throw from this place!

The realisation struck him like a physical blow. *How can I have been so stupid?* he asked himself. Why, if Grad'ur had made those marks, was the stuff on his clothes but not on his skin? Kelewulf recalled how Grad'ur had slammed his head into the cage bars when the evidence of the stained clothing had been recalled. He had been holding out his bound hands before him, as if to make this exact point!

Elafir spoke to her servant again, mirroring her words in sign language. 'You had no right to kill Mamur in the way you did.'

Hrol went to reply, but he had barely formed his first shape when the high priestess cut him off.

'No! Do not try to say you did this for me. You did it for you. And you bungled it. Because of your poorly planned, badly executed crime, I was forced to dream up a way to frame Grad'ur. Thank goodness the boy Kelewulf was so

229

gullible that we could use him to clear ourselves of any suspicion.' She glared across at him. 'Do you think I wanted to risk exposing myself in this way? To dirty my hands and abandon the painstaking plans I have made. I was *this* close to taking that throne without the need for bloodshed! When you took it upon yourself to do what you did, you nearly brought the whole house of cards down on top of us!'

Again, the slave tried to answer by forming words with his hands, and again the woman cut him off before he could finish.

'Stop. You think ending slavery was my sole purpose in wanting to become empress? Are you truly that naive?' She paused before going on. 'You murdered Mamur because you thought the only hope to stop slavery in Hasz was to make certain I could take the throne. And because I have not only refused to reveal that you are the real killer, but also framed another man to die for your crime, you have made me an accomplice to the deed. The reason I insisted we meet here and not in my citadel is because there is no longer any place for you there. You are no longer in my employ.' She held a purse out to him, forcing the thing into his hands when he refused to take it. The man was crying and making low moaning sounds. 'You are to leave the city, never to return. Never.' Stepping forward, she grabbed the man's chin in her right hand, pulling his face up so that he stared straight up into her own. When she spoke, she enunciated each word slowly. 'If you do, I will have you killed before you make it through the outer walls. Do I make myself clear? DO I?'

The man managed a nod, but Elafir kept her grip on his face, staring into the slave's eyes as the tears still streamed down his cheeks.

Kelewulf could hardly believe what he was seeing. He did his best to unscramble both the jumble of thoughts and the different emotions he was experiencing. When he shifted his weight a little to try and take some of the pressure off his arms, the crate beneath him made a small creaking noise. It was the tiniest of sounds, but he saw the high priestess stiffen at it. Knowing all pretence at quiet was hopeless now, Kelewulf threw himself backwards at the precise moment Elafir swivelled her head towards the opening he'd been peering through. Dropping to the floor, the crate crashing down behind him, he winced as his knee twisted and sent a lancing pain up through his leg.

'Who's there?' he heard the high priestess call out. When she spoke again, it was clear she was addressing her ex-servant. 'You were followed, you fool! Get out there. If someone overheard us, we will both pay with our lives!'

Casting all thoughts of caution and stealth aside, he turned and ran, grimacing with each step. He turned the first corner just as the squeal of the door's rusted hinges registered in his ears. Forcing himself to greater speed up the cobblestone passageway, he glanced back only when he'd made it to the top and rejoined the main path, blending into a throng of people outside the royal palace. The crowd were in a state of high excitement and agitation, all of them pushing and shoving at each other as they stared up at the small balcony over the huge doors at the front.

Kelewulf saw the slave emerge from the passageway behind him. His hands were covered by the leather gloves once more, but now, held in one of them down by his side, was a short, curved dagger. Hrol scanned the throng, searching for any clue as to who the eavesdropper might have been, and Kelewulf was forced to look away and turn his head to the front to copy those around him. He instantly wished he had not. Because at that moment, greeted by a horrified gasp from the crowd, the flayed pelt of Grad'ur was draped over the entrance.

Kelewulf closed his eyes, but it was too late: the image was inked into his mind and he knew he would never be able to remove it. He had been a part of the man's demise, tricked into bearing witness by building a picture of guilt – a picture that Elafir had helped to compose.

Do you still think your high priestess is so marvellous now? the lich whispered inside his head. *No? Good. Then let us work out a way to make her pay for using us like this. Let us show her she is not the only one who can bend others to their will.*

Stromgard
16

King Erik looked up at Fariz as he approached. The ship captain looked nervous and out of place as he was escorted through the Great Longhouse by two guards on either side of him. When he was a short distance from the dais, Erik addressed him.

'You are the man who sailed my sister and Jarl Gudbrandr to the Sölten Isles?'

'I am, Your Grace. My crew and I delivered them safely under the flag of parley, as per your orders.'

'And you have returned with news for me, I understand?'

'I have. Brundorl is assembling his flotilla as we speak, adding to it all the time as other vessels return to the Sölten Isles. He awaits your instructions as to when to attack the Hasz'een fleet, which is currently still at harbour.' Fariz gave a small shake of his head before continuing. 'The marauder king wants you to understand that he assembles his ships not for the gold or the royal pardon you offered, but because of the actions of the princess and the jarl. He will attack Hasz if and when you give word to do so. He also wants you to acknowledge that, should such an order be given, the losses on his part will be great. With this in mind, he will consider his debt to you paid in full, and has no wish for his territories to be recognised as part of the Kingdoms. He asked me to quote him: "The Sölten Isles are not for sale. We are brigands and pirates, and as such we will not be tied to any king or queen. We do what is asked by Strom to fulfil our obligation, nothing more."'

'The actions of the princess and the jarl?'

The captain swallowed and gave a little nod of his head.

'We – my crew and I – come here fresh from a *second* request for parley, this one instigated by the pirate king. He thought it best that the message should be delivered in person and not by a messenger bird that may have gone missing in a storm or to a predator. After talking with him, I had to agree.' He paused and met the king's gaze. 'I am the bearer of grave news, I'm afraid.'

Erik couldn't stop a tiny shiver of dread at how reluctant the man appeared to go on. A myriad of possible scenarios played out in his head, from Brundorl kidnapping his sister, to the possibility that she had been hurt by the man. But if that was the case, why would he have asked for a second parley and then sent the merchant ship's captain back with a message. 'Well?' he eventually asked.

'The news concerns your sister and the young jarl, Lannigon Gudbrandr. They are no longer in the Sölten Isles.'

'They have continued on to Hasz?'

'No. They have … disappeared.' The captain held up his hand before the monarch could interrupt. 'Everything I know is from the eyewitness who was with them at the time, but having met the man during my conversation with the pirate king, I have no reason to doubt him.' Fariz took a deep breath before continuing. 'Upon arriving at Brundorl's court, the jarl and the princess discovered that the pirate king's son had been abducted. Jarl Gudbrandr was convinced the boy had been taken by some terrible monster – a draugr – and succeeded in persuading the king to let him try to find him. Lann and your sister located the boy and saved him, but in doing so the princess was … taken.'

'Taken?'

'The eyewitness says she was dragged through a mysterious black hole by the creature. Lannigon Gudbrandr gave orders for the boy to be taken back to his father before he jumped through the same hole after her.'

'And nobody followed? Nobody else went after them?'

'From what I have been told, the hole disappeared as soon as the young jarl jumped through it. Besides, there *was* nobody else, Your Grace. Lann had insisted Brundorl only send two of his men, arguing that the more men were sent, the more would die. No one has seen or heard from either Jarl Gudbrandr or your sister since.'

Erik sat perfectly still on the throne and tried to grasp everything he'd just been told. Darkness and danger in the form of unnatural events seemed to dog his sister at every turn, and despite all his own power he was utterly unable to protect her as a brother or as a king. A part of him wished he and Astrid had never met Lann or his witch aunt.

How his sister coped with the things she had encountered was beyond him. And now she had been dragged out of this world into another by some undead monster! He offered up a silent prayer to the gods that his beloved Astrid was still alive. His only comfort was in knowing that she was a formidable fighter and that their friend had gone after her. If anyone could bring her back, it was the wielder of the Dreadblade.

'I see.' Erik stood, a signal that the conversation was over. Almost as an afterthought, he said, 'Thank you for your news, Captain Fariz.'

'I wanted to say how sorry I am. Despite the dangers he has caused me, I have grown fond of Lann.' Fariz gave a little hopeless shrug. 'I am just a simple sailor, and I know nothing about the terrors Lannigon and Astrid might be facing right now, but I hope they can stay safe and find a way to return – together.'

'Let us hope so, Fariz. If they do not, I think all of us – simple sailors, kings, and everyone in between – will be in danger in the times that lie ahead.'

Gematik's Citadel,
Eastern Hasz

17

Kelewulf paced back and forth in his room, trying not to succumb to the twin feelings of panic and anger that were threatening to unravel him.

Why was it that every time he put his faith in someone, they turned out to be the very opposite of what he believed they were? Elafir had made him think that she was better than the people around her, that she had principles and values that set her apart. But instead of exposing Hrol's crime as soon as she became aware of it, she'd let an innocent man be blamed for it. She'd framed Grad'ur and let him be killed for the crime, killed in a terrible, terrifying way that made Kelewulf shudder each and every time he thought about it.

The question was, what he should do next? Betraying what he knew about the high priestess was next to impossible; the only person he might have been able to tell was dead. Everyone else he knew in this country was either a student or a colleague of the high priestess.

Could he carry on as if he knew nothing about the murder, and continue to learn under Elafir's tutelage? No, that was impossible. He could never look at the woman in the same way, much less pretend he hadn't seen and heard what he had at that window.

The knock on his door made him jump and spin about to stare in its direction. His heart beating quickly in his chest, he was unable to answer at first.

The knock came again, and this time Alwa's voice followed it.

'Everyone in the citadel is to be downstairs when the next bell is sounded. The high priestess is returning to say goodbye.'

'Goodbye?' he managed.

'She's leaving the citadel. She has an even grander place to call her home now.'

Kelewulf didn't need to hear Alwa's next words to know what she meant.

'She'll be in the imperial palace. They've just announced she is to be empress!'

The Rød

18

Astrid had hardly taken her eyes off the figure of her unconscious friend since they'd journeyed out of the mist-covered domain, a host of vælkyrie carrying them up into the clear skies above. But when their eventual destination loomed up out of the red-blanketed landscape she couldn't help but stare at the giant tor of black glassy rock, its sheer sides thrusting up vertically from the ground so high that the only way to reach the top was by flying there.

The huge longhouse atop the tor looked out of place in this nightmare world. It was a thing Astrid might have expected to find back home. Smoke was drifting slowly up from the chimney at its centre, suggesting that somebody was home. It was into the dimly lit interior of this building that the vælkyrie ushered Astrid. Lann, who was still being carried in one of the vælkyrie's arms as if he weighed little more than a child, was placed on one of the many low bunks occupying one side of the building.

A large screen divided the longhouse in two. This end was clearly a dormitory for the vælkyrie, and it reminded Astrid of the shield maidens' lodgings back in Stromgard, but she could also hear movement on the other side of the divide – the unmistakeable sound of pots and pans clinking together, as if somebody was preparing food.

Despite the strangeness of her surroundings, and indeed the world, she found herself in, Astrid's only thoughts were for her friend as he lay, unmoving, in the cot. She knelt close beside him, holding his hands in her own, an anguished expression on her face as she watched him.

Lann stirred, and mumbled something. When he gave a little shake of his head, Astrid reached forward and wiped away some of the sweat that glistened on his forehead. As she did so, he opened his eyes. But he didn't return her gaze. His stare was faraway, as if he could see through the beams and the roof suspended over them to something outside.

'Where are they?' he asked, his eyes full of panic. He tried to raise himself up but collapsed back down again with a groan. 'The draugr! Where …' As Lann slipped back into unconsciousness, Sigrun entered the building and approached the pair.

'This is Vestrilla,' she said, gesturing around her. 'I suppose it is, for us, what you would call "home".' When she looked at Lann, a small frown creased her brow.

'Will he be all right?' Astrid asked. 'He woke just now and I think he might be hallucinating.'

'It is good that he has passed out. At least, like that, the terror that infects him is not driving him to madness as I have seen it do to others.' Sigrun saw the alarm her response caused and added, 'But, yes, he will be all right. He has hidden strengths, this one. Magorlana will look at him soon. She will also try to help you both get back to your own realm.'

'Magorlana?'

Sigrun gestured towards the screen, the hint of a smile playing at the edges of her mouth. 'She is an Ancient, and has been here even longer than we vælkyrie. She was here before the dark god was banished to this place to infect it with his evil, and because of that she has no love for Lorgukk and those who support him. She treats the vælkyrie like we are her children, and, in a way, I suppose we are. She will know what to do, she always does.' She lowered her voice and stepped closer. 'She is a little … odd. Try not to be too alarmed when you meet her.'

This last, coming from a towering colossus of a woman whose skin was covered in strange symbols and pictograms, struck Astrid. 'I want to thank you, Sigrun,' she said.

'For?'

'Helping Lann rescue me.'

The vælkyrie frowned, as if thanks were a notion she struggled to understand. She gestured in the direction of her winged companions outside. 'We are vælkyrie. We serve the gods in guarding the Rød. We have always done this. When that creature, the draugr, brought you here, it was only able to do so because we failed in stopping it from crossing over to your realm in the first place. My sisters and I should thank *you* for helping us to put that right. Besides, there's nothing we like more than an excuse to enter the Murrke and kill the foul creatures that exist there.'

Astrid was about to ask another question when the sound of the screen being drawn aside made her turn in that direction, her eyes widening and her mouth forming a small circle at the sight of the figure who came shuffling through.

Magorlana was the oldest living thing the shield maiden had ever laid eyes on. The woman must once have been truly huge in stature, but now she was crooked and warped out of shape, like a piece of wood left out in the rain for too long. Her head was a great block that seemed too big for the hunched and twisted frame beneath it to support, and her hair – a shock of pure white that stuck out on all sides of that great dome – framed a face so wrinkled it might have been fashioned from tree bark. Her fat, purple-coloured lips stood out starkly against this snow-white mane. These opened and closed repeatedly with a wet, smacking noise as she shuffled over in their direction.

'Magorlana,' Sigrun said with a nod of her head.

The greeting was waved away by the ancient creature. 'So, these are the ones, are they?' she asked. She peered at Astrid and Lann through rheumy eyes the colour of storm clouds, one big and bulging, the other small and hardly open.

'The young woman was brought here by a draugr—'

'Foul creatures! I trust they are all properly dead now?' She smacked her lips in appreciation of Sigrun's nodded response.

The vælkyrie continued. 'When the girl was brought through, the boy—'

'The boy followed. Of course he did. Who wouldn't follow such a ravishing creature as this?' The woman reached out and took Astrid's chin in her hand, turning the shield maiden's face once to each side as she inspected her. The fingers of that hand were ice cold, but Astrid did her best not to flinch from the touch.

Magorlana's eyes fell upon the black blade hanging at Astrid's waist. 'Hmm. So the girl was infected with the darkness, and the boy saved her by placing the sword in her hands. Clever.' She looked down at Lann. 'But in doing so, he opened himself up to the fear and terror that comes from the Blakk. Not so clever.'

'I should give him back the Dreadblade. It will recover him,' Astrid said.

'Foolish nonsense,' Magorlana replied, tutting and waving away the suggestion in the same manner she had Sigrun's greeting. 'You have already experienced the Fear once. If you were to do so again so quickly it would be the undoing of you. The lad is strong, sword or no sword.' Her lips smacked again and she stared down at Lann, nodding her head once at whatever she saw there. 'He is in no immediate danger. Besides, I would like a word with him.'

'He's too sick to speak,' Astrid pointed out.

'Pah!' Magorlana turned away and started back through the dividing screen. 'Bring them, Sigrun,' she said over her shoulder. 'And don't try to slither off once you've carried the lad in. I can see how badly wounded you are. You need old Magorlana's help just as much as they do.'

That help came first in the form of a thick and hearty soup that reminded Astrid of a vegetable stew she enjoyed back at Stromgard. It tasted as good as it smelt, and she found herself wolfing the stuff down while Sigrun had her wounds tended to by the ancient.

'The smaller pot hanging on the stove? It contains a herbal tea,' Magorlana said, turning her eye on the shield maiden momentarily. 'Foul-tasting stuff, I'm afraid, but I've sweetened it a little with shinke roots. It should be done now. Drink some for me.'

'No, thank you. I'm fine. I'll just—'

'Drink some.' The instruction was delivered in a way that suggested further argument was pointless. 'It will help fight the effects of the Blakk. You might have that sword hanging from your belt, but the Fear has been in you. It can stay inside you for a long time, if you're not careful, reinfecting you, way into the future, when you least expect it.' Magorlana watched as Astrid lifted the ladle out of the pot and sipped at it, screwing up her face as she did so. 'More.' She nodded her approval when the shield maiden did as she was bid. 'We must get some of it into the boy too. We can sit him up and spoon it into his mouth.' She wrinkled her bulbous nose and peered down at the stitches she'd put into the flesh of Sigrun's leg. Happy with her work, she slowly hoisted herself upright again before making her back way over to Lann.

'What's in this stuff?' Astrid asked, glancing towards the pot as a strange feeling, like a warm blanket of calm, began to creep over her.

'You are better off not knowing, trust me,' Sigrun said, helping to lift Lann upright so Magorlana could squeeze his mouth open with one hand and ladle the liquid into it with the other.

Whatever was in the foul-tasting stuff worked fast, and Lann opened his eyes, frowning at first, then managing a smile when his gaze fell at last on Astrid.

'You're OK,' he croaked.

Magorlana looked from the young man to the young woman with the merest hint of a chuckle as she hoisted herself upright again. 'Sigrun, I have a balm in the small room at the back that I'd like to apply to that stitched wound of yours. Come.'

'It'll be fine. I don't need—'

'Come!' the old woman said, shooting her a look that swept from Lann to Astrid and back to the vælkyrie again.

'Ah, right. Yes.' Sigrun nodded and made her way out, Magorlana following along behind.

'How do you feel?' Astrid asked.

'Like I've woken from a terrible nightmare that still lurks there, in the back of my head, just waiting to fill it again. You?'

'I'm OK. Thanks to this.' She patted the sword at her side. 'Thanks to you.' She saw how he looked at the sword. When she started to remove it from her belt, he lifted a hand and stopped her.

'No. I don't think that is a good idea. Keep hold of it for now. It will tell me when it's time for me to take it back.'

'How does it feel, to be without it?'

247

Lann paused, trying to put his feelings into words. 'Like a part of me has been ... detached. It reminds me of a story I heard once about a man who had to have his leg removed after it was damaged in battle. He said he could always feel it there, underneath him, even though he knew it wasn't.'

Despite Magorlana's tea, it was clear to Astrid that Lann was still struggling with the Fear. 'We need to get back to our realm,' she said.

'I want to go to Hasz. I need to find Kelewulf and stop him before he can get the heart. He has no idea what it is he seeks to unleash on the world. We do. We know.' He shook his head. 'The Fear would destroy everyone if Lorgukk is returned to our world. It would—'

'There's another reason you need to leave,' Magorlana said from over by the screen. There was no telling how long she had been there, listening. 'And it's the same reason the Dreadblade has to stay in the shield maiden's possession. For now.' She shuffled over to them. 'Lorgukk knows the dark blade is here. He senses it every bit as much as you feel the darkness that leaches out of him in this realm. While it is in Astrid's possession, he is ... confused. He knows she is not the true bearer. He's asking himself if you are dead.' She made her way to the side of the fireplace and began rooting for something in one of the many drawers there. 'You say you want to go from here to Hasz?'

'Yes. It is my destiny.'

'Ha! Destiny. How I hate that word. Destiny, indeed. What is that, hmm? Have you learned nothing in your recent trials?' She turned to them, holding out what looked like two small eyeballs. 'Take. Eat.'

'I'm not hungry,' Astrid said. 'The stew filled me.'

'I don't feed you these to fill you.' She stood perfectly still and gave them a look that made both of them uneasy. 'Eat.'

Lann and Astrid reached out and took the small round things. They were soft to the touch, and the more they looked at them, the more they were convinced they really were eyeballs.

'Eat!'

They did as they were told.

'This tastes every bit as bad as it looks,' Astrid said around the food, her expression perfectly portraying her disgust. 'What is it?'

'A means to an end,' was the reply, but Magorlana's words seemed to blend and merge into one another, floating in the air to form a smoky cloud that seemed to mutate into a face that winked at Astrid before disappearing in a shower of sparkles that popped and fizzed before they extinguished.

'I don't feel so good,' the shield maiden managed to say, putting a hand up to her face. 'My lips aren't working properly.' Hands gently took her by the shoulders, lowering her back down on to a seat. 'H-have you … have you poisoned me?'

'You'll be fine soon. Both of you will,' Magorlana replied, her voice the colour of the sky on a warm summer day. Her words were butterflies now, yellow and green, that fluttered up into the air in front of Astrid's eyes.

'I can see rainbow people,' Lann muttered from somewhere not far away. 'And a giant flower. I like the flower.'

Astrid floated around as if she were underwater, unfazed by everything, until somebody came along and helped her to her feet again. Supported by this unseen other, she walked a short distance before being brought to a stop again. Everything was soft and grey. In the distance, out beyond the cloud, Magorlana was mumbling something under her breath in a strange language, the words alien to Astrid's ear.

Then a gleaming circle of white appeared, shining brightly enough to make Astrid's eyes hurt. In the same instant, Lann and Sigrun snapped into sharp focus beside her, as if they too had materialised out of nothingness. They were joined by Magorlana and, with Sigrun supporting Lann, all four stood before that blinding circle of light, the noise from which was like a giant waterfall that threatened to engulf them at any moment. With her awareness suddenly returned, she also became aware of the Dreadblade's voice; the weapon was filling her head with a high keening wail that reminded her of the hunting dogs her father had kept when he was alive. She groped for the sword belt, fumbling with the buckle that fastened it around her torso. Pulling it loose, she held it out before her.

Sigrun stepped forward. She was still supporting Lann with one arm, but with the other she reached across her own body and unclipped the small bone horn she wore at her side.

She handed it to Astrid. 'Take this. You will need it at some point in the future. It can only be used once in your world, but when it is sounded my sisters and I will leave our realm and come to help you in yours. We will listen for your signal and come the instant we are summoned.' She paused. 'But know this – once we leave this place we can never return, and the vælkyrie will no longer guard the wall between the realms.'

Astrid met the vælkyrie's eyes. 'I will only use it when it is most needed, you have my word,' she whispered.

Sigrun greeted her response with a single nod of the head.

'They need to leave,' Magorlana said. 'Sigrun, strap the Dreadblade back on its real owner's waist. Without it he will not have the strength the make the crossing. Even then, I fear it may not be enough.'

The vælkyrie did as she was bid. When the belt was in place, Magorlana reached across and took Astrid's hands, placing them firmly around the handle of the sword. She did the same with Lann's hands, folding his fingers down around Astrid's and interlocking them tightly with her own.

'Where are we going?' Lann asked Magorlana.

'Where you need to be next –' she gave a humourless chuckle – 'to fulfil your destiny.' She turned to Sigrun. 'Now, before it closes!'

Astrid went to say something to the ancient being, but was stopped from doing so by Sigrun stepping forward and shoving her forcefully through the bright opening. Spinning as she fell away into the light, she just caught a glimpse of the vælkyrie doing the same to Lann.

And that was all she saw before the whiteness filled her head with its terrifying beauty, folding itself in and through her as it transported her back to her world.

One second Astrid was at one with the whiteness, a thing of light and magnificence, the next she was collapsing down on to a cold floor of packed earth and scattered straw. The loud thump beside her could only be Lann falling to the ground a split-second after she did, but Astrid didn't have the strength to raise her head and look. Every part of her hurt. Muscles felt tender and bruised, bones and joints ached. Her stomach lurched and she threw up, not caring that the vomit was pooling next to her face and hair. The foul taste of the tea Magorlana had made her drink filled her nose once more.

'Lann?' she managed to say, a thin stream of watery drool running from her mouth.

There was no response. Somehow she managed to stretch out her arm behind her, and sought out his body with her hand. He was lying on his side facing away from her and she felt a flood of relief when, resting her palm on his back, she could feel it rising and falling, albeit barely, as he took in short, shallow breaths. The sound of a door opening over her head gave her more hope, but her heart truly soared when, blinking through eyes that refused to stay open for more than a moment, she saw her friend Maarika hurry in and drop down to her knees beside her.

'Astrid? Lann? What are you doing here? Where did you come from? By the gods, what has happened to you both!'

'The Rød,' Astrid whispered. 'We … came back from the Rød.'

'We're in Stromgard?' Lann muttered, the anger and frustration clear to hear in his voice. 'Why? Why has Magorlana sent us here when Kelewulf is in Hasz?'

And that was the last thing Astrid remembered before a black curtain – the complete opposite to the beautiful one of light and wonder she'd experienced minutes ago – wrapped itself around her and dragged her down into nothingness.

Hasz

19

It was no great surprise to Elafir that following Grad'ur's trial and execution almost everyone who had previously opposed her ascent to power changed their minds and rallied to her side. The enthronement ceremony was a lavish and opulent affair that saw heads of state from all over the empire descend upon the palace bearing gifts and well-wishes for her 'long and prosperous reign'.

Sitting on the throne she'd so long coveted, the empress stared down at the great queue of dignitaries, her heart sinking at how long everything was taking. She greeted each person with a nod of her head, lifting her left hand so that they might kiss the Ring of Hasz, the symbol of power now firmly installed on her index finger. How many times had she performed this action today? Two hundred? More?

Whatever the figure, her left shoulder was aching and she was no longer registering the names of each new visitor.

Every one of them was keen to speak with their new imperial leader and impress on her the individual problems their region was experiencing. Elafir had heard tales of everything from poor harvests and civil unrest to disease and disorder. In one case she was implored to send soldiers to help resolve a dispute over the theft of a herd of sheep! Her courtiers and advisors did their best to suggest these requests should be put forward at another time, but the attendees seemed intent on airing their grievances.

And all the time she was wondering about the identity of the person who'd spied on her and Hrol during their meeting. Her ex-slave had failed to find the eavesdropper before she'd carried out her threat to banish him forever. In all likelihood the listener was nothing but a local street urchin, and if that was the case they wouldn't have understood a fraction of what had gone on. But if it wasn't some destitute brat? Not for the first time, she cursed herself for letting Hrol go in the way she had. In choosing that path she'd left herself open to danger. She should have killed him, not exiled him. But her path to the imperial throne was already strewn with bloody footprints, and she had no desire for any more.

'I beg your pardon, Empress Elafir?' her chief advisor asked.

Had she spoken any of her thoughts aloud? 'I asked how many more?' she replied. 'These proceedings are taking forever.'

'Only about forty or fifty.'

'I want this to end. Soon. Get a message to those remaining that I will not be entering into any discourse with them. Tell them I'm weary, or that I've lost my voice. Tell them anything, I don't care. Just get them to kiss the blasted ring and move on.'

Despite his dismayed expression, the man did as he was bid. Even so, it took almost another hour before the last two waiting dignitaries – a small, thin couple who looked as exhausted as their empress at having been made to wait so long – were done with.

Elafir watched the man and woman go, the latter nervously glancing behind her and making little curtsying motions all the way along the route to the large doors on the left of the throne room. As they swung shut behind them with a low bang, she let out an exasperated sigh and slumped down into the uncomfortable throne. Her chief advisor reappeared by her side, making the little throat-clearing noises he always did when he was preparing to speak.

'What is it?' she asked.

'The evening celebrations start in a little over two hours, Your Imperial Majesty.'

She groaned. 'This is a day without end. I'll be in my rooms. Send somebody to get me just before the feast.'

As the empress stood, the man bowed low at the waist. His action was repeated by the few remaining palace attendants present. They stayed like that until Elafir left the throne room, waving away the guards that would normally accompany her.

With the throne room doors closed behind her, she leaned back against them, shutting her eyes and taking a moment to collect her thoughts. When she opened them again she was startled to find a man, dressed all in black leather, standing in front of her. He was unarmed, but there was something about him that put her on guard, and she reached out for her spells to defend herself if she needed to.

'Majik will not be necessary,' the man said. 'I mean you no harm.'

'Who are you?' she asked, her fears about Hrol and her role in the cover-up resurfacing.

'Merely a messenger who has been charged with bringing you before his masters. It's not far. If you'd like to follow me, Imperial Majesty.'

'And who are these "masters"?' she asked, staying where she was.

'I'm to take you to the Council of Four.' He paused. 'You're in no danger, I assure you.'

'Council of Four? I've never heard of them.'

'That is because you've never been the imperial leader of our nation until now. The council has been in place for as long as anyone can remember. Only the wisest and holiest are called to a position on the council,' he said with a small reverential bow of his head. 'It is regrettable that we have to introduce you like this – the incumbent holder of your office usually prepares their successor for this moment. But on this occasion, we have been forced to do things a little differently.' The man's lips twisted into a shape Elafir thought might have been a smile. Then he turned away from her and walked towards the wall on his right, stopping in front of it. She watched as he raised his right hand, extending his forefinger to sketch, in a fairly wild and stylised manner, a majik symbol that she dimly recognised. As he finished, a section of the wall seemed to disappear into shadow and he stepped to one side, gesturing for her to enter.

She understood the powerful conjuring at play here, just as she understood that the doorway was much more than a connection between this wall and the space just behind it. No, the 'door' was a bridge to somewhere much further away. Despite this, and because she was intrigued by the skill and knowledge of the Art on display, she stepped through the opening …

… and found herself standing in a small, bitterly cold room in front of two men and two women. All of them were dressed in black cloaks. The messenger who had created the portal had not followed her through, but she could feel the dark opening still open at her back. The four stared at her unblinkingly. They were standing close enough to each other that their shoulders were almost touching. Elafir guessed the youngest of the quartet must have been in his eighties. But while their bodies were old, the intensity of their stares suggested minds that were sharp and astute.

'Welcome, Empress,' one of the women said, looking the newcomer up and down. 'Majik runs in your veins. That is unusual for one wearing the Ring of Hasz.'

'Why am I here?'

'You have been brought here so that we might reveal a secret only the Council of Four and imperial rulers of Hasz have been privy to for centuries. Something that has been at the heart of our society for all of that time.' She narrowed her eyes at the empress. 'Perhaps you can guess what it is?'

Elafir shook her head.

'Behold.'

In a move that looked rehearsed, the four parted to reveal the elaborately decorated pedestal behind them. On top was a heavy glass dome.

Stepping forward to peer inside, it slowly dawned on Elafir what she was looking at. 'Is that what I think it is?' she asked in a small voice.

'It is,' the woman said, her tone matching Elafir's own. There was a pause, as if she were waiting for more from her empress. 'You see what it means, don't you? It means that we are not like the other races and nations that lie on this continent and others beyond the seas. We, the Hasz'een, are the chosen people! Why else would we have been entrusted with its safekeeping? It is proof that we have always been right to go forth and conquer the other nations of this continent, and why we must push on beyond the seas. You, as our imperial ruler, must ensure the Hasz'een are all-powerful in this world. The Heart of Lorgukk demands it be so!'

Elafir's amazement vanished almost as quickly as it had formed, and the powerful emotion that replaced it took her completely by surprise. The laughter that escaped her was just a chuckle at first, but it quickly transformed into a harsh and raucous sound that filled the small space.

'What is so amusing?' the woman asked, the anger in her voice clear to hear. 'This is a sacrosanct place, Empress. Your behaviour is unacceptable!'

But Elafir was unable to stop straight away. The laughter had become a thing all of its own now, an uncontrollable force that would not be quelled. Tears ran down her face and she swiped them away as she sought to get a grip of herself. After what felt like an age, during which the Council of Elders stared furiously back at her, she was ready to speak.

She looked into the face of each council member in turn, registering the pious outrage of their expressions. And as she did, her own feelings changed yet again.

'That … thing. *That* is the heart of the dark god? That shrivelled-up and shrunken piece of offal!'

'Hold your tongue,' the woman hissed.

'NO! YOU HOLD YOURS! I am the ruler of Hasz now, and I will not be told what to do by the likes of you.' She stared about her, daring defiance. 'For centuries you have guarded this secret, and you, or others like you, have told my predecessors that *we* were the chosen people. Did you ever stop to consider what that might mean? Did you ever wonder if the dark and terrible things our people have done to others, killing and enslaving entire nations and believing we had every right to do so, might have been as a result of that way of thinking?'

'Empress Elafir, you need to understand that—'

'Do not tell me what I need to understand! Because I understand perfectly what it is you were trying to tell me a moment ago when you said that the Hasz'een were the "chosen people", and how being "special" means that others are somehow beneath us.' She shot the four a furious look. 'And if they're beneath us, if the heart being in these lands shows we're superior, well, it's acceptable for us to subjugate and enslave them, isn't it? What did you hope to get out of this meeting, hmm? Did you hope that I, like those before me, would look upon that … *thing* … and follow in their footsteps?' She paused, scanning their faces again. 'Well, if that was indeed the case, I can assure you that you will be bitterly disappointed. I am not like Mamur and those before him. I have no love of war and ruination. I may not be proud of everything I have had to do to get to the Hasz throne, but now I sit upon it I can promise you that a new era is upon us, an era that has *nothing* to do with your precious heart!'

When the woman spoke again there was the merest hint of trepidation in her voice. 'Your Imperial Majesty, we only wish to serve Hasz and—'

'Enough!' Now she had begun to speak, Elafir's words would not be stopped. 'I am your imperial ruler and I will decide who best serves the Hasz'een people. I will also determine what symbols represent our power and might.' She paused, as if weighing something up in her mind. When she spoke again, her voice was flat and devoid of the emotion that had hitherto filled it. 'As of this moment, there is no Council of Four. You are all absolved of whatever it is you believe your responsibilities and obligations to be. You are no longer the keepers of this … object.'

The second man spoke out for the first time. 'You cannot do this! Who do you think you are?'

Elafir dipped into the anger that was blooming inside her, and allowed it to fuel the majik she summoned. A darkness formed around her, a darkness that also shone through her eyes as she stared back at the man and the others. The air inside the chamber crackled as if it were a living thing. 'I am your empress. I am Elafir, first of my name, and I will change the lands and the people of Hasz forever. I will not be thwarted in this, and I will not be told by the likes of you what I can and cannot do! Obey me now and leave this place, and I will spare you. Defy me and you will die.'

'What of the heart?' the woman asked. 'What do you intend to do with it?'

'That is no longer your concern. Now go, while you still can.'

Elafir stood perfectly still as the four made their way past her and exited through the gateway. Only when she was happy they had all gone did she allow her majik to abate, a wave of exhaustion rolling over her as she did so. Then, with one last glance at the object beneath the glass dome and a shake of her head, she too turned and left the tiny chamber.

The messenger was waiting on the other side of the portal. Of the Council of Four, there was no sign.

'This gateway,' she said, gesturing towards the shadowy opening. 'The majik symbol you used to create it is known to me. It is not complex enough to make such a powerful thing. So how did you do it?' She saw the man's hesitation. 'I would warn you not to lie to me, I am in no mood.'

'The empress is right. The pictogram, in itself, is not enough. You must also have the key.' With that, the man withdrew a green polished stone from the pocket of his robe. It was inset with signs and symbols of its own. Unlike the desiccated heart she had just been shown, the majik in this new item was obvious to anyone with even an inkling of the Art.

The man made no move to stop her when she reached out and took it. 'Thank you. I did not get your name.'

'Fornack, Your Imperial Highness.'

'I will keep this for now, Fornack. I'm afraid that you are no longer in the employ of the Council of Four because, as of today, there is no council.' She allowed this to sink in. 'However, if you are willing, I would like to offer you a position in my court. I need good men and women to advise me in certain matters, and I value people of majik as more than just … doormen.'

The man's mouth twisted into that peculiar shape again and he bowed from the waist. 'It would be an honour to serve you. If I may be so bold, I think Hasz is on the verge of great change under its new empress.'

'I think you're right,' she said. 'I will see you tomorrow morning in the throne room. Oh, and Fornack? If you should hear of any dissent from your former employers, it would benefit you to inform me of it.'

'The empress's ears shall be the first to hear anything of the kind.'

'Good.' With that, she pocketed the key and walked away, still eager to grab whatever brief rest she could before the evening's celebrations began.

The citadel was in a state of confusion. Elafir's successor had been chosen by the empress herself, and there were more than a few surprised faces up and down the corridors at the news that Master Larghal had been elected to take the role. What with his age and poor health, many suspected that his appointment was only ever envisaged to be a short one.

Two days had passed since Elafir's inauguration, and despite sending numerous requests for an urgent audience with her, Kelewulf had still not heard from the former high priestess. Desperation and anxiety were beginning to gnaw away at him, and yesterday he'd finally allowed his frustration to get the better of him. It was no coincidence that he'd been in the library at the time – the place where he'd discovered that wretched book on poisons. For reasons he couldn't fully recall now, he'd felt an overwhelming anger take hold of him and he'd laid waste to the place, kicking books here and there, tearing manuscripts, and finally barging Larghal's reading desk with enough force for the thing to topple over and break.

He couldn't tell whether it was this act of vandalism or his messages to the palace that pushed the empress to grant him his wish to meet with her the next day.

With an hour to go now, Kelewulf paced back and forth, working through everything in his head and trying to assess his options. The plan he and the lich had devised meant he would be treading a treacherous path. Any slip would result in death. Despite everything, a part of him wanted nothing more than to forget what he'd seen in the alleyway that day, to erase what he knew about Elafir and go back to the way things were.

She murdered them both, the lich whispered inside his head. *An emperor and an emperor-to-be! She dragged you into this mess, and made you an accomplice to lie in court for her.*

'I didn't lie.'

That's not how it would appear to them. The lich paused. *She thinks she's got away with it.*

'She has got away with it! There is nobody left to challenge her and nobody to expose her for what she is.'

Nobody but us.

'Us? I'm the only one that might die as a result of all this. I don't need to remind you that you have already suffered that particular indignity.'

All right, you.

'I am a foreigner here. A foreigner who is about to accuse the Empress of Hasz, the most powerful person in this empire and perhaps the world, of murder.' Kelewulf stopped and stared towards the door, aware that he had spoken out loud and was in danger of being overheard by passers-by. When he continued, it was in a more hushed

266

and deliberate tone. 'I am about to threaten this deadly woman, suggesting that I could expose her to her people, a people who do not exactly take kindly to foreigners. So you'll excuse me if I seem a tad anxious!'

You don't have to expose her to the people of Hasz. You just have to let her know that we know what she has done, and that we could expose her if we wanted.

'Yes, but—'

Elafir has so much to lose now. She finally has what she's always sought. Never underestimate what people in power are willing to do to hold on to it. I should know. I gave up everything, even my soul, for the chance to attain it again. You can do this, Kelewulf. You have walked a road every bit as dangerous as this before and managed to escape without harm. When the lich spoke again, its voice was a low and sinister whisper that filled the young necromancer's head. *The heart is here, in Hasz. I know it is! I have always known it is. And now that that woman is empress, she will know where it is. This is our chance. This is what we came here for! She has no idea who was at that window, but knows that* somebody *overheard her talking to her slave. We have to use that.*

'And what's to stop her killing me the second I do?' It was a question he'd asked himself a number of times. Because if the empress knew it was him at the window that day, she would end his life without as much as a second thought. 'Or perhaps she'll decide to torture me instead. Make me reveal what it is I claim to know. Because that's what I'd do if I were in her position! I would make sure a threat like that disappeared.'

We've discussed this. We have to convince her that we have spoken to the eyewitness, that we know where they are and that we can have them speak out against her at any time. We also tell her that we have insured ourselves against any move against us, and that should we 'disappear', the truth will be revealed. She has to believe that you, Kelewulf, are equal to any threats she makes. She must be made to think that you can bring her reign to an end even before it has really begun!

'How stupid was I? To think I could make a home in this place. To think I belonged here.' Kelewulf thought about how everyone's attitude towards him had cooled since the high priestess had left the citadel.

We don't need them. We don't need Hasz. We don't need anyone. Because they all let us down in the end, don't they? Even your precious Elafir has left you behind now. It's time for you to do what you came here to do, Kelewulf, and find the heart.

Kelewulf, his travel sack containing his possessions on his back, was brought to the palace by a single guard. The man had instructed him to follow and then walked ahead in stolid silence without another word. Kelewulf had been expecting to be taken to the throne room, so he was surprised when they proceeded to a smaller entrance that led them through a number of small and dimly lit corridors until they came to an iron-studded door.

His escort turned and left, leaving the young necromancer no choice but to open it and enter by himself.

The empress was sitting on a low seat with her back to him. As he closed the door behind him, she bid him approach.

Taking a chair opposite Elafir, he took in the empress for the first time since she had been given that title. She looked tired.

'It fits, then?' he said, noting the tiny frown lines that momentarily creased her forehead as she sought to understand what he was referring to. 'The ring.'

'Ah. Yes. And it always does, regardless of who becomes emperor or empress.'

'Majik?'

'There are five rings, all of different sizes. One of them is guaranteed to fit.' She lifted her hand and looked down at the item, giving a short sniff. 'Who would have thought it? The Ring of Hasz, the empire's most unique symbol of power, is actually one of five.' She moved her finger so the ring caught the fire's light before returning her arm to rest on the chair. 'I have discovered many such surprises since taking the throne.'

'Things are not always what they seem, are they, Your Imperial Majesty? Take people, for instance – who strive to appear to be one thing when in fact they are something quite different.' He noted the flicker in her eye as he said this, but it was gone as quickly as it appeared.

'I'm sorry that I could not see you earlier, Kelewulf. Matters of state have meant I have very little time to do anything but what is required of a new ruler. But I am glad we are able to talk now.' Kelewulf went to respond, but the empress continued. 'You are to leave Hasz. Immediately. It has been decided that you are no longer welcome as an acolyte, and therefore you have no place on these shores. The decision has been made by our new high priest.'

Kelewulf met her stare, an amused expression on his face. 'How odd that a pronouncement that I should leave Hasz should come at the same time I have made up my mind to do precisely that.' He gestured towards the travel sack at his feet. His smile slipped away. 'It is one of the reasons I asked to see you, to inform you of my decision. I'll go just as soon as I get what I came here for in the first place.'

'And what would that be?'

'You don't know?'

'I do, but I would like to hear it from your own lips.'

'The heart. I came here for Lorgukk's heart.'

The empress let out a short, humourless breath. 'I'd hoped you would change your mind. That, by showing you kindness and acceptance, you might turn away from a goal that is driven, ultimately, by hatred and sadness. But you have let the world darken your soul, Kelewulf.'

'Coming from someone who murdered their only opposition to achieve power, I could say the same about you.' As he delivered these words, he noted how little effect they had on the woman across from him. Instead, she sat unmoving, unruffled by his revelation. He felt a slight pang in his chest as he acknowledged, not for the first time, why he held this woman in such high regard: Elafir reminded him of his own mother. Not in looks or bearing, but in the way she conducted herself in the face of adversity. In another world, at another time, perhaps they could have truly been friends.

'So, it was you at the window.'

Kelewulf kept quiet, biding his time.

The empress brushed at an invisible speck of dust on her skirts. 'Would it surprise you to learn that I did not know the item in question was in the keeping of my people until very, very recently? And that, as far as I am aware, I am one of only six people alive who know it exists?' Still Kelewulf remained silent. 'It's true. I, like so many other Hasz'een, believed the legend of the heart making its way into the care of our people was just that: a legend.'

'But that's not the case.'

'No.' She regarded him for a moment. 'No, it isn't.'

'Then the question you have to answer is ... which is more valuable to you? Your newly discovered relic? Or my silence?'

'There is more than one way to guarantee someone's silence.' Something seemed to move behind her eyes, a darkness she'd half summoned, showing it more as a threat than anything else.

Kelewulf held her gaze. 'I thought of that before coming here to meet you today. How my life was at risk, and how I might easily end up meeting the same fate as poor Grad'ur. I considered telling you that I had taken steps to ensure you could not harm me without harming yourself. But then I considered what I have learned about you during my time here, Elafir. How you want to change your world and the people in it. How you hate the idea of another war every bit as much as you loathe the practice of slavery.' He paused, noting how the darkness behind her eyes had gone now. 'You saw attaining the seat of ultimate power as a means of achieving these things, and though your path to the throne became a tainted one, you kept to it. You could kill me now, but what would that accomplish? How would it benefit Hasz?'

'And what is *your* goal, Kelewulf?'

'I want people to look at me and know that I too am a person of power. Because that is all this world respects.'

'That isn't true. Not everyone—'

'It is true! My father's father was a tyrant who raided other countries far and wide to extend the lands over which he ruled. My father followed in his footsteps. Both sat on a throne forged with blood, and both were beloved by their people. My uncle's approach was different, but he too never hesitated in striking down any enemy that dared defy him. The people of the Six Kingdoms still sing songs about them all. These men were killers – brutes who knew the power of the sword and axe, little more. But because of that they were powerful. I want to feel what that is like, but I'll do so without the need of something as crass as a steel weapon.'

'By unleashing chaos on our world?'

'By having the power to do so if I choose. You see, my ambitions aren't so different from yours, really.'

'But the outcomes, should we see them through to the end, are. Very different.' The empress rose to her feet and moved away a few steps, deep in thought.

Sensing she was faltering, Kelewulf pressed his advantage: 'Think on this: my majik is growing all the time. I have learned much during my short time here, plus the lich and I have come to a mutual understanding that means I will have access to Yirgan's knowledge without having to worry about his undead spirit's treachery. When I leave Hasz shortly, I will do so as one of two things: a powerful ally, whom you have helped and whom you can call upon

273

in the future, or an enemy that has brought about the ruination of your reign and wrecked the dreams you had for
your empire and the people in it.'

'You will not be leaving Hasz at all if you're dead.'

'That has always been a possibility, right from the beginning of my time here in these lands.' Kelewulf offered her
a smile when she turned to look at him. 'You knew why I
was here in Hasz, from the moment I foolishly allowed
you inside my mind to help return the lich to its confines,
but you allowed me to stay because it made the most strategic sense. Now, as I am about to leave, I find myself in the
same position. I hope that now, as then, you will make
the right decision.' He paused and then he, too, stood.
'There is one last thing that you might wish to consider ...'

'Yes?'

'During your visits to my cousin, King Erik of Strom,
did you really believe you might be able to broker a true
and lasting peace between your empire and the Six
Kingdoms?'

'How did you—?'

'The lich. It sensed the majik you used to transfer your
form between here and Strom. It piggybacked on your last
journey to see what you were up to.'

'As you seem to know about my visits there, you must
also know that, yes, my intention was to make a pact with
King Erik.'

'And you believe you can trust him as a peacekeeper?'

'I do.'

Kelewulf smiled. 'Interesting. Because, you see, the lich has been inside Erik's head in the past and, once it had tagged along with you on your "visit", it wasn't too difficult for it to slip inside the King of Strom's head again.'

Elafir waited.

'Perhaps you should ask yourself why, if King Erik is so set on peace, he has a huge armada of ships making their way here to sink the Hasz'een navy in its harbour.'

It seemed to Kelewulf that, for the first time, the calm demeanour the empress had maintained throughout their conversation crumbled a little at this revelation.

'How do I know you are telling the truth?'

'I have told you no lies since coming here to meet you, Empress Elafir. I think you know that.'

'If it is the truth we are concerned with here, then perhaps you would be interested to know I had no idea about my servant's murder of Mamur until the deed was done. Hrol knew that my becoming empress was the best chance to stop slavery on these shores. As the victim of brutality at the hands of slavers, it is something he was willing to risk his life to stop. He took it upon himself to ease my passage to the throne. But the murder attempt almost did the opposite. Some of my former supporters looked set to change their allegiance to the hardliner

Grad'ur. It was only then that I became involved and helped Hrol frame the nobleman.'

Kelewulf gestured towards himself. 'Oh, I know that. The problem you have is expecting the Hasz'een people to buy it. To them it will look as if you simply murdered your way to the top.'

The pair matched each other's stare as a long silence stretched out between them. It was the empress who broke the impasse.

'I need more than your word,' she said. 'I need something more binding.' She walked over to a desk in the corner of the room and took out a scroll of paper that she proceeded to write upon. Kelewulf could feel her connect with the Art and her lips moved as she wrote, weaving whatever majik she was calling upon into the words. When she was finished, she brought the thing over to him and held it up so that he could read it. 'It simply says that in return for the heart, you will never reveal what you know about Mamur's murder. It also says you agree to come to Hasz's aid should the nation need you on any one occasion. It is a blood contract.' The former high priestess reached into the folds of her finery and brought out a small dagger. Drawing the blade across her palm, she smeared the scroll with her blood before holding the weapon out for Kelewulf to do the same. 'The spell woven through these words ensures that if either of us break our oath, death will be the result. It is dark majik, deadly majik. And only a fool or a madman would think they could break the promises it is married to.'

Kelewulf stared at the scroll for a second or two, then he too drew the dagger through his flesh and added his blood to Elafir's.

The smile she gave him unsettled him. He watched as she turned towards the wall at the back of the room and drew a symbol in the air, creating a shadowy door-shape that opened to reveal a man on the other side.

'Fornack, take our foreign friend here through to the chamber and give him the heart. Once you have done so, kindly escort him down to the harbour and see to it that he is put on the first ship out of Hasz.' She still had her back to Kelewulf, but the next words were directed at him nonetheless. 'I wish we'd parted on happier terms.'

'As do I, Empress Elafir.'

'Then go. Take your wretched heart and never let me see your face again.'

Kelewulf sighed. Despite their meeting playing out precisely as he'd hoped, he hadn't anticipated the unwanted realisation that struck him now: how he didn't want to leave this place with her still angry at him. This woman's opinion of him mattered far more than he cared to acknowledge.

Go, whispered the lich.

Kelewulf did as he was bid and stepped through the doorway.

The man called Fornack was standing in a small chamber. The only other thing in the place was a stone plinth, on top of which was a great glass dome.

Kelewulf's pulse raced hard and fast inside him, and he realised he had been holding his breath. The lich, too, seemed unable to speak, but he could sense its elation.

He stepped forward on unsteady legs and peered at the artefact beneath the glass.

'Wh-what is that?' he asked, turning to glance at Elafir's manservant before returning his gaze to the shrivelled and desiccated thing.

'It is the heart.'

'That? That … is not the heart. It cannot be! *That* is a … that is … It cannot be!' Kelewulf spun about, looking for the entrance they'd come in through. 'Take me back to Elafir. I demand to see her!'

'Those were not the empress's orders. You were to take the heart and leave Hasz. And you are only ever to return if called upon to do so.' The man made a strange, lopsided grin as he lifted up the glass cover and gestured for the young necromancer to take his prize. 'I doubt that invitation will ever be made …'

Kelewulf's head was spinning. He boiled with a mixture of hate and humiliation. How could he have let himself believe he could ever achieve power in the way he wanted? He was a failure. A fool.

He stifled the sob that threatened to escape him and grabbed the dried hunk of offal from the plinth. Staring down at the thing, it was all he could do to stop himself throwing it to the floor and grinding it to dust beneath the heel of his boot. Instead, he shoved it into the pocket of his trousers.

Gathering himself as best he could, he managed to meet Fornack's smirking face.

'Take me to the harbour,' he said. 'I have no use for Hasz any more.'

Stromgard

20

It took almost a day and a half for Lann to fully recover from the Fear and be able to get up out of his bed. Astrid made sure she was there almost from the moment he did so. Coming in to his recovery room, she found him walking towards the heavy curtains that were keeping the daylight out. He had the Dreadblade in his hand, as if, she thought, it had been the first thing he'd thought of upon waking.

'Hey, let me get those,' she said, pulling the drapes open and grinning as he blinked at the sunlight coming in through the window.

Lann looked out on to the streets below. 'Are we where I think we are?' he asked, frowning and looking back round at her.

'Stromgard, yes.'

'Gods, no!' he said. His clothes had been placed on a chair on the other side of the room, and he moved towards them. When the world spun sickeningly about him, he would have fallen to the hard wooden floor had Astrid not caught him and forced him to sit back down on the edge of the bed again. 'What are we doing here? We have to get to Hasz.' He shook his head as if to clear it. 'Has there been word from the Sölten Isles? The young boy. We should—'

'Sebastien is fine. He was taken from the barrow and reunited with his father. Captain Fariz delivered the news to Erik himself.'

It was clear from the confused expression on his face that Lann was having a hard time piecing together everything that had happened to them both since they'd set off for their parley with Brundorl.

'How much do you remember?' Astrid asked.

'I remember going after you and that creature. Sigrun and the vælkyrie … we found you and the draugr. They were waiting for you to die. There was a fight.' He frowned and shook his head. 'I'm afraid there's nothing much after that.'

'You saved my life.'

'How?'

She nodded down at the Dreadblade. 'You put the sword in my hand. It gave me the strength to fight the fear of that place. But it opened you up to that same fear in a way that almost killed you.'

'So how did we get here? And why, of all the places we could have come back to, did we end up in Strom? We are further back from our goal than if we'd never gone on your brother's mission!'

'And had we not gone, that small boy would have been taken to that terrible place instead of us. He would have died and been possessed by one of those things.' She reached out and rested her fingers lightly on his wrist. 'The Dreadblade goes where it is most needed, where it can do the most good. Besides, it was not my decision to come here.'

'Then whose was it?'

'Magorlana's.'

'Who?'

His question produced a strange smile on Astrid's lips. 'She got us out of the Void, and this is where she sent us. I've been thinking about it whilst waiting for you to recover, and she would only have sent us here if there was a good reason to do so.'

'She should have sent us to Hasz! That's where *he* is.'

'I don't think you understand how ill you've been, Lann. The physicians were concerned you might not recover at all. If she'd transported us to Hasz, where do you think you would have been able to recuperate? And how do you think we would have survived if we'd been attacked, or some other mishap occurred? Stromgard is a safe place for us. It's where we needed to be and Magorlana understood that.'

Lann tried not to show his frustration. Despite everything Astrid had just said making sense, he wished he'd not ended up back here like this. He turned to look at her again, noticing the item hanging from a leather thong at her belt. 'Is that what I think it is?'

She nodded. 'Sigrun gave it to me before sending us through Magorlana's portal. She warned me that I was only to use it in situation of dire need and how, if it was heard by the vælkyrie, they would come from their realm to this one.'

'How long have I been in this bed?' he asked, looking across at the rumpled covers.

'Just under two days.' She pointed to the sword. 'You kept that thing with you throughout.' She paused. 'When I had it about me – back in that other place? – I could feel the weight of it. And how heavy a burden it is for you to carry it.'

'And yet it saved you.'

'It did. You both did.'

'I think it's high time I got dressed, don't you?' he said, getting back to his feet more carefully this time. Another thought occurred to him. 'Are the kitchens open? You would not believe how hungry I feel right now.'

Her laugh was like medicine to him. 'Then let's go and see what we can get you, shall we? But I warn you, my brother has already announced plans for yet another of his famous feasts as soon as you are fully recovered. If you eat too much now, you will not have room in your belly for later.'

'I wouldn't count on that. Give me a minute to get changed and we'll go.'

As he went towards his clothes, Astrid gently hooked his elbow, stopping him.

'I said this to you before, when we were at Magorlana's, but it seems you don't remember. So, let me say it again now. Thank you, Lannigon.'

'For?'

'For coming after me. That place … it was …'

'Why wouldn't I have come after you? There's no way I could have left you in that place. You mean too much to me, Astrid.'

She stared back at him, her eyes glassy as tears threatened to fall. When she leaned forward and placed a kiss on his lips, he was more surprised than he could imagine. It was only the briefest of kisses, her lips barely grazing his, but it sent him dizzier than that first attempt to get up from his bed had.

'Wow,' he said, swallowing hard and not knowing where to look. 'Er, thanks.'

'Now let's go and see what we can find to put in that empty belly of yours, eh?'

King Erik was feeling exhilarated when he returned from the hunt he'd led out that morning. The wild boar that the hunting party had chased down had been a magnificent beast, and he was pleased with the way they'd dispatched it quickly – a swift, well-delivered thrust of a spear to ensure the creature hadn't suffered unnecessarily. Re-entering Stromgard with their kill, Erik had laughed and joked with his huntsmen as if he were simply one of them, and for the first time in a very long while the young king felt released from the pressures of his position.

His delight at having Lann and Astrid safely back home, and Brundorl's promise of help secured, was only tempered by a creeping unease that he had not heard from Elafir in days. The high priestess should have contacted him by now, and he was keen to hear how things stood in Hasz since the assassination attempt on Mamur.

Having insisted on stabling his own horse, Erik made his own way back to the Great Longhouse and ordered the servants to take the evening off and leave him to his own devices. Alone in his own rooms, having bathed and changed, he warmed himself in front of the roaring fire that had been set for him. Standing like this, with his back to the room, the uncomfortable feeling of being watched slowly crept over him, and despite the warmth of the fire he gave a little shudder. Turning round, he was only half surprised to see the figure of Elafir standing a short distance away. 'You startled me. But it is a welcome surprise. I had been beginning to wonder what had become of you, High Priestess.'

'It's Empress Elafir now.'

'My congratulations! That is indeed great news. You must be delighted.' Her eyes never left his, but the normal warmth in her look was absent. Indeed, her demeanour and expression seemed to him to be bordering on hostile. 'Is there something wrong?'

'I thought we had an agreement, you and I?'

'We did. We have.'

'That agreement, as far as I can remember, was to ensure neither of our nations acted in an aggressive manner towards the other. In short, that we would do everything to avoid a war between us.'

An uneasy feeling crept over Erik as it slowly dawned on him what she might be alluding to. He chose his next words with care. 'A king, or an empress for that matter, must consider all possibilities and act for the good of his or her people. I have not attacked Hasz, and I have no intention of doing so, especially now that you—'

'You have an armada of ships heading to Hasz to sink my navy at harbour!'

'No! I have ships making their way towards Hasz in case you failed in your bid to become empress. I had to consider that anybody else who took the throne would likely decide to carry out Mamur's plans for war.' He matched her stare. When he spoke again, it was in a softer tone. 'I am truly glad for you. I know how long you have desired the chance to change your nation and its attitudes.' He moved towards her. 'I will call back the ships, and I hope you can understand why I took the precaution of readying them at all. We have no desire for war with Hasz. Sinking your navy, if I'd been forced to do so, would have been a last resort. I hope you can believe me when I say I never meant to deceive you.'

There was a brief silence before she spoke again. 'I want to believe you, Erik, I really do. Just as I want you to believe me when I say that Hasz has no intention of warring with the Six Kingdoms. We want peace.' She glanced at something to her left, as though, wherever she truly was, she had been disturbed. 'I have to go.'

'One last question before you do. What news of my cousin Kelewulf? Is he still in Hasz under your watchful eye?'

'He is not.'

Erik gasped. 'Where is he?'

'I don't know. And if I am honest, I no longer care. Perhaps he is coming home to his family.' No sooner had she spoken these final words than she disappeared, leaving the king alone again.

The Blakk

21

The hammock swayed in time with the movement of the ship as it made its way over the Norderung Sea. At first, Kelewulf had found it hard to find sleep; the humiliation and anger that raged away inside him made it all but impossible. But eventually, when fatigue got the better of him, he'd drifted off. Fast asleep in his cabin now, a restless Kelewulf stirred in his slumber, a small, anxious whimpering noise escaping his lips.

The darkness in which he seemed to float was absolute: a perfect nothingness, devoid of all light and sound. The emptiness made him feel tiny and insignificant, like a dust mote under an airless, starless sky. But there was something here; something that slowly filled him with terror as he waited for it to reveal itself to him.

When the voice entered his head, he couldn't help but flinch.

'The time for me to return is near. I have been exiled for too long, and the human realm has slowly forgotten me.'

'Not all of it.' Kelewulf's thoughts became words that floated out into the darkness.

'You know what I am?'

'You are Lorgukk. The dark god.'

'I am.'

There was a moment of pause, that awful, perfect silence crushing in on Kelewulf until the god's voice filled him again.

'The Dreadblade has been returned. Not only that, but its bearer dared bring it into my realm! They didn't dare stay, oh no! But such an event cannot – will not – go unanswered. That one of the gods would dare to come here, taunting me by bringing that devil weapon into my domain, is inexcusable. The dark sword has no place here, and the god that bears it shall be made to pay for their—'

'No god bears it.'

'Then who?'

'A boy.'

There was a moment as the god seemed to take this in. 'It would not be wise to joke with me, young necromancer.'

'I am not foolish enough to do such a thing. I speak the truth.'

A sound like boulders being hauled over one another filled Kelewulf's head, and it took him a moment or two to realise that the dreadful noise was the dark god's laughter.

'You must not deviate from your path now. You are closer to your goal than you know. You must return me to the human realm. If the gods have so little regard for me that they would give such a thing to a mere boy, I will bring them to their knees.'

'And what do you offer me in return?'

'Ah, yes. What is it you want? Riches? Fame? To rule?'

'I want the world to know it was I who brought you back. I want to be at your right-hand side when you unleash your hellish army on my homelands. And when you have my cousins, the king and his sister, on their knees before you, I want them to see that it was I who was responsible for their downfall.'

'Is that all?'

'And Hasz. I want Hasz and the empress who rules there destroyed.'

'Agreed,' the dark god said. 'This boy who wields the Dreadblade. He can be no ordinary human. He is a threat to us.'

'No. I will deal with him.'

Kelewulf woke in a cold sweat. With shaking hands, he fumbled with the lantern beside him, struggling to light it. When the glow from the flame pushed back the shadows of the small cabin, he clambered down from his hammock.

Fishing in his travel sack he found the item he sought and removed it, placing it on the floor and sitting cross-legged over it so he could make out the words penned in elaborate letters on the parchment's surface. There were surprisingly few. Despite this, or perhaps because of it, he understood the difficulty that was woven into the spell and the effort required if he was going to be able to perform it when he reached his destination. The majik itself would require he go into a trance-like state, and he'd need to consider if it might be safer to do so in a circle of protection. Even so, just reading the words on the scroll now, silently imagining intoning them aloud, caused the inside of the cabin to change. The light grew dimmer and an icy draught sprang up from nowhere, making him shiver inside the heavy cloak he'd draped around his shoulders.

'Will it work?' he asked aloud, despite being alone in the small compartment.

It will.

'And if it doesn't?'

It will work.

Stromgard

22

The feast to celebrate Lann and Astrid's safe return was held in the banquet room at the rear of the Great Longhouse. Lann was still feeling tired, but Astrid had insisted he make the effort to dress up and accompany her. By the time the guests of honour arrived the room was already packed to the rafters. Erik seemed troubled by something, but he welcomed them both with great hugs, demanding they sit at his side. After calling for drink and food, he pointed out that the wild boar he'd helped to kill in the hunt was among the dishes.

Finally, with the celebration well and truly under way, Erik turned to speak with them again.

'Your efforts in the Sölten Isles have put a halt to any chance of war.'

'You ordered the attack?' Astrid asked.

'No. Other things have come to light that make it no longer necessary. I just wanted you both to know that your hardships were not for nothing.'

'I'm glad we could be of service,' Lann replied, the coldness in his voice difficult to miss. 'However, our primary objective – to get to Hasz and make Kelewulf pay for the terrible deeds he has committed against all of us – is no closer to us now than when Astrid and I first arrived back here.' He put down the piece of meat he was holding and pushed his plate away, wiping his hands on his trousers. 'With the king's leave, we will depart again for Hasz in the next day or so, and make sure—'

'Our cousin is no longer on those shores.'

The revelation came as a shock to Lann and Astrid, each of them staring first at one another and then the king as they took the news in.

'Then where is he?' Astrid asked.

'I'm afraid I have no idea.'

'You told us there was nothing he could do in Hasz without you knowing about it,' Lann said, his anger clear to hear.

'And that was true, *while* he was in Hasz.' The king shook his head and took a drink from a goblet. 'It will not be long before he reveals himself again.'

The loud scrape of the chair on the flagstones as Lann stood up made those closest to the king's table turn round and gape. 'He escaped?' Lann hissed at the young monarch. 'You have allowed the person who killed my aunt and your father to flee our grasp! How could you? How could you be so careless?'

'I do not like your tone, Jarl Gudbrandr.'

'And I do not like to be used as a pawn in trifling matters of state when there are far greater threats to be dealt with.'

'You consider averting war to be trifling?'

'If Kelewulf is allowed to open the door between this realm and the one that your sister and I have just returned from, and if he does so in such a way that the dark god himself is able to return, wars between different nations will be the last of our worries.' As he spoke, the Dreadblade wailed inside his head, fuelling his outrage. 'You did not see the things we did in that other realm. You did not experience the paralysing fear that flows out of Lorgukk to infect everything there!'

Astrid placed her hand on his arm. 'Please, Lann, sit down and we can talk about—'

'Both of us nearly died in that place because of the terror that infected us like a disease. They call it the Fear. And it's something that your cousin wants to unleash here! And you – YOU – let him escape!'

'How dare you talk to your king like that?' Erik too was on his feet now.

Lann managed to bite back his reply. Kicking over his chair, he stormed away through the doors into the empty throne room behind them.

Astrid watched him storm out. She understood his frustration, just as she could understand Erik's fury at being spoken to that way in front of his subjects.

The musicians had stopped playing, and it seemed to Astrid that every face in the room was turned their way.

'I'll go to him,' Astrid said, gesturing to her brother to stay where he was. 'He is not himself. He didn't mean some of the things he just said.'

She waited a moment until Erik's anger had subsided and he nodded his consent. Tapping his hand with her own as a thank you, she rose and made her way to her friend.

The throne room was dimly lit. Scant moonlight fell through the windows and the smoke holes high up in the roof. The only other illumination came from the glowing embers in the long fire pit that ran up the centre of the room. Lann was standing not too far into the chamber when he heard Astrid come in, but he did not turn to face her.

'Hey,' she said. She kept her distance and he knew she was doing so to allow him the space she thought he needed right now. The acoustics of the place, usually so busy and full of bodies, was weird, and her voice sounded small and fragile. 'You OK?' she asked.

'I lost control of myself back there. Your brother's right, I shouldn't have spoken to him like that.'

'Erik understands.'

'He doesn't understand. How could he? He hasn't seen the things we have, hasn't experienced the things we have.'

'No. But do not forget that he too has been the victim of Kelewulf's sinister majik. Being under its influence almost led him to his death. Perhaps he understands a little better than you give him credit for. Like you, he is trying to do his best in a world that's not quite what he once believed it to be. None of this – gods and monsters and majikal weapons – none of it is easy for any of us.'

Lann let out a small sigh. He turned and made as if to go out again. 'I'll go and apologise.'

She stepped forward and put her hand on his chest to stop him. She smelt of wild flowers. 'In a moment. Let me step back into the banquet hall and smooth things out a little first.'

He looked at her and remembered the kiss they'd shared earlier, his heart beating faster beneath her touch as he did. She gave him a small smile, then turned and exited again.

'Well, wasn't that sweet?'

Lann spun around to face the source of the voice. At the other end of the fire pit, his face illuminated from below, was the last person he would have expected to find here.

'Kelewulf,' he said in a whisper so low it was almost inaudible.

'Isn't she lovely, my cousin? Beauty and strength are not always found together, but she has them both in abundance. You seem to be quite taken with her.' He gave a little sniff, his eyes taking in Lann's face. 'I'm afraid the two of us have never been properly introduced, although we did *almost* meet in the not too distant past. At Vissergott, wasn't it?' A cruel smile played at the edge of his mouth. 'Yes, you were the young man I saw charging down the hill towards me brandishing the terrifying-looking weapon currently hanging at your hip. Remind me, how did that turn out again?' He made a point of frowning theatrically, as if trying to recall the memory. 'Ah yes. That terrible creature emerged from the portal and killed the witch. You were a little too slow to save her, as I recall.'

As Kelewulf spoke, Lann had very slowly begun to make his way round the long fire pit, moving towards his right. Kelewulf moved too, mirroring his pace until the two were facing each other across its middle. The embers were still hot enough to make the air dance between them, distorting their features.

'That "witch" was my aunt,' Lann said, slowly drawing the sword from its scabbard. 'She was a good person. She was everything to this world that you are not.'

If Kelewulf was frightened at the sight of the Dreadblade, he did well to hide it and continued to stare across at his challenger.

Lann felt a flicker of confusion. As he'd drawn the sword, he'd expected it to come to life in his head and in his hand, its voice and power filling both. Instead it remained mute in the face of this evil.

'I've taken the liberty of finding out a few things about you,' Kelewulf shot back at him. 'A poor farm lad turned hero. A boy chosen by the gods themselves to wield a mighty weapon. But you're not, are you? Not a hero at all.' He sneered across the flames. 'You are nothing. A failure, not worthy to bear the weapon you hold.'

Lann strengthened his grip on the sword.

'You're a nobody! A joke! If you and your divine sword were worth a damn, you'd have stopped me before I killed your precious aunt! You're a phoney and a—'

The rest of his words were cut off by the loud bellow of fury that came from the other side of the fiery pit. Surging forward, Lann pushed off his back foot and threw himself through the shimmering air, the Dreadblade held high over his shoulder.

Time seemed to slow for Lann as he allowed his rage to consume him. Even the searing heat that licked at his feet and legs couldn't distract him, and he kept his eyes fixed on the face of the young man responsible for so much of the pain and anguish he'd experienced in his short life. With his adversary at his mercy, he swung his arm round and down, noting how Kelewulf made no effort to move or defend himself in any way. Indeed, the look on his rival's face in that moment took Lann by surprise. There was none of the fear or panic he might have expected. Instead, after goading him into attacking in this way, he was wearing an expression that could only be described as ... satisfaction.

Goading. That's what he'd been doing. Kelewulf *wanted* Lann to attack!

The realisation came too late. The sword was in full swing, scything the air until it met the point where Kelewulf's shoulder joined his neck. As the blade bit through the flesh, Kelewulf turned his head towards the weapon and smiled. Suddenly it was no longer a face of flesh Lann was looking at; it was a thing of straw and string and leaves, feathers and mud and small sticks. The thing Lann had attacked wasn't a human being at all, and it certainly wasn't Astrid's cousin.

In the small loft room in a guest house a few streets away from the Great Longhouse, a sweat-drenched Kelewulf sat on the floor inside a circle of salt. Naked, with his eyes closed, he let out a little grunt.

His suspicions had been correct – the Black Shield spell he'd stolen from Master Larghal had been dreadfully hard to perform, and had left him spent to the point of utter exhaustion. In this state he'd doubted he could maintain the majik necessary to control the gölem for too long. Luckily, he hadn't needed to. The young man, Lannigon Gudbrandr, had risen to his taunts and struck out at the mannequin with a death-dealing blow.

Lann felt the Dreadblade bite home, cutting through what should have been flesh and sinew. The sword strike was a good one, the deadly blade, sharp as a razor, easily cutting through the person of straw and string until it hit the thing buried inside its chest, where its heart should have been. The black stone that Kelewulf had picked up from a beach not far from port was the only thing of any real substance in the gölem, but it was the majik that Kelewulf had woven into it that made it more than just any old rock.

Astrid had almost made it back into the banquet room when a terrible feeling of unease crept over her. Instinctively she placed her hand on the bangle around her upper arm, but there was none of the sharp tingling she felt whenever it was warning her of danger. Even so, she could not shake off the creeping sensation of menace.

Lann.

Turning back, she hurried in the direction she'd just come from, entering the throne room just as the Dreadblade struck the black stone buried at the heart of the gölem. A sound like a giant hammer hitting an anvil filled the room, the noise so painful to her ears that she cried out and threw her hands up to the sides of her head.

The sound was accompanied by another sensation: a wrenching feeling, as if something were being dragged from her – some part of her being that had been bound up with the dark blade during her brief time with it in the Void. Staggering as if from a physical blow, she cried out at the sight of Lann as he collapsed to the floor, his body completely limp as if the life had suddenly disappeared from it.

Groaning, she stumbled over to him, her fear for her friend driving her forward.

There, on the floor beside Lann, was the Dreadblade, its blade broken neatly in two as if it had been taken up and snapped over the knee of one of the gods themselves.

'Lann?' Astrid was already beside him. There was no blood, no sign that bones had been broken, but he was not breathing. She shook him, gently at first and then more violently, her desperation clear to hear as she said his name over and over again.

She couldn't collect herself. The inside of her head was a scrambled, jumbled mess. She started to get to her feet, and then dropped back down, unwilling to leave his side. Tears blurred her vision, the world swam out of focus.

When her hand fell on to the horn fastened to her belt, she knew what she had to do. With trembling fingers she fumbled clumsily to untie the leather thong it was attached to. She raised the horn to her lips.

'Stop.'

It was a man's voice, but Astrid knew it was no human uttering the word that filled her body and mind all at the same time. Doing as she was bid, she moved the horn away from her lips and turned towards the speaker.

'Now is not the time to call our winged sisters from their realm.' The voice and the figure standing before her were well matched. The former was strong and commanding, difficult to ignore or disobey, and it originated from a figure whose beauty and bearing were almost painful to behold.

'Wh-who are you?'

'I have many names. But you might know me as the god Rakur.'

Astrid let out a humourless bark. 'You! You come in a different form this time, I see. Look at what you have done. You gave the Dreadblade to Lann. You made him bearer of that terrible weapon and the demands it placed on him.' She gestured towards the unmoving figure at her feet. 'Are you happy with your work?'

She glared through her tears at the deity when he remained silent. 'Are you here to revive him? Are you? To return him to me? Because, if not, I see no reason for you to be present.'

Rakur stared down at Lann's prone form. 'This was not foreseen.'

The look on his face made Astrid groan in despair. 'Foreseen? You're a god! You don't get to hide behind meaningless words like "This was not foreseen". Lann needs your help! Please tell me you can save him.'

'I can revive him. But the wielder and the blade are one. Until the sword is repaired, Lann will not be the person you knew before.'

'Who can repair the sword? Who? You?'

'No. Only the original creator of the weapon is capable of that.'

'Og? The first god?'

Rakur shook his head. 'Og had the swords made, but he did not fashion them. No, the god of fire, the blacksmith god Egrep, was their creator. The two of you must journey to him before the sword and its bearer can be fully restored.'

Astrid moved away from Lann for the first time. Hardly able to believe she was doing so, she pushed her face towards the god's and snarled her words at him. 'Where will we find him, this Egrep?'

'He dwells in lands far to the north of here. In the Lands of the Ice People. But you will not be the only ones making that journey.'

'What do you mean?'

'Kelewulf is travelling there too.'

'Why?'

'An item he seeks is there.'

'The heart?'

Rakur shook his head again. 'Your cousin already has that in his possession. No, he needs an ancient staff, an object of dark majik, if he is to have any chance of doing what he wants to do.'

'Why don't you gods stop him?'

'We cannot get directly involved in human matters. Not in the way you are suggesting.'

'I want *him* back,' she said, pointing down at Lann and glaring at the god. 'I want you to bring him back. And don't you tell me you cannot get involved!'

The god looked at her, hesitating.

'He has done everything demanded of him since that devil blade was put in his hands. He rid this world of monsters when you gods lifted not a finger. I'm not asking you, Rakur, I demand you give him back to me!'

The hint of a smile touched the edges of the deity's mouth. Rakur blinked.

There was a loud *pop!* and Astrid turned to look at the fire as it spat out a wooden ember, the small glowing thing describing an arc in the air before landing on Lann's chest, where it smouldered and began to burn through his tunic.

With a shout, Astrid dropped to her knees and beat at the little glowing cinder until it was snuffed out. Sitting back on her heels, she turned her head to find that the deity had disappeared.

The gasped intake of breath next to her made her heart thump in her chest and she turned her eyes back to Lann, whose forehead creased as he met her gaze.

'You're alive,' she whispered.

'Where am I?' he said. 'And who are you?'

North of Stromgard

23

Kelewulf slumped to the side and almost fell from the saddle of the horse that continued to walk along beneath him. The pair had ridden hard and fast through the darkness to get away from the capital. Kelewulf's exhaustion was so great that he resigned himself to stopping to make camp for the night, despite the lack of any obvious shelter. In the end he chose to curl himself up behind a small rock formation that had thrust itself up out of the earth. He lit a fire, despite knowing it might be spotted by those who were undoubtedly out searching for him, hoping they could capture and return him to Stromgard to face justice.

The meagre flames did little to stave off the cold winds blowing across the land from the sea to the west. He huddled inside his cloak, pulling the blankets up around his chin to stop himself shivering.

He closed his eyes, but fought the desire to to sleep immediately. Instead, he channelled his mind in another direction, seeking to commune with an infinite blackness that struck terror into his heart.

He was standing on a mountain path in front of a cave entrance. Fear poured from the cave mouth, and he wanted nothing more than to turn his back on it and run away. Instead his feet made their way inside, seemingly of their own volition, until he was standing in an impenetrable darkness, all alone.

Kelewulf turned around and saw that the entrance no longer existed.

'The greatest threat to your return is no more,' he said into the dark.

'The Dreadblade? How?'

'I destroyed it.'

'That cannot have been easy. And the one who wielded it? The boy?'

'Also destroyed.'

The silence that followed stretched out until it was eventually broken by the dark god. 'You journey to the Ice Lands? To fetch the Staff?'

Kelewulf tried to suppress the anger he felt. He'd expected Lorgukk to praise him, to tell him how impressed he was that he had defeated such a powerful weapon. Instead, he'd brushed it aside as if it were nothing.

'I do.'

'Then soon I will be free.'

'Yes.'

'And I will reign.'

'And I will bathe in the glory of your power, know it was I who brought it back into the world.'

Kelewulf woke with a start. Breathing rapidly, he stared about him for a moment, trying to recall where he was. His horse snorted somewhere nearby. Something had happened to wrench him away from the deep slumber he'd been in, something momentous. An idea nagged at him from a place deep in his mind, and he fumbled inside his cloak, pushing his cold hand into the pocket of his trousers until his fingers closed around the object there.

Feeling the dry, leathery flesh of the heart, he wondered if he was being foolish. If the dream had been just that – a dream.

Then it happened again. It was so weak it was almost undetectable, but it was there …

Lorgukk's heart pulsed.

Acknowledgements

I'd like to thank everyone who has made this book possible, and for the help they have given me in making *Dark Art* the best it could be.

Thank you to everyone at Bloomsbury – a great publishing house that continues to produce fabulous works – for everything they have done.

A special thank you to Hannah Sandford, my editor, whose love of fantasy shines out from the pages of this book. *Dark Art* would not have been half as good as it is without Hannah's insightful advice and suggestions.

Catherine Pellegrino of Marjacq is my agent, and deserves a medal for her patience and understanding. Thanks for your kind words and reassurances when I'm in the doldrums (which has been quite often during the writing of this book).

Finally, a thank you to my wife, Zoe. You are my anchor in the storm. x

About the Author

Steve Feasey lives in Hertfordshire with his wife and children. He says he didn't learn much at school, but he was always a voracious reader. He started writing fiction in his thirties, inspired by his own favourite writers: Stephen King, Elmore Leonard and Charles Dickens. His first book, *Changeling*, was shortlisted for the Waterstones Prize and became a successful series. He is also the author of the acclaimed Mutant City series. Following *Dark Blade*, this is his second novel set in the world of Stromgard.

stevefeaseyauthor.com
@stevefeasey

HAVE YOU READ

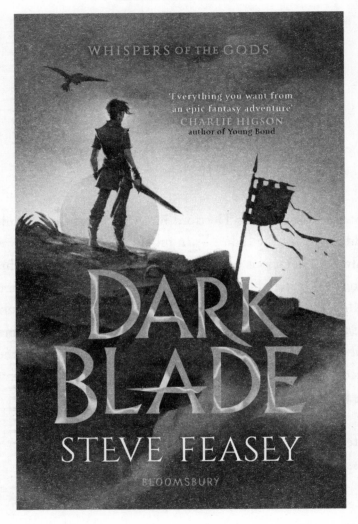

The first epic fantasy set in the world of Stromgard …